I0703093

Praise for The Rain Artist

"An otherworldly, Atwood-esque dystopia."

—O: The Oprah Magazine

"From covering the lavish rain parties to the hectic underworld, the prose is deliberate. Its rhythm is engaging, too, pulling the story along even through the unsettling moments. Strong social commentary overlays the grim dystopian novel The Rain Artist, in which creativity and humanity are at risk of excision."

—Foreword Reviews

"Intriguingly eclectic ... cathartic."

—Publishers Weekly

"The Rain Artist offers us a glimpse of a mad-hatter, horror show of a future that feels all too possible. Foster is a more soulful Philip K. Dick, as focused on the inner lives of the troubled, colorful characters who inhabit this novel as the high-concept, adrenaline-fueled mystery that will keep you turning the pages."

—Benjamin Percy, author of The Dark Net,
The Dead Lands, Red Moon, and The Wilding

book one * the clepsydra series

The Rain Artist

MOONSTRUCK BOOKS

Moonstruck Books
Portland, Oregon
moonstruck-books.com

ISBN (paperback) 979-8-9888154-0-2

ISBN (eBook) 979-8-9888154-1-9

Interior formatting by JP Painter
Cover illustration by Don Smith
Cover image: "Central Park Plaza: Hotel Sherry-Netherland (center), Hotel Savoy Plaza (right), From 58th Street and Fifth Avenue," New York Public Library Digital Collections. The Miriam and Ira D. Wallach Division of Art, Prints and Photographs: Photography Collection, The New York Public Library.

in memory of Brian G. Foster

August 22, 1958 - July 2, 2021

who taught me how to read a pattern
& made the world a more beautiful place
through his goodness, patience, and verve

The rain it raineth on the just
And also on the unjust fella;
But chiefly on the just, because
The unjust steals the just's umbrella.

From the oral tradition, attributed to Charles, Baron Bowen (1835-94) by Walter Sichel in *Sands of Time: Recollections and Reflections*, published in 1923.

Midtown

1

Paul Anahera believed most problems could be solved with flowers; not because human conflict was simple, but because beauty was the remedy for everything. Flowers cured grief, infidelity, frigidity, and regret. He sold flowers from the front room of Celine Broussard's umbrella shop—celluloid, virtual, hydroponic, and living blossoms—to people who knew that words weren't enough. Actions spoke louder, and flowers, loudest of all.

In the morning, when the pavement still leaked chemical mist, Paul unlocked the roll-up grate of Broussard's and stepped into the narrow, refrigerated room where he'd worked fifty, sixty hours a week, every week, for the last however-many years. The cold cases where he kept the roses were fogged. Variegated petals pressed against the glass like fingers, exploring, looking for an escape. Hardier varieties, from tough-stemmed ranunculus to trimmings of Australian eucalyptus, waited in knee high white buckets that nearly covered the black and red tiles. He stepped through them, as though through a vast garden, and flicked on the lights.

One of the tubes sputtered, only igniting halfway. He squinted up at it. Last time, he had nudged it back into alignment with the power prongs with a broom handle, but this might be its last gasp. The faulty light turned the back corner of the shop dim, but nobody went back there but himself; it could wait a day.

The first commuters dawdled by as Paul snapped on the storefront neon and lugged yesterday's bouquets to the display rack by the door. The awning was worse for wear, its vinyl cracking at the seams. The city's atmosphere corroded fabrics, even synthetic ones; Paul replaced the cheerful green-and-pink panels annually. Traces of ammonia in the air leached into everything; the shop was so close to the subway that it picked up the hydrogen chloride and methylamine sprayed on the tracks to keep infection and pests subdued. It was bad for the flowers, Paul thought as he rotated a spray of green snapdragons and fluffed the carnations. Maybe everything in this life was perishable, but still—it was a shame to hurry it along.

After Paul had shooed away the pigeons sheltering on the ledge above the shop, he went back inside, washed his hands, and arranged the catalogs of to-order boutonnieres and corsages by the register. A faded stand-up of Marilyn Monroe stapled against the wall beamed at him from the depths of an artificial, heart-shaped wreath. He winked at her frozen, angelic smile and went into the back room. This was where his real business operated.

Paul, among other things, was a trafficker of stolen goods. A black market trafficker, he kept the flower shop open as a front for legitimate trade. What came in the back door in one condition left through the front as something completely different. He could care less about the merchandise itself. You could put in a rabbit and out came a dove; it made no difference to Paul, as long as he got his percent. He loved two things: flowers, and a deal.

He had once worked in the fields where real flowers grew, and knew they came from open fields, grown in rows as packed as densely as subway riders. Back then, he picked pharma-grade poppies which were genetically engineered to blossom over a few weeks. In comparison, he handled the shop's decorative flowers with more care. They were shipped into the city in refrigerated vans instead of destined for maceration. Each stem was distinct; flowers with unusual defects, like torn or missing petals or even small bruises, could still be sold-as is, rotated in a bouquet to conceal any shortcomings, wrapped in cellophane, and pushed into the hands of someone eager to get back in his wife's good graces.

Flowers were the language of appreciation of the milestones that studded even the dullest, most ordinary life. They were meant to be temporary and had a shelf life of three or four days at most, for hardier varieties. The delicate ones, the short-lived lilacs or violets, only lasted through one night. Living flowers were real, and their authenticity gave them a hint of doomed romance, a nod to an earlier time, when people used to die for love. Digital flowers cost less and were practically meaningless, purchased only to spruce up the bare offices of lawyers who were always in court. Paul knew a dozen ways to delay the inevitable decomposition that turned leaves to slime, tugged petals from their sockets, and dulled fresh hues. He could refresh most commercial varieties indefinitely, dyeing and even painting some of them, or threading a hair-thin wire through the fleshy bulb at the base of the petals through whatever fiber was left of the deteriorating stem. He could soak the flowers in sugar solution to make them perk up, or keep them so cold that it suspended animation. A new flower was all excitement; an old one, apathetic, its promise expiring before your eyes.

Hothouse production extended a flower's life, but more people preferred the much-cheaper artificial ones—you only bought those once, Paul thought, but if only once, what was the point? The flowers he sold were the best quality in Midtown. Some living, some synthetic, he kept a full stock on hand and did brisk business. A lesser crook would have skimped on flowers and only kept enough around to maintain appearances. Paul knew this kind of place: they kept a few brittle, shrink-wrapped roses on the shelf, or plastic daisies dyed tacky shades to match whatever holiday theme the month brought along. A front was not, by definition, a money making proposition. The more it cost, the more you lost, but Paul thought flowers were worth it.

He liked to joke, "If it doesn't work out, I can fall back on bouquets full time."

Of course it worked out. The black market was shrink-proof; people always wanted something that was a little out of reach. Besides, he had his security in Celine, who rented him the flower shop—their business was protected by the ultra-wealthy folks she served. She was above suspicion and, by extension, so was Paul. Without her, the rich might have money but they'd never have class.

Celine Broussard was the only umbrella maker in the world. Her work was both exceptional and peerless, which gave her immense freedom—with the fringe benefit of protecting Paul from scrutiny.

For nearly a century, generations of Broussards had owned the stout, stucco building near the finance district, coming down from their apartment upstairs to make umbrellas in the shop. It was in an odd spot tucked behind a sandwich take-out on a cobbled alley that stank of either onions or the coppery pellets that subdued the city's dust, depending on the season—not the kind of place a person might expect to find a master craftsman. But Celine was free from the pressure of attracting new business; because her mother left her the building, she never had to think of moving. There was no need to advertise her umbrellas, which had a reputation of their own. Anybody who needed one would already know the shop and its wares, and how to contact the owner. Aside from the awning, the only marker for Broussard's was a white pressboard cat on the sill of the display window, which was soaped with gray paint. The cat had a circle around its eye like a monocle.

Celine once told Paul that the rain parties, across the decades of her career, had become unrestrained spectacle. In exclusive clubs and specially designed rooms, rain still fell down the collars and saturated the shoes of wealthy men. It was cheaper to sprinkle your guests with freshwater pearls for two hours, she said. She described the debauchery she'd witnessed at these events—the food, the clothes, and above the melee, her umbrellas, blooming like peonies in the artificial rain.

The back of the flower shop was separated from Celine's studio by a low, blinding light box of a room, tiled from floor to ceiling in irregular white slate-work, like a mosaic of human teeth. A few drains breathed a chilly wind from the irrigation tunnels that ran parallel to the subway nearby and kept the room frigid in both seasons. Paul could tell anyone it was perfect for keeping the flowers fresh; in fact, the hand-stained irises and glassy tulips he stored in long troughs, their full roots immersed in bubble-pods of hydrolyzed peptides, kept hold of their bright petals days past normal expiration. The cold room captured scent and noise and also acted as an airlock between the florist and the loading ramp out back. Passing through this room, Paul sensed the tang of frost in the air and shivered in his buffalo-weave jacket. The second door's rubber lip sealed to the frame when he shut it behind him. Celine would be arriving from upstairs in an hour or so—he was doing a delivery for her for the Weiss rain party, an order for two hundred and twenty-one umbrellas.

The Weiss family owned eighty-six percent of the world's remaining icebergs and was said to have a chunk of glacier in each room so that guests could lick the ancient ice and suck the polar water directly into their mouths. Money was the opposite of rain, Paul thought: It only trickled upward.

He checked the dock for bugs, taking an old rake and scraping along the hidden ridges. A few loose screws, a roach that sauntered along the lip of the ramp like a tipsy streetwalker, and a rime of dust came loose under the rake's teeth. No devices. Some landfiller graffiti decorated the lip of the ramp, and he reminded himself to paint over it when he had time. Those people were vermin; their slogans irked him, and he growled to himself as he worked, thinking of the squalid warrens that tunneled into the recesses of the city. He shook the rake off and returned it to its rack by the door, carefully scraping his polar-felt moccasins before he went back through the airlock.

By the time he got back to the register, a few customers were perusing the ready-made bouquets. One of them leaned like a condemned man against the counter, clutching his device in a sweaty, shaking hand.

"Anniversary?" Paul guessed. The man nodded.

"We all forget 'em when things are going good."

"She said something when I left the house," the man said. He rubbed his temples so hard that deep wrinkles of exhausted skin enfolded his eyes, making them vanish momentarily. When he took his hands away, he looked even more tired than before.

Paul paused, a lily clamped like a baton between his fingers. "How bad is it?"

"Bad."

"You let this do the talking," Paul said, giving the flower the gentlest possible shake. Its stamen glittered. Motes of saffron-gold powder dropped onto his sleeve, each one infused with linalool and benzyl alcohol. "When I'm done, it won't matter if she caught you with her sister."

He twisted a laminate ribbon around the lily arrangement and handed it to the sweaty man, who mopped his brow with his sleeve and grimaced.

"These'll do," the man said, half in question.

"You come back next time and there won't *be* a next time," Paul said, appraising his own work. The lilies were streaked with palest pastel pink. A few sweetheart buds peeked out of the arrangement, among the hosta leaves and tender ferns that Paul used as filler. The wrapper was the same pink, the color of an exhausted toddler's cheeks. Paul used pink for apologies; it struck him as less presumptuous than red or white, the colors that comprised it.

"Costs less than a divorce," the man agreed. He paid without looking at the receipt and went out, holding the flowers high, as though carrying a torch.

In the hours between commuter rushes, Paul sold a few bouquets and a nosegay of carnations tinted a hideous green. He sold tuberoses to a woman so pregnant she could barely stand; she pressed the blossoms to her face, wishing she could eat them. He stacked celluloid dahlias in translucent coffins for the scooter boy to take to offices over in Flatbush. Days when he was planning for one of Celine's umbrella deliveries went fast; in no time, traffic had thinned out and only a few slack-faced, exhausted people shuffled by, barely giving the florist a glance. He dragged the buckets back from the awning and patiently swept the quarter inch of city grit back toward the curb. He knew it was pointless to clear it out, but he couldn't leave anything untidy for long. The glass cases in the store were free of fingerprints and the white airlock in the back was aseptic enough for surgery—he should know, he'd done it in there, held the guy down while someone else gave him a second dose of chloroform. Nobody had ever found out. To this day, he had never told Celine about the extent or the filthy underbelly of his business. He made sure she had no reason to inquire. There were advantages to keeping things neat. He'd never regretted taking time, as much as he needed, for these simple, endless tasks.

When Celine came down to her studio, he would lay out the umbrellas, wrap them like bouquets, and transport them to the party. It was a routine they'd done a thousand times. But there's a first time for everything, Paul thought. You could never be too careful. The day that started normal was the one that wrecked your life.

2

BEAUTY BEGETS BEAUTY; anyway, Celine loved flowers. From the back room of her studio, she caught a whiff of Paul's shop every time the electronic chime over the front door sounded. The fragrance energized her. A colorful smear of pollen on her trousers made her look as though she'd walked through a field, rubbing against the blossoms. She took a deep breath, tasting the green in the air. There was no proof that cut flowers did anything to improve air quality, but just having a few stems in a room was scientifically shown to relax a person. Flowers made you forget what was wrong; they glossed over the hard parts of living, the words that were impossible to say.

The final umbrellas for the Weiss rain party were nearly finished. She worked her curved needle around one piece's ribs, stabbing gently through the fabric. She was too experienced to make mistakes, but it didn't hurt to be mindful. Shoddy work vexed her; if her stitches were sloppy, she felt their defects physically, as though itching against her skin. She smoothed the seam, taking pleasure in its uniformity.

A single umbrella took four hours to make, from its hand-stitched canopy and handle guard to the time Celine needed to fasten the stretchers to the ribs with pin-sized, golden screws. She turned out three umbrellas a day or sometimes four, when her hands weren't misbehaving. Her joints were the only aging part of her body. The rest of her was still young, pushing sixty-five. She sat on a tall stool over a table protected by thick silicon mats, which were covered in razor cuts, rulers, and cross hatching. Leftover gores cut from gray suede and butter-colored silk were draped in neat plastic tubs. Her clothes were tailored from the same fabrics; she pieced them together herself, saving yards of discarded cloth and transforming them into one-of-a-kind suits and blouses in gentle shades that reminded her of the long-lost, aqueous sky.

When she reached the end of the gore, she laid the panel on the table and slipped a lily leaf out of her cardigan—stolen from one of Paul's bouquets. She'd gently detached it from the stem and tucked it into her pocket. She stroked it, assessing the fibers in the deep ridges of its parallel veins. The natural predictability of its form soothed her. Some things were already exquisite, she thought, while others merely aspired to perfection. After decades of designing high-fashion umbrellas, she was at the peak of her craft—but she would never sew anything as flawless as a lily-leaf.

Still, the Weiss' special order was as immaculate as her two hands could make it. She turned the panel to one side, then the other, inspecting the uniform, near-invisible stitches along the rib. This would suffice. The party was a winter fantasy theme:

white, everything white. Instead of the water-repellent neo-nylon Celine usually worked with, they requested a special, hand-waxed, washi-texture canvas for their umbrella canopies. Once, the bespoke umbrellas were porous, plain, and monochromatic; now, minimalism was considered old-fashioned. The natural markets and trade put billions in these families' pockets, and true to form, they were desperate to outdo one another in their displays of outright wealth.

Making umbrellas taught Celine some things about the rich. First, they were not as clever as people with fewer resources. Second, they were deeply insecure and protected their assets the way an ordinary person protected their reputation. Third, there was no innovation among financiers, which was why the rich copied one another slavishly. For example, if one family placed an order for umbrellas with gold-spattered canvas panels or umbrellas shaped like ginkgo leaves, Celine inevitably received dozens of copycat orders. The Weisses, apparently, were more inventive than most. Their party would feature a wall of ice blocks with gifts frozen inside them. The rain would be warm: a tropical downpour that turned the ice wall to water so that the sealed, plastic gift boxes inside floated like coffins rising in a flood.

She smoothed the multi-colored scarf around her neck in a solemn meditation. It had been her grandmother's, and its goldenrod border seemed to hold the sunshine of Celine's youth in its dye. The women who had raised her and indoctrinated her into the art of umbrella-making would have been thrilled by the innovations of the rich—and the higher price tag that went with them. Each rain party seemed to push the limits of what Celine knew about sewing; each order was more fanciful than the last, from rare dyes to bugle beads to appliques that sparkled under the rain, dissolving into secret patterns that spelled out the guest of honor's name. Celine was not fond of excess, but accepted innovation as part of her calling. The art of making umbrellas had an aristocratic history, and she felt beholden to that, even as the parties people used them for became superabundant bacchanals.

The Weiss order was for two hundred umbrellas of one pattern and another twenty of a different design for a planned flash dance routine, which would be performed by hired entertainers. As was rain party tradition, there would be a final umbrella for Robert Weiss to carry: a special design, to commemorate his retirement. But that wasn't all. His sons, Henry and Laszlo, had placed a second, secret order for two identical umbrellas with an unusual set of features: hollow aluminum tubing, oversized gores, and a spiked ferrule, like a bayonet designed to shed blood instead of water.

An order of this size took her months to assemble. By the time it was done, Celine's hands ached and her eyes swam with fatigue. Paul's display of LED-dotted house cactuses wavered, their individual lights coalescing into fractured stars. She was nearly finished; only a few more adjustments to go.

With no daughter of her own, she sometimes worried about passing the business on. Who would learn these skills, when her hands were too rigid to demonstrate a flat-chain whipstitch or how to hold the pattern tracing wheel? She knew the value of her craft, and her clients paid it, knowing they were buying her discretion as well. If she'd been less cautious, she would have found an apprentice. But it was too risky. Working alone, Celine beheld the secret, rain-soaked world of the ultra-wealthy. She saw their excesses, took their money, and kept her mouth shut.

Robert Weiss' retirement party was going to be an affair to remember, and they'd paid for it accordingly. The old man had overseen the family business for a century. Now, he was said to be stepping down from all his responsibilities but an emeritus position on the FlinCorp board. His eldest son, CEO-elect Henry Weiss-Broms, would continue overseeing the vital work of harvesting brine for salt from the shallow northern sea. The transfer of power from one generation to the next would shift the global markets; speculators anticipated a downturn, anything from a blip to a partial collapse. But that was just guessing, Celine reminded herself. Greed or fear drove markets as much as real commodities. It would all come down to Henry.

Henry himself was a cipher who rarely spoke to the press and was more austere than his father, who was single handedly responsible for driving natural water brokering into the stratosphere, in the literal sense—he'd funded the first water extraction tests on Mars and was said to be testing a way to manufacture water in a molecular collider that slammed gas particles into one another with such force that they exploded into rain. His half-brother Laszlo was even less creative: he only made money, never rain. Henry, the gossip went, was no innovator. But do the inheritors of parental wealth ever need to improve on the impulses of the past, or just see them through to their natural conclusions? Celine rubbed her bleary eyes with the back of her hand and picked up her needle again. The final umbrella was the most complex, and she needed to give it every ounce of her attention.

She attached the panel to the piece and gave it an experimental swirl, to test the ribs for tensile strength. She had never made one quite like this—it felt barbaric to her, and she hoped it would be a one-off design, unrepeated in its ugliness. The gores were the same color as the other washi canopies, but the rest of the design included hardware that Celine had to cadge from Paul. God knows where he got it from—she had the sense never to ask, and he'd given her the same courtesy. Even if Paul wondered, what could Celine possibly tell him? The facts bewildered her.

She screwed the ferrules into place and laid the two umbrellas side-by-side on the mat. At first glance, they blended right in with the others. Only the bearers—and their maker—would know the potentially lethal secret hidden in plain sight, between the ribs and canvas petals of the piece. She stuck a pair of cork dice on the pointed tips to keep them from losing their edge.

It was no business of hers what the Weisses planned for their father. Maybe it was nothing; maybe this was another way for them to gild the lily, improving on a time-tested design perfected by the artists before them. Or maybe not. Celine created what she was paid for. Who was she, to question the caprices of the rich?

3

The morning of his father's murder, Henry Weiss-Broms lifted his nose to the morning mist in Otzara, the family's garden outside Lansing. The garden was his best friend. Everyone should have such a friend, he thought. He interlaced his fingers with the fronds of the sword fern that guarded the gate that marked the entrance to the family estate. Even at the height of the morning, the thick canopy overhead created a perpetual pool of shade that protected the garden's slopes from the ferocity of the sun. While the leaves at the tops of the maples cooked in the unfiltered rays a hundred feet up, their roots were cool and damp. Henry felt cradled in his friend's chilly arms. He loved the garden and he was sure it loved him back.

Centuries ago, when the Weiss family acquired the first acreage deeds out West, it was not clear whether the planet would turn hot or cold, wet or dry. The ice caps were melting and days-long dust storms covered the sun. The family preserved Otzara as a pristine empire with their own future in mind, preparing for a time when the majority of the earth was either submerged or so parched that technology would have to fill the gap left by soon-to-be defunct natural processes. They created networks of drainage pipes that could irrigate their crops and saved warehouses of pre-served seeds, genetic samples, and clean water—enough to last for decades, and then be replicated and regrown so that the estate would be a forever Eden, a place the crisis of the outside world could not touch. They were ready for the creeping collapse of the ecosystem; when it came, it was a feather-touch on their land.

Over the years, the sea had become a dehydrated, saline slime bed that receded from the former coast; rivers dried up and were filled in by canny land developers who built new high rises in the soft beds, making it impossible for the water to ever return. Groundseep hydrated the surviving crabgrass and tree species adapted to hyper-arid conditions, but it was not enough to sustain life without artificial support.

Because of this, the Weiss-Broms' gardens were reinforced against increasingly erratic water supply, historic droughts that lengthened in each progressive season, and deadly natural patho-gens that crept in on hands, boots, and the backs of flying crea-tures. The family combated agrochemical cross-contamination and preserved the land, ensuring that Otzara was the only place on earth without GMO plants. Real greenery fed naturally bred meat. The garden began as a retreat, but after years of climate col-lapse, it had become a shrine to the world-that-was—to be enjoyed by the only people who could afford to walk its heavenly paths and breathe the purest air left on the browning sphere people once worshiped as a fertile goddess.

Henry plucked a pygmy forget-me-not and brought it to his nose. In a few hours, he would have to fly back to New York for the rain party and get this whole thing over with. He was not anxious; like any growing thing, he'd moved with deliberation and in silence, trusting that his actions were the outcome of his nature. He reached up to stroke the fuzzy carpet of moss that dribbled between the pint-sized clay lions whose open mouths studded the edge of the entry-gate roof. The moss stretched tiny, golden spore-sprouts toward the sky, as though aspiring to the maples' height. Below, an azalea bush crowded a trimmed huckleberry hedge that was threatening to blossom twice within the season, tempting the house finches out of the branches. Smooth river stones meandered in a path through the gate and up through the first cultivated land-scape. A slender trillium marked the eastern edge of the region that used to be part of Michigan. Nothing bad could ever happen here, Henry thought.

It was the only part of this wretched world worth saving.

A distant clunk touched his ears as he passed through the gate. Some of the gardens contained shishi-odoshi fountains with cut bamboo in them that filled and tilted in a secret rhythm, scaring off the deer from the delicate new shoots. Other sōzu flowed through troughs of brilliant yellow irises and fed the pocked lotus bulbs that crowded the lily ponds. The lotuses were Henry's favor-ite—not just because of the bright, fez-shaped sepal in the center of each flower's massive, pointed crown or the delicate stems that supported each blossom, which seemed as weighty as a full-sized human head. He was enchanted by the plants' broad, green leaves.

Each one was as tough as Teflex but soft to the touch, the texture of the skin in the jugular triangle of a person's neck. The leaves opened like gently sloped Saturday temple hats toward the sky; no matter how brutal the heat was on certain days or how intensely the unfiltered sun shone, the lotuses seemed to be immune. They sucked up the heat and transformed it into neon-blazing chlorophyll that glowed even in the dark. Once or twice a month during his visits to the garden, Henry was able to venture into the eastern acreage to observe the sōzu renovation—a water test that subjected the pipelines and ponds to flooding conditions.

Not that a flood was likely. At least, not a real one.

The water that drained through the galvanized pipes was pure spring water, clean enough to drink from the cups of your hands. It filtered through the massive network of tubes and tunnels, feeding the thirsty roots of the garden. Walking through the lush gardens and farms, Henry found it easy to forget that elsewhere, people sold their own children for a handful of edible buck-meal. They sucked moisture from mass-produced gel packs and chewed on bottled hydration slurry. They would never taste water of this clarity.

In Otzara, Henry had flowers, dew, and quiet. If he wished, he could have walked all the way from Michigan to Montana without leaving his family's estate. Otzara represented real wealth—value that exceeded the trillions he and Laszlo shuffled between shell corporations, gambled on exchange rates, or laundered into tech bonds. That was all speculation. The garden was undeniably real. The reserve held thousands of re-natured acres that stretched north, through what was left of the finger lakes and the agricultural land preserved for livestock and crops. Robert Weiss-Broms' great-grandfather bought the pieces that would become the core garden and his children and their children added, generation after generation, new swaths. There were more than ten gardens—from a millennia-old core landscape to the newborn areas that a crew of botany technicians babied into stability. The more established sections, like the one near the Lansing Gate, were always in danger of lapsing into weakness. The pollution that assaulted the garden's borders from every angle—sky, roots, even the air that filtered through the pines—toxified the soil and leaves. Encouraging growth was a complex task, and Henry, being who he was, preferred it all be done silently and out of sight, with tools that worked by hand.

For years, the main gate had acted as a transition from the filthy outside world to the tranquility of the border garden. But now, the gardeners spent more and more time pushing back against the invading forces of acid fog and corroding runoff. Henry bent down to inspect the mouse-print pattern of rot that sprinkled across the azalea's leaves. All of these spots would need to be color-corrected and misted with a neutralizer. The longer they waited, the sicker the plant would get. Pruning was the least desirable option for treatment, since it ruined the symmetry of the branches. The Weiss-Bromses were particular about aesthetics—Henry especially. When he was chosen by the family board to take the CEO role from his father, he was presented with a tin hori-hori knife in recognition of his devotion to the land. The first thing he'd done with it was plunge its razor edge into the turf between the pavers to lever a stone loose, certain a sick root was moldering underneath it. He knew that creating the illusion of an untouched, natural space required great attention to detail. Each element had to be cultivated, trained, corrected, and cared for.

Unlike his half-brother Laszlo, who never came here—always busy in the city, never giving this place a single thought—Henry knew every leaf and flower in his favorite section of the garden and gave each element the doting attention a parent lavishes on a delicate child. He turned the corner of the cedar plank teahouse and skirted the white camellia bushes, which were just developing their new growth tips. Their dense foliage was a convenient screen for the pit that backed the sand and stone garden. The carapace of a broken pipe protruded from the mangy soil. The old system was finally surrendering to the toxins in the soil. Replacing its segments with reinforced, galvanized steel without disturbing the plantings on the surface was achingly slow work. The entire system was underground, but serious repairs took most of the previous year and were still ongoing. Even the Weiss-Bromses couldn't accelerate the pace of such a major overhaul. Drainage lines, like gravity, were the province of nature; they were up to the character of the soil and depended on whether the earth felt like yielding to human whims on any given day.

Otzara had its own logic, its own special nature. Here, the shifting ground broke the pipes and shuffled the paving stones. The cumulative effect was acres filled with only plants, where gardeners performed repairs that couldn't possibly last. They trimmed the trees and tended plants with longevity in mind, although sustainability was an illusion. Plants lived sunbeam to sunbeam and moment to moment, Henry thought. It was human hopes that were the problem—yes, human expectations.

When the last remaining natural resources dried up, or were recycled to the end of their usefulness—pumping out gray liquid too saline for farming, the air turning a poisonous shade of amber—these acres would be truly priceless. Miles away, millions of voices would cry out in thirst, while the water they craved ran over the smooth rocks of Henry's streams.

But only if the investment was protected. Robert Weiss gambled with these resources by keeping them in the open market, trading on the family's legacy as though it was a common commodity. Brokers who'd never seen this place—who would never even stand in the azaleas' shade—profited off Robert's bush-league trades. He cut in outsiders, sharing profits that should have been his sons' alone. At the same time, the Weiss corporation bankrolled industries that churned out poison dust, killed the tender saplings, and changed the pH of the soil. Robert drove up the garden's value with one hand and chipped it away with the other. Henry frowned.

It all had to stop. It was the only way.

In a few more days, this would all be over.

4

To MAKE PAPER, you needed paper. Yochanna Rother had tried and failed so many times that the drains in her apartment were permanently glutted with shreds of pulp. A single broadside could be processed and replicated into several smaller sheets like a mother into chicks, but who could afford the first one?

Instead, she made do with what she could find. Anything, everything. But so far, she had no luck. The cornflake wafers that lined the walls of Yochanna's closet melted into soggy wads when she tried to extract their cellulose. Edible bubble casings made of seaweed extract degraded into limpid shreds, like newborns' nail clippings. Worn-out clothes refused to yield their fibers. She considered filching one of the cardboard signs people flew on the sidewalk, but she was afraid to get too close. She read what it said on those signs; she worried their words were contagious.

Collecting powders was more generative. At home, her kitchen was spattered with blots of wild colors she foraged from all over the city. A dab of blue came from a crumbling traffic divider, while a bright yellow came from the irascible-looking urchins growing on her bedroom window's sash. There were innumerable shades of soft, pigeony gray that seemed indistinguishable until Yochanna set them next to each other; then, their diversity blossomed in delicate hues. Some concealed a delicate pink blush while others were grimy orange and walnut-husk amber. Her stove was covered in stained pots and pans, each a home to a different, vibrant concoction.

Since she had no paper, she smeared test patches of her inks on the walls of the apartment. The landlord-approved eggshell primer was perfect for it, and from across the kitchen the walls had taken on the look of a deranged impressionistic painting. The short, multicolored brush strokes were aligned in no particular orientation and made no image, but the fluid variation between colors soothed Yochanna and made her feel that, even though she could not really call herself an artist, she could at least point at the mess and say with confidence: *I made that.*

The cell she thought of as 'home' looked out on the dismal wreck across the alley, its windows coated in dust and chicken wire, so she explored the alchemized spaces between human and city with color. She could identify any of the swatches on the wall by location, from memory—from the crusting brown dab of raccoon blood she sponged up from a roadkill, to the aquamarine liquid that hid inside a daisy's stem. When she looked up from her work bench, she was sometimes surprised to see the city shimmering back at her from the once-blank kitchen wall.

It was one step closer to what she wanted to make, but without paper, what was the point of ink? In school, she learned that medieval monks abandoned the idea of paper and made their strokes on squares of vellum or other scraped hide. The idea of finding some animal and skinning it, much less tanning its hide and smoothing it into a usable surface was revolting to Yochanna. The rats in her neighborhood were big enough, but also dangerous. They carried diseases, they bit, and they were covered in coarse, raspy hair that repelled foxes but not parasites. She could not bring herself to do it. All she needed was a sheet of paper, so she mixed the torn pieces of whatever she could salvage and tried to strain it—over and over—on a laundry sieve saved from the trash.

Nothing she did worked.

She had spent so many nights staring into the sieve as her plans dissipated through its metal sluice. Each time she thought she'd found the formula that would give her a blank surface to work with, it slipped away before her eyes, leaving her with a clogged sink and handfuls of soggy mush to muck out of the basin. It wasn't supposed to be this hard; ancient people made paper from papyrus and river reeds. They skinned lambs and ornamented the peeled fleeces with the innumerable names of God. These skills were perfected over generations and then died out within a century. For a while, only artists knew how to make paper and ink; then, only academics. When the whole world was digital, books were kept as specimens or curios. Nobody needed those relics except people like Yochanna, who longed for media that didn't change when you looked away from it. She wanted to make paintings that preserved time and emotion. She wanted to create movement in the viewer; those static images could transmit something between the artist and the person regarding the art with a magical connection that seemed to have been broken by the overconnectivity that surrounded her. Technology was as inescapable as the dust that filled the city streets. You could see anything you wanted at any time, buy anything, sync with anyone within your open source. But, in all of it, something was lost.

Where had wonder gone? Yochanna watched the failed paper swirl in the throat of the drain. It seemed impossible to make something entirely by hand; machines interceded in the holy process at every stage. Her whole life, it seemed that she had been born at the wrong time.

At night, she dreamed of a life filled with beauty. She thought, if I had money, I would buy a bouquet. A whole stack of paper. Flowers, rich with fibers. Both things, at once. She had imagined thick, creamy slices of paper dotted with violet petals and tinted with the sap-green of springtime pistils. Even hothouse blossoms and conventionally grown plants had enough cellulose to hold together a handful of pulp. She'd never wanted to be middle class so badly. Her desires were embarrassingly bourgeois. She fantasized about soft, mass-manufactured sofas, picture frames with glass in them, and imported cheese. Drawing all day, with no screens chirping at her. Cherries dipped in real chocolate. When she woke up in her dingy studio, she was seized by despair, a hunger that would never be satisfied by what was being served to her.

She didn't want access to everything; she only wanted *enough*. As she prepared for her morning commute, she imagined the blank spots in a healing brain, slowly filling with images that lixiviated in and separated into layers. Yochanna could not remember the last time she dreamed in pictures that had nothing to do with the world outside her head. Instead, *she* was the one who got stuck, the last to leave the nest. There was no way out and nothing to look forward to; she was, for the first time, truly poor. Walking to the bus stop in the morning, she turned her tote bag design-side out, so the Georgetown logo showed. As if to say, *I don't belong where I've ended up.*

Yochanna chose a seat on the left side of the bus, so that she would at least catch a glimpse of the sun. The only view she saw was at the peak of the bridge, coming and going. At the highest point, she caught sight of the skyline that sprawled beyond the overlapping racks of billboards and glossy screens that told her what to buy. At this altitude, New York was a vast, glittering island of spires, skyscrapers, and transit lines, packed so densely that they knit together in a single fabric, no single element discernible from the others. Most mornings, Yochanna took comfort in this view. She felt her own insignificance, her place in the middle of everything, the rich potential in every point of light.

This morning, she saw the city's shimmer recede and pull away as the bus plunged back down into the artificial dusk, dragging her into the underworld of Brooklyn. The bus descended into the morass of crowded, partially sunken buildings piled on top of one another like impacted molars; it was a swamp of people, a mile and a half of litter and bodies, the shapeless, unfinished bones of new construction, its scaffolding converted to temporary housing, where tattered tarps fluttered like wings in the wind the bus made as it blustered past. Heaps of trash choked the alleys; in the drainage ditches, deltamethrin dust hung thick as fog, subduing pests and disease.

Yochanna pulled the cord for her stop and stepped onto the curb. A few pigeons, pecking fries from an abandoned McDonald's carton, scattered as she passed them. It was half a block to her office—an ugly walk. She was glad she'd bought a pair of blocker glasses. She turned up the volume on her device and made sure she had a good grip on her tote bag. Her route took her under a filthy overpass, past a trash drop-off, and around one of the smaller East Side encampments in Brooklyn. She told herself she wasn't scared, because she didn't want to be a person who was afraid of the world she lived in, but all the same she felt her pulse elevate until it was keeping pace with the synth beat in her headphones. Both sides of the sidewalk were already lined with beggars sitting on cardboard squares. Yochanna walked stiffly, feeling many eyes on her. A few of them propped up handwritten signs, or put out battered hats and bowls for food donations. One sign said, *Reparations.* The gutter was clotted with clumps of filthy hair. A man in American-flag pajama pants argued with a woman wearing a policeman's cap. Two people, so thin that their sex was indeterminate, fought over a wheelchair, yanking it back and forth. Yochanna was glad she couldn't hear their voices. The tents were covered in white streaks of bird shit. Pigeons nested against the beams of the nearby freeway overpass. She could smell a fire, meat cooking. The homeless caught rats, sparrows, and lost cats, and ate them. They ate anything. Everything.

Yochanna edged around the encampment. This block smelled terrible, even though there were community showers and two bathrooms. Nonprofits provided sanitation, plumbing, clean syringes, personal care and paper products, but it didn't seem to make a difference. Everything was dirty. Soap dispensers and outdoor sinks immediately acquired a layer of grime. Orange caps and syringe tubes crackled under her feet. Every day, an ambulance loaded out another overdose.

Ask Not What Your Country was branded on the subway rollups and the billboards that blasted their messaging down at the tents. Yochanna read the slogan dozens of times on her way to work. It replaced last month's *Pitch In For A Better America*. People like Yochanna were encouraged to spend their time giving. The basic income drip created a volunteer state. Subsistence wages, universal healthcare, and food stamps for everyone promised people a chance to do what they really loved. Everything needed was provided, but beyond that? Seemed to fall from the sky, enriching some people but not others.

Yochanna once believed the slogans, which said to create art, live your passion, contribute to a better society. She'd set her sights high. She was still paying for her naivete with student loan interest that quadrupled every month.

Yochanna stepped around a body wrapped in a brown, flayed tarp. She held her breath, as though poverty was transmittable, an airborne virus. Still, the smell stuck to her clothes; muffled shrieks that made their way through the padding in her headphones. She shied away from the vacant slots between panhandlers: the spaces that suggested, *you are not as far from this as you think.*

There was always a crack to fall through, no matter what the billboards said. Their message was obscured by ornate graffiti, which reminded Yochanna of the medieval illuminations she studied at Georgetown. The multicolored spray paint and complex signatures reached as high as the artist's arm would go, making a colorful, chaotic ribbon that wrapped all the way around the block. Sometimes, a familiar letter or word leapt from the disorder, tempting her to translate it; it was the only thing she used her education for, these days. She had learned the Latin names of every species the ancient monks had inked on vellum and could identify the special combinations of chalks they'd mixed with goat urine to blend the colors. Graffiti was a distant cousin of the manuscripts she'd pored over so she stuck close to the hedge of spray-painted thorns until she got to the recessed entry to the Brooklyn Urban Bird Society, tapped her security code into the keypad, and set the door to lock behind her.

This morning, nobody was sleeping in the stairwell, which felt like a small mercy. They were usually hung over or strung out or just plain sick. Loud but not combative. Yesterday, one of them had spat directly at her face when she asked him to leave. The phlegm splattered over the left lens of her blockers and smeared when she rubbed them with a tissue. Yochanna's boss Mitch had found her in the stockroom, looking for the alcohol swabs.

"You should probably make sure your vaccines are current," he said. He was so much bigger than she was, and he blocked the stockroom door when she said she wanted to go back to her desk. His hand grazed her body as he reached for the shelf beside her, procuring the box she'd been looking for. By the time he moved aside to let her pass, her work-appropriate shirt was soaked with nervous sweat and the top two buttons were mis-aligned. She could feel herself becoming thinner, like a sheet of tin rinsed again and again in a sluice of acid wash.

Whatever was in Mitch's saliva was making her sick too, but she couldn't tell if it was nausea or anxiety. In a few more weeks, she could go to a clinic—usually, she only spent her benefits on the things that soap and hydro-packs couldn't fix. This month, she'd sunk her credits into a mental health module. She was considering a new antidepressant called Acedia: it was supposed to be effective for malaise and melancholy, the two strains of depression she had the most trouble with. A pay-per-minute therapist diagnosed her with "recurrent nostalgia for anachronistic experience," which described why she couldn't stop missing a time that far predated her own years on earth. She didn't want to be here or now; no amount of mindfulness exercises would ever be able to change that. A pill didn't take away her hour-plus commute or the boss who wouldn't stop pawing her. No medicine could change the situation or even make it bearable.

As if manifesting her anxiousness, her compulsive scratching had come back this month. She clawed the insides of her own thighs, the grout in the shower, the gray flank of the Hudson overpass, the disintegrating lichen on the undersides of benches. She carried a paperclip so that she could etch notches in porous surfaces and collect the dust that flaked off them. Sometimes, she sank the clip's discolored tip into the soft part of her inner thigh and watched the single drop of blood congeal slowly on her skin. She didn't tell the therapist about the collection of powders that dotted her kitchen counter or the pulp that clogged her sink. In her pockets, she spirited pinches of rust, gravel, and drywall, the urban colors that surrounded her.

In the office, she filled the water compartment from the dispenser, then loaded the double pods into the coffee machine. It huffed and puffed. Last year's model, already breaking down. Nothing came with a warranty anymore. The reasoning was, *you have a basic income: can't you just buy another one?* She mixed in a few spoonfuls of powdered milk from the cardboard canister. The coffee turned the color of faded pajamas. Next to the dispenser, a poster of New York pests: deer, raccoons, pigeons, sparrows, Canada geese, rats, and squirrels. All seven species were gray, the shade of concrete, evolved to blend into places without grass or trees. They were scavengers and nuisances. They survived because they took whatever they found, and left no trace behind. Even their nests were temporary.

Yochanna set her mug on the neutral pad next to her audio set. Both sides of her desk were cluttered with soylent wrappers. She cleared them into the trash hamper and sat down facing her monitors. The surface tablet, awakened by the proximal temperature of her body, lit up under her elbows. She let her tote flop gently on the floor. The screens flickered, updating. She watched them, munching a handful of pistachios out of her snack drawer. The communications panel blinked. Answering the phone wasn't her job, but like locking up, making coffee, and keeping the doorway clear, she ended up being the one to do it anyway.

"Yochanna," her boss said, flipping the lights on. "What are you doing here in the dark?"

"Just getting organized."

The blue tubes in the ceiling clicked overhead as the gas inside them warmed, casting a glow that was supposed to mimic the natural light spectrum. She watched Mitch go into his office. Through the door, she could see the faux wood paneling, walls crowded with award plaques and framed prints of local, native songbirds. Every year, he convinced another major donor that they could revive the Baird's Sandpiper population; that the East River district's arsenic levels had subsided and its cement banks were habitable by shorebirds; that donations now would erase the damage that past investments had already done. Mitch told Yochanna once that his job was telling a story that someone wanted to believe in, whether it was true or not.

"It's all fear or greed," he'd said, an avuncular hand creeping north of her knee. "They're afraid of not getting what they want, or greedy with what they've already got. But everyone likes songbirds. One guy gave us a million because I could whistle like a scarlet tanager."

Yochanna heard the familiar clunk of his personal device landing on its neutral pad.

"Is that coffee I smell?" he called.

She brought him a cup, with a packet of white sweetener stirred in. He thanked her, face pointed towards the cascading icons on his desk screen.

"Did we get that Audubon grant off last week? The deadline's tomorrow," he said.

The *we* made her bristle.

"I stayed late Friday," she said.

He picked up his coffee, blew on it, and stood by the window, looking down into the street. "Look at this."

The tent city was on fire. Yochanna saw a few structures shaking, as though someone was trapped inside and desperately trying to escape. One of the tents vomited a column of dull orange smoke. The dwellings were packed together: it was difficult to see between them. A blue tarp, rigged up as an awning, sagged into black, smoldering holes as the heat ate the plastic away. A raccoon, cub dangling from her mouth, bolted for the safety of the overpass. From the window, Yochanna could see that the settlement was mostly cardboard, shanties improvised from packing materials, and old camping equipment. All flammable.

"Did you call 911?" she asked.

Mitch shrugged.

He put her arm around her and pointed down at the people standing on the sidewalks. They wore filthy backpacks stuffed with things that couldn't be left behind. They clutched each other, hands holding heads and shoulders and bodies close. One man, jacket smoking, rocked back and forth. Yochanna couldn't hear sirens, though Emergency Services was less than three blocks away.

"They all have exactly what we have up here," her boss said. His grip tightened and she sensed the familiar tension of his frustration. "What do they spend it on? People like this. You give them what they need, or you take it away, and the outcome is the same."

"The same?"

"No, worse. That place they're squatting used to be a park before they ruined it. Three species of sparrow migrated through here, and now we've lost that habitat. What's the point of protecting something that doesn't make the city more beautiful?"

"Ask not," Yochanna recited, like you were supposed to. People liked birds because they were undemanding: reminders of a simpler time, when people hung clear tubes of seed outside and watched the cardinals gather, sing, eat. Birds were beautiful, not like these ragged humans with their matted hair and filthy, darkened fingernails.

"I work here all day, looking down at this trash," he said. One of the little houses, nailed together from sheets of discarded plywood, ignited. The people on the sidewalk flapped their arms. They were not migratory. They weren't going anywhere.

Yochanna heard the first squeal of sirens.

"It's a short drop," her boss said. Then, he looked up, as though seeing her for the first time. "Having enough isn't enough. Food, water, healthcare, shelter. What about the rest?"

"The rest?"

"You're young. You're lucky you don't know what you're missing."

She knew, though. She felt the missing pieces acutely. Keeping up the momentum of this normal-ish life was full-time and the dullness wore on her. She was tired. She was glad the only real window was in her boss' office, because she would have spent too much time staring out it, wishing she was somewhere else.

Mitch either ignored her or treated her to the full, nauseating force of his attention. She could not say no to him; if she did, she would lose the little bit she had. What he did to her in the paneled room wasn't explicitly in her job description. It was cold comfort to think that plenty of other young women were complying with the exact same stomach-turning invasions in private offices all across the boroughs.

His hand was heavy on the top of her head, pressing her down until her knees hit the carpet. She obeyed out of habit and let her mind wander, leaving her poor body behind to choke and drool on its standard morning task. Her body was a series of toggles, and Yochanna watched dispassionately as Mitch flipped them one at a time in a series that never failed to sicken her. She felt her kneecaps riveted to the seedy carpet while her obedient mouth hinged open. There was no off button and no escape. When her boss was finished, he stuffed himself deep into the pocket of her cheek and caressed her throat with his hands until she swallowed. At no point had he even looked down at her—his focus was out the window, on the smoke and fire engines.

When he let go of Yochanna's hair, she backed away from him on all fours. There was a dark puddle on the rug between his feet, sticky with the same stuff that drained from the sides of Yochanna's stretched and aching mouth. Her jaw hurt and her ankles throbbed from kneeling. If she cut her hair off, he would have nothing to pull, she thought—but she liked her hair, why deprive herself of the one pretty thing she owned, just because some bastard put his hands on it?

While she swiped at the mess in the corners of her mouth and the wet spot on her blouse, Mitch refastened his pants. He didn't even smile at her this time, but turned away whistling under the pretext of refilling his coffee. Her whole life would be this, until he got tired of her and replaced her with another failing-dream art student, another mound of debt, another indentured girl who was too impoverished and afraid to do anything but comply.

When she got back to her desk, she could hear the shouting outside, mixed with the fire services' horns. Her screens were all dark. She gazed at her own reflection for a long moment, hardly recognizing the face reflected back at her in the surface tablet.

5

BEFORE, WHEN PAUL worked in the poppy fields, the other pickers swapped stories about people who fell into the gleaning machines or were shot by drones for breaking curfew. It was a fast way to go. Painless, almost. Better than what many of them lived with.

Harvesting poppy heads was delicate work and had to be done by human hands—one of few non-automated tasks, since android eyes struggled to differentiate the pod from the plant's buds and could destroy a crop by deadheading too soon. After four years of picking, Paul could sense the sap in the stem with his hands and knew every shade of green in the poppies' spectrum. Drug tests no longer worked on him; his system was saturated with airborne opioid oxygenate. He felt no pain when he knelt in the long rows of plants and crawled among them like a supplicant, collecting pods.

The change came over him gradually, but once inoculated, he stopped singing prayers with the others at night and withdrew into himself like an animal into its scrape. He was the biggest in the labor pool and the strongest and claimed the most productive plants for himself. He was not above protecting his share with his fists or the curved blades they used to trim and cauterize the milky stems.

One day, he had filled his quota early and received a dispensation for recreational time: two hours instead of the customary fifteen minutes of leisure. There was nothing to do on the farm, so he climbed the deteriorating fence that marked the edge of the field and ascended the gentle slope that protected the vast, red-petaled, fragrant meadow that stretched over the hills. It was noon, or later. The sun, high and fiery, scorched the back of his neck. His stomach lining stuck to itself, growling with hunger. His sneakers scuffed through the dog stickers and soft earth covering the gopher mounds.

The rattlesnake grass, the tiny blue flax flowers, and taller strands of wild wheat parted before him. He liked to look up at the crisp edge of the sky where it bent down to kiss the distant silhouette of New York, many days' travel in the distance. He loved to see it shining there, impervious to the sun and accelerated rhythms of harvest and planting. Like a glittering token, it helped him forget that, under the ground, a million crawly things ate and puked and writhed in a vile dance of creation.

He found a spindly deer trail. It led away from the poppies and took him out of sight over the first sky-bleached crest. The sun touched him through his shirt and he felt it at the roots of his hair.

He felt the first whisker of sweat nose its way through his armpit. He stumbled over a runty fern and swore, turned to kick it.

The grass was thick around the plant's base and full of dead, dry sticks. A flat place showed where a field mouse had gone in and out of the tangle, nipping the soft green fiddleheads with the precision of a florist. At the center of the fern, as though by arrangement, there was a skull, which gleamed like the sticky pistil of a lily.

There was a skeleton in the grass.

Paul knelt down to look at the dead thing's grinning pearly teeth. A few black places showed on the forehead, and on the broad plate of mandible where the muscle and skin had been scraped away. An irregular fissure ran down the nose and trailed into the left nostril. He examined the shape of the head and the way the incisors came close together under the upper lip. Who would skin a dog and leave its carcass here, picked clean, in a field under the sweet-scented sky?

Foxes and dogs were close enough, Paul thought.

He held the skull's two halves in his hands and stared at it as though it was going to disclose to him a secret. He lifted the skull's carapace, its helmet of bone, and let the lower jaw drop into his hand. This is where the tongue would have been, the black-rubber lips and whiskers, all the parts of the fox's mask. He raised it to his eye to look into one of the oval eye sockets.

"Don't," said a voice behind him. Paul started. He tightened his grip on the two pale plates of bone.

"Turn around."

He complied, lost his balance halfway. The fern that tripped him rustled in the small of his back. He saw now the complete circle of dried bones. The irregular pattern was a ring the size of a dinner platter. Ulna touched femur, touched the delicate row of vertebrae and splayed scapular bones and each separate knucklebone, all laid out like a necklace. Paul's toes nudged the pelvis, which had been broken and half-buried in the ground.

A hot, small thing brushed against his hand. He recoiled. He couldn't see—his eyes hurt, the sun was too bright. The skull was snatched away before he could do anything about it. He squinted at the stranger and perceived that she was not only young but also poisonously pale. A landfiller. She frowned at him. She was half his age, dressed in a ratty gray camisole and faded black jeans mended with dental floss. Her collarbones protruded like wings— her hair was dull and dark, her eyes the shade of copper pellets. She put the skull in the drooping pocket of the stained sweatshirt she'd tied around her waist.

"You're just a kid," he said. The girl set her boot in the center of his chest and kicked him onto his back. He scrabbled over the fern and the white-greasy bones. She planted a foot on either side of his chest and squatted low. Her haunches touched his belly and her knees doubled up as high as her shoulders. She stroked his cheek with her closed hand. Her nails were ragged and dotted with dirt and mica.

"Want to see what I've got?"

She held her hand over his face and opened it, one finger at a time. He flinched, expecting some nasty surprise, maybe a lizard or a clod of dirt. Then she laughed.

"It's nothing!" she shouted. She slapped his shoulder.

"You tricked me," he said.

"You're easy to trick. When's the last time somebody touched you like this? Your wife?"

He couldn't remember.

"I'm not married."

"Yes, you are. The married ones don't try to get away."

He could hear the skull click its teeth in her pocket when she shifted her weight. His euphoria from being away from work was evaporating. His stomach groaned, needy. She was small—a quarter his size. He squinted, gauging whether she'd put up much of a fight. She had a tiny red birthmark the color of cough syrup on her neck. That birthmark was the brightest thing on her body. He had a sudden, ravenous urge to cover it with his thumb, wrap his fingers around her skinny neck, and crush against her in the jagged nest of bones.

Her fingers crept up from his shoulders and tugged his earlobes. Her teeth were yellow and sharp, too crowded in her mouth. Paul thought he saw an extra incisor, a double canine.

She was hungry.

Well, he was, too.

He had heard that there were landfillers out here who lived off the grid, scavenging from the farms. They were considered vermin, the last and lowest form of humans—no connections at all, undocumented. If one was shot by the guards or found strung on the razor barbs of the electric fence—fists full of stolen pods and charred tongue jabbing through a burn-hole in its cheek—nobody cared. It was only a landfiller.

"Let me up," he said.

She shook her head.

"I'll hurt you," he said. He slapped her hands away. "What the fuck are you doing to me?"

She leapt off and landed in the grass. She swiped at the dog stickers and low, bright blades of grass. Her boots were threadbare and sodden. Her sock showed through the Teflex of one. The other was patched with a shred of duct tape. He sat up and brushed the gray dust off his shirt.

"Why did you leave the poppies?" She ripped up a tiny bunch of wild violets.

He stood on wobbly legs. Standing over her, he could see down the front of her sagging camisole, both nipples and her belly exposed to the air as though she wore nothing at all, nothing more than an intoxicating huff of smoke.

"I don't like this game." He took two steps, stopped. Turned.

She plucked a stem of rattlesnake grass and swizzled it between her fingers. "I can help you if you take me with you. Back to the city."

His laugh was a curt bark. "I don't even know you."

"What if I said I could help you cross the desert?"

"You're a child. Skinny little kid."

A pair of crows flew over their heads. Their twin shadows dashed between Paul and the girl. For a moment, Paul saw the silhouettes, clean as cut paper, each feather stenciled on the yellow stalks of flax and renegade barley and witches' wheat and dog stickers and the tiny low plants that make golden burrs that clung to Paul's sock like foolish promises. He saw, in that instant, a dark place exposed.

"I bet you'd do anything to get to New York. I bet you'd give a finger."

She waggled her digits at him, a coy wave at odds with her withered, flat mouth. When she leaned over and put her face against his cheek, he was surprised by how warm she was. Even through his clothes he could feel the heat coming off that pale skin, as though she had a furnace burning inside her. Her lips grazed his ear. The tiny hairs inside stood up as though electrified.

His tears burned him like venom. His throat closed and spasms racked his chest. Her skinny fingers tangled in his hair. The girl fondled the nub of each vertebra, the atlas and axis and the powerful cradle of muscle that cupped the back of Paul's skull. Her fingertips wormed their way across his skull, feeling the pits and lesions that blossomed on his cheeks, the amphetamine crust of his nostrils and the drying fissures in his cracked lips.

"Life's a mouth," she said. "When you get what you want, you have to swallow."

She snuck a finger into his mouth, then two. She probed deeper, feeling his molars and the bloody places where his gums were starting to recede from the surface of his teeth. He sucked on her hand, pulling it deeper into his mouth. She tasted like bleach and salt, and something sweetly rotting. Her rough nails were gritty, and scratched his tongue.

"Sit on my lap," she said, arranging herself cross-legged. He was too big to fit, but he lowered his rump between her legs and she wrapped her skinny arms around him, cradling him. His cheek rested on her collarbone. The heat rose off her, carrying the stink of rotting blackberries and sulfur.

She slipped down the strap of her camisole. Her breast was a tiny bud, fat and firm and flower-sized. She toyed with it until it swelled. Her skin was so pale he could see the blue veins through the milky skin over her heart. She guided Paul's face down to her nipple. He took it in his teeth, then opened his mouth to suck her in deeper. To his surprise, he tasted sugar and melons. A squirt of cantaloupe-flavored milk seeped from the corner of his mouth. He pulled back, but she caught the back of his head and pressed his nose into her flesh. He choked on the sweetness. Milk as thick as honey ran down his throat.

"On the treetop," she sang. "When the wind blows, the cradle will rock."

She stroked his hair. He snuffled at her, rooting like a pig. Then he seized her and sucked hard, drawing out the long swallows of hot, vanilla-sweet liquor. She did not gasp or shudder, the way a normal woman would, or reach down to touch between her legs. She rocked Paul, side to side, and she sang as she nursed him.

"When the bough breaks, the cradle will fall—and down will come baby, cradle and all."

When he was finished, she covered herself and rubbed her thumb across Paul's swollen lips. Milk-drunk, he wiped his mouth and looked down at his hand, expecting it to be stained with a smear of blood.

He grabbed a handful of her clothes and drew her closer and his teeth found other, softer places. He would have put her into his mouth whole if he could. She tasted like the meadow, a handful of clover and soaked in sun-rich sap, a place where seeds found life and fed the thousands of creatures that breathed and died and let their bodies go to rot in the soil, turning themselves over to the next generation that pushed out of their graves and sought the sky in turn.

She could not fight him off forever. In a few minutes, he had what he wanted from her. For the first time in months, the pit in his stomach settled, though it was not a feeling of satisfaction. The milk and meat curdled inside Paul as he sat quietly, bargaining with his hunger.

He plucked a strand of wheat and tied the stalk in a knot. The coil lay in his palm. He looked at it for a moment, then snapped it into pieces and put his fingers to his tongue to taste the bittersweet sap. He sat on the hill alone for a long time, watching the wheat's shadow move like a clock's hand across his skin.

When he slunk into the labor trailer, it was long past curfew. Security scanned his identity chip and noted that he would be docked for the missed hours, but he did not care. It was close to midnight and he could not have said where he was or what he'd done. *Abuse of trust,* they wrote in his disciplinary chit. He wouldn't be allowed out again.

He chugged endless jars of liquid from the communal sink. The girl's blood lay thick in his stomach and he could not purge or drown it, no matter how much fluid he poured down his neck. He gagged on a mouthful and dropped the jar in the sink. The others stared at him from their bunks, eyes wide and glossy in the dark, afraid of him. Looking at his own hands, he saw the lilac patterns under his skin, weak and distant, the shape and color of summer lightning. He had to eat, he thought. If he did not eat, he was going to die.

She had offered to take him to the city.

The next morning, he could not make himself concentrate on the poppies. His teeth seemed larger in his mouth. As he was working the rows, a thread of drool leaked through his filtration gear and dribbled over his gloves and the bouquets of opium pods. He was deaf and blind and his hunger was a flood of sensation that turned everything to taste, a flavor, a hunger that overpowered his other senses.

The drones found the girl's body halfway up the hill, her slender remains half-buried in the wild golden grass. Her bony arms stuck stiffly out, as though still trying to fend off her attacker. Putrescence wafted down the crest of the rise and brought security into the perimeter, scanning for evidence of her killer.

She was not undocumented after all, but a runaway. The pickers whispered about it among themselves, saying she was a princess—an ice drinker, not a landfiller. She had wandered away from her family's vineyard, spun on some mystery hallucinogen. Lived underground until her skin lost its pigment. A pint of her blood soaked into the earth, more precious than a hundred seasons of opioid sap. It had a value that had to be repaid.

The authorities came for Paul while he was on his knees in the picking field, his hands full of red opium poppy flowers. The petals crumpled like crepe paper in his grip and when they subdued him and scanned his molars to confirm the dental evidence, the robotic tongs separating his clenched teeth cut the edges of his lips so that he tasted blood again. The other pickers, many of whom had felt his fists or the edge of his trimming knife, watched dispassionately. His bunk—the best one—would be left empty. Someone else could sleep there now, undisturbed.

Trials were for the rich, like real meat and resting. The death penalty had been abolished for being inhumane, but the alternative made you wish you were dead. Paul had heard from the others that incarceration was not time without work: it was worse. There was no difference between night and day in prison, no seasons. Few people survived: they found ways to execute themselves, rather than be crushed in the mandibles of fate.

At Lakeshore Corrective, classical music seeped through a speaker in the ceiling and gas jets jutted like flower buds from the edges of the floor. Rough hands stuffed Paul into a too-small aerating vinyl coverall marked with the prison's logo, strapped him to a barber chair, and shaved his head to the skin. The intake room was bathed in a pale green light that some psychologists proved had a sedating effect on the brain after extended exposure; the guards' eyes were covered in translucent shields that sat between their eyeball and lids, filtering this light out so that they remained unaffected. A candy-colored mural of demonic-looking sheep with human faces and flattened teeth wrapped around the room; the monsters danced gleefully on a rainbow, trampling the colors so they fell in technicolor rain on the fields below them. *Soothing.*

Paul flexed his muscles, testing the strength of the restraints, which were stained with former inmates' perspiration and blood. The barber's chair was sticky and as he wriggled in his seat, sweating, he thought of the people who had preceded him in this position, and wondered how many of them had shit themselves in fear, ceded all control of their minds, and flailed in terror in the radial straitjacket.

A guard with a single, perfect curl of red-blonde hair adorning her forehead approached him with a cattle prod in one hand

and a blunt device the size of an electric razor in the other. She was tiny, compared to Paul, with proportions like a doll: the peak of her cap barely came up to his seated shoulder. Her oversized head bobbled on the delicate stem of her neck. Her legs were abnormally slender, with knees that bowed outward, as though accustomed to gripping a body or a moto-bike. Her uniform concealed her secondary sexual characteristics; the double-layered cloth, generative pads, and taser-toed control boots were fashionable on her, not threatening. She looked like a little girl dressed up in her papa's riot gear.

She stuck the prod's lethal snout next to Paul's head and deployed the volts. His eardrum crackled and he jerked back. The static charge lingered in the chamber of his ear.

If he had not been restrained, he would not feel afraid of her at all. He had battered smaller people. He could crush and subdue the guard without the use of his arms. When not afraid, he was impossible to control. But under these alien conditions, his body was ungovernable. He was so focused on the cattle prod that his eyes felt like they would rotate inside his skull, following the woman as she prowled around him.

He heard her tiny feet on the tiles as she crossed behind him, light as a dancer. He did not need his hands to kill her. If he was not bolted to the chair, he would bash her with his leg so that she flew into the hellish mural and then he would rush into her and smother her by covering her with his body and driving his knees into her belly and her lungs until her ribs were smashed and she either drowned in her own blood or fainted from the pain. He had developed a rare sensitivity to the anatomy of the human head and, even through thick boots and over the sound of screaming, knew the exact moment when the interlocking plates had failed and the first runny squirt of jelly spurted through their broken hinges.

However, his legs were locked into the footbrass and the restraints cow-clipped him to the spine support pad. He took a deep breath, willing himself to focus. The guard stalked where he could not see her. He heard her tap the prod on her boot and then drag it over the tiles. The sound itched. He stuck his tongue out, as though that would help him turn his head further. Undignified as a dog, he floundered in the chair with his mouth flapping open and his eyes rolling.

A zinging bolt of electricity made his kidneys quiver. Paul felt his body spasm as a deep, involuntary twitch quaked through him. Saliva ran from the corners of his mouth and soaked the already-discolored straitjacket. The guard darted forward and jammed the syringe shader into his back so that all ten needles went through his skin and pierced the deltoid muscle. His body, primed with adrenaline, surged with panic and pumped the FDA-approved supplements—anti-infectives, placebo meds for double-blind studies, and an mRNA serum that would bond to Paul's white blood cells for the duration of his sentence—into his body. He was fully inoculated in under 45 seconds.

He woke up on a narrow bunk in the block reserved for Violent Offenders. His coverall was designed to collect and neutralize uric acid—inmates pissed themselves all the time, or were denied access to sewage points and had to make do in their clothes. Paul's uniform sucked up the urine that soaked him from waist to knees. In a moment, and other than a vague sense of shame and a smattering of welts on the back of his neck, there was no evidence of the intake process at all.

He rubbed his newly bald head and felt the tender, chilled apricots of his ears. He did not know what time it was: he was sentenced to a thousand days of incarceration, but without a clock or calendar, there was no way of knowing how quickly these days passed. The entire sentence would be a miserable blur punctuated by sleep, meals, and other men's faces.

The correctional center was constructed to constrict. To discomfit. They did not have the authority explicitly to shoot you or flood your body with voltage but they could make you stuff your hand all the way down your esophagus, past the wrist to the forearm. That was a popular one, in here. To die eating yourself, with the final breath released only when the pathologist hacksawed through the ulna and pulled the whole ragged stump out of the throat.

Without sun or darkness, Paul began to measure time in the rubber-sheeted bodies that rolled feet first out of their cells. It was common for inmates to deliberately aspirate the pureed, colorless paste served in the cafeteria to fill their lungs or choke, or contract a walking pneumonia vicious enough to smother the breath from them. One man paid his friends to smuggle laundry powder to him, enough to eat, and he died with lavender-scented soap bubbles burbling from his melting trachea, tearing at his own stomach as the floral micelles melted his digestive lining. Another jammed his head into the corner of his bunk and threw himself sideways so violently that he snapped his own neck.

At first, this seemed unthinkable, but after a while, Paul found himself prodding his gums and slipping his fingers against his soft palate, probing past his gag reflex. There was a faded purple starburst on the wall of his cell and after the first dozen suicides, he realized that it was not a discoloration in the concrete but the splatter that follows impact. Some former occupant of Paul's bed, his same square footage, was a person so desperate to escape that they had bludgeoned their own head against the wall hard enough to mash their brain out in a florid halo. Sometimes, its gelatinous rays seemed to stretch out to Paul, like the tendrils of a poppy's petals. They beckoned him. *This is how you do it. You put your head right here.*

He considered it, knowing that even if he was capable, he was not insane enough to bypass his brain's survival instincts. Besides, there were other barriers. After the injection of mRNA metabolized, it made his body adversarial. A prison in itself. The protein came from farmed jellyfish and made Paul's skin react to the bars and bricks as if they were charged with a current. They stung like acid if Paul touched them, either by accident or when he forgot how to feel pain. The jellyfish protein left feather-white scars on his fingers, but the nerve damage it inflicted was negligible.

He would not give up. He could still make a fist.

The blanket was warm but scratchy, the coverall was too small, and the slippers issued to him melted when touched by moisture. The only time he was around the other inmates was when eating or showering, not long enough to exchange more than a few words. Within six weeks, he was testing negative for opioid compounds and his nervous system was ragged and bald. He was always hungry, in here—the food units dulled his hunger but could not erase the taste of the girl's milk or the freedom she had tempted him with.

As the days passed, he was convinced that she had wanted to be eaten.

She wanted him to go north, to the city, away from where the poppies bloomed.

She offered him a way to go, and he had taken it.

He exorcised his fears with violence. In dreams, his strength was magnified and he could bend metal with his hands and shatter bones with a single blow. He started to honor his faith again, praying to whatever would sustain him through the sentence. That his will might become intractable as God's.

In prison, he lay on his bunk and raised his head thousands of times, nodding until his neck was a thick tire of muscle. His already broad shoulders expanded until the coverall seams split and his bunk was too narrow to hold all of him at once. When his incarceration was complete, he would start life over again. He would go to the city and get a clean identity chip. Never pick on his knees again. Never burn under the sun, seeking relief in the shadows of the machine gun watchtowers. He could do odd jobs, and in a place with so many people he was sure to find some kind of work.

He sprawled on his wafer-weave mattress with his toes jutting through his slippers, skin stinging as the mRNA pricked him with its ionic needles. He nodded and nodded, assuring himself that at the other end of incarceration was a life in Manhattan.

He would get there—if he did not die or go mad first.

His first act when he reentered society was to hotwire a van and sleep in it until he was not tired anymore. He woke three days later. His clothes were plain but shabby, pieced together from scraps salvaged from a dumpster outside a uniform shipment center. They hung on him. He was large and gaunt, and even in New York, his hunger never eased. He walked into a shop in an alley off Canal Street, pocketed a bean sandwich, and carried it off, hoping the deli owner wouldn't notice the theft. As he crouched under a storefront soaped with pale gray paint, a white pressboard cat on the sill glared down through its monocle. He ate quickly, stuffing the stolen food between his jaws. It was the first hot food he had eaten in days.

The woman who opened the shop door walked out backwards, holding a stack of long, ribbon-wrapped parcels that slipped out of her grip as though greased. She lost one and it bounced off the cobbled street and landed with a slap between Paul's legs. He picked it up and rose to his feet, filling the doorway and the awning like a golem. He offered the woman her package and noticed how wide her eyes were and how her hands trembled as she snatched it from him.

"Thank you," she muttered. She was frozen to the spot.

"You look like you could use some help," he said in his gentlest tones.

Her name was Celine Broussard and she made something called an *umbrella*.

6

THE DAY OF the Weiss' rain party, Celine emerged from her studio with an armload of umbrellas. It was time for them to go. The containers of flowers surrounded her, high as her belt, as she waded through an impenetrable hedge of fragrant, juicy stalks. Her hair radiated from her head like the bristling crown of a sunburned thistle. She wore stripes of silver eyeshadow that made her look as though she had two robotic oculi instead of human lids. Her mere presence was enough to draw anyone's attention, but just in case, she called out her friend's name.

Paul looked up from the virtual bird of paradise he was fine-tuning; the shimmer was off, the three orange whiskers at the top of the flower kept flickering. He set it on the charging pad on the counter and its pixels refreshed in uneven threads, redrawing themselves.

He only needed a few moments to lock up the shop and collect the Weiss' order from the back room. It was a simple job—Celine paid him to come with his van, load the order, and take her to the skyscraper in Midtown where the rain party would be. As they lifted the long boxes of finished product into the van, Celine winked at the white cat in the window for luck. She had found it years ago on a curb in Queens, where a film crew was cleaning out a bedroom-sized set. Nobody noticed her sliding it into her bag and vanishing down the street with part of their movie. The cat, implacable in its self-satisfaction, looked perfect in the window—as though it had always belonged there.

Celine was not concerned that anyone would steal her umbrellas. In the absence of rain, they had no practical value—each one essentially a museum piece or a novelty. The average thief would not even know where to resell one, though you could get practically anything else on the black market, from fresh lilacs still covered in artificial dew to new organs, grown in an agar stew offshore and smuggled into Dumbo by fishermen. All the same, Celine felt a twinge of anxiety when Paul's van stalled at an intersection and was surrounded by commuters, anonymous in their filtration masks and goggles, swathed in layers of reflective insulation. Someone slapped the broad side of the van, and she jumped.

Midtown was packed with ghosts, some benign and some not. She watched a group of investment bankers in identical padded vests and illuminated high-tops gather around a tamale vendor, who pressed plastic-wrapped packets into their outstretched hands. At the curb, a pigeon tried to lift a hot dog bun that was nearly as big as itself. Forty-foot electronic screens scrolled on every building, advertising new data plans, library events, musical and theater performances, awards, and civic regulations. Nobody looked at the pop-ups, but they filled the street with an eerie, pink and blue haze that hung in the permanent twilight of the city. Dry beams of sunshine sometimes slipped among the skyscrapers. Between the tall towers, shadows adhered to pavement that was cold and thick with grime.

Paul drove gripping the wheel, peering through the grit on his windshield with the focus of a sniper. The streets were dark, even at two in the afternoon. Pedestrians in day-glow jackets skittered across intersections; the colors of their clothes popped into high relief when Paul's high beams passed over them. Many of them wore headlamps or had added safety trim to their bags and backpacks.

The van eased toward the Flatiron through a river of humans who did not yield to traffic or acknowledge the encoded signals marking crossings and corners. Periodically, a distinct feature would emerge and flit like a moth before the busy, fragmented movement of the crowd subsumed it. As soon as Celine caught a glimpse of a naked eye or a strip of patterned fabric or a logo-marked pocketbook, it was gone, and she forgot what she had seen as instantly as the feature had caught her attention. Street life was the opposite of her studio. By the time they arrived, a mild stress headache pinched her scalp. It was not a consolation to think of other passengers in other cars going to other destinations. From long communication with their family stewards, she knew that the Weisses traveled on four wheels only when leaving the city. For intraurban travel, these ice-drinkers used independent helicopters or other sky transport to take them from one place to the next. For the party, they would arrive in a charter sky bus en masse as the event was starting. That was the function of money, to go from comfort to comfort, bypassing the inconvenient parts of being human.

Paul helped load the umbrellas into the service elevator on a luggage rack provided by the building.

"Safety first," he said, which was their own lucky ritual. He patted Celine's stack of cartons.

"I'll be back in a couple of hours," she promised.

"Don't take any wooden nickels."

Neither of them had seen real wood, just the pressed laminate made into umbrella handles and high-end tables and chairs. Even Celine's umbrella designs were a relic, an opulence beyond the reach of all but the wealthiest. Most people would never see or feel rain; they would never even hold an umbrella. Celine grew up hearing about an older New York, a city where people lived like small sea crabs, scuttling from peel-paint cold-water apartments to the subway to the packed soup of open-air offices and then home again, with umbrellas clamped in their hands to protect them from the nearly constant rain or intense humidity. In the days of rain, her grandmother used to say, you could get a cheap, disposable model at any news stand; many of them were made from corn fiber or other biodegradable matter that gradually lost its integrity and leaked or melted on the plastic frame. But that was back when rain was everywhere, so much of it that the Hudson Canal was filled past its rim with floating droplets of pollutant-rich water. Celine thought these were fairy tales: tall, living trees that cast cool shade on lawns watered with natural rain. Her grandmother was also the one who told her about the wooden nickels, though what a *nickel* was, was never clear.

Order loaded, Paul shook Celine's hand and stepped back, disappearing into the electronic smog. The elevator rose with a clank. The main cars were set on titanium rails and ran silently, operated by people who wiped the glass doors clean at every stop so the wealthy never had to see a fingerprint or filthy smudge. Workers were not allowed to use the main elevators. The service elevator was for everyone else; it had no attendant and groaned and creaked as it slowly ascended to the mezzanine. Its panels were stamped aluminum, uninsulated, with a square cut into each side. The floors slid by; the tubes' green cast segued into natural-frequency bulbs that mimicked what sunshine used to be like. Celine caught glimpses of offices and people: swatches of hanging art; plastic plants with vivid rubber leaves; a digital fountain that streamed HD footage of moving water; and broadcasts of stock updates, weather reports, soft colors, and repetitive tonal music designed to calm the mind and lull people into forgetting that their environment was unnatural.

At the mezzanine, an attendant met her, rolled the cart to the second elevator, and swiped the security passcard so she could ascend to the room where caterers were staging the tables and flatware for the Weiss' rain party.

She waited with the umbrellas near the honey wagon where the dancers were getting ready. A sliding screen, partially transparent, offered Celine one-way privacy; she could look at the caterers, the dancers, and the other performers, but not be seen herself. Each cell had mauve, quilted walls and brownish pink carpeting that reminded Celine of a scab. She watched one of the dancers fidget, finally perching on a free chair with one leg tucked under, to offset the thin padding on the seat. The single outlet under the shelf charged her device.

Celine was an expert at waiting. Time passed differently backstage at rain parties: there was nothing to do, and then everything happened at once. Everyone was either hanging around or had already disappeared. Through the pale screen, she could see that the honey wagon was full of performers in nylon encasement suits, hoods pulled back so they could breathe and blink and sip their almond milk matcha lattes. The walls of each cell were thin, so Celine could hear them gossip—most of it dull, solely about themselves. One told a story about "accidentally" spending a full day with a C-list star. Another recounted an interview that turned into a hostage situation when they were stuck inside a hotel lobby with the paparazzi out on the sidewalk. Another one claimed to have been mistaken for a famous predator's girlfriend, precipitating a mini media hurricane of attention. This celebrity sought out partners so immature they didn't even have body hair yet. His wife, it was said, ran up a horrendous electrolysis bill, fending off the inevitable mammalian qualities of her body and the divorce that would go with it.

"I was younger then," the dancer said.

"You're so young now," purred the makeup artist, adhering latex fish scales under the other woman's eyes. "You can't even tell the difference."

"I was so pretty."

The others reassured her that she was still pretty, would be pretty forever. It made Celine grateful that she had been born sturdy and plain, into a family of craftsmen. She would never have to earn her place in the world with her beauty, or suffer the procedures that other women did. *Classic* was the word for the few female-bodied people who aged profitably in show business. With the right amount of facial fixative and tasteful adjustments to hair and wardrobe, performers had a chance to work into their mid-30s. After that, it was "character" parts, catalog modeling, and brothels. Some made the ultimate career move and married men who wanted beautiful wives and could afford to keep them up. A few dozen women in each generation had long trajectories. The men, on the other hand, matured into new and versatile roles, unconstrained by fashion trends or beauty standards. Masculinity was timeless, distinguished, and iconic. A non-woman could collect wrinkles, extra pounds, and gray hairs and still be celebrated. The same wasn't true for the others.

The dancers in the honey wagon all knew this: it was the reason they were called "extras." They sat in their individual cells, gazing at their phones, praying to their mirrors, touching the edges of their mouths, worrying over the places the lights would touch, refract, brighten, and expose. Each cubicle contained a gorgeous, single, anxious body, each finding clever ways to numb their fear while they waited for their little bit of limelight to dissolve. The hallway where Celine waited buzzed with the extras' movements and the things they murmured to one another, promising that this would not be the last party. They were still desirable, at least for now. The anxiety of beauty was unavoidable; Celine pitied them.

A man with tall hair and an illuminated tie helped guide Celine and her cart past a table laden with chafing dishes. They'd lit the blue propane flames and set the heating lamps over the laminate boards that would hold cutlets of wild game meat. The Weisses had an animal reserve in Montana that kept cows, sheep, antelope, bison, deer, giraffe, and ibex for the family's personal use. The meat was flown, fresh, into the city. For this dinner, they would serve their privately raised antelope steak, truffled giraffe bites, and prime rib. Seafood wasn't safe unless it was farmed in filtered water—which the Weisses had in abundance. The menu included a hundred domestic lobsters, pulverized into flavored puffs. Ordinary people ate ground cellulite and vegan fillers; it was even possible to get slices of petri dish steaks, pink and flaccid and round as the containers where the muscle fibers were cultivated, but those were prohibitively expensive. Celine could eat curls of stained cartilage, styled as faux squid pasta, any time she could afford it. The Weiss family got the real thing: shreds of cephalopod doused in natural butter and garnished with a frisson of crispy tentacles.

The only time she'd ever had real chocolate was at these rain parties. Its rich, acid flavor was one of the many reasons she looked forward to the lavish celebrations. The "chocolate" she bought at home was derived from the Weiss' private stores as well—their naturally grown cacao plants were used for food research and contributed to the taste libraries used to customize the flavors in ordinary people's meals.

The catering manager swept the handful of menu cards off Celine's table just after she snuck a piece of dessert into her purse.

"We put you as close as possible to the wall. You'll be in the splash zone, but you can move back once things kick off." He grudgingly handed her a card. "If you stay, there's a full meal provided for staff. You weren't in the head count, but we have enough."

"Thank you," she said. Nobody liked working these things, no matter how good the money was. There were rumors that some of the rain parties devolved into orgies, with guests compelling service workers to take part. The tips were never what they should be for cleaning up after a handsy gang of plastered executives. Like anything else: the pay was inadequate, but who could afford to turn it down? The catering manager had the fifty-yard stare of a veteran events planner. Celine squared her shoulders.

"You have ten minutes," he said, and she nodded, one professional to another.

She laid out the umbrellas on the table beside the wall of ice. Its tender chill seeped through her garments and caressed her skin, making her shiver.

Each commemorative umbrella was white and embroidered with tiny Swarovski crystals that glittered like dew drops on the treated, waterproof, dupioni silk. The three unusual ones with the spiked tips, she set aside, tied with a simple white ribbon.

As Celine looked over the banquet settings, she saw the catering manager struggling to set Robert Senior's chair on the dais. Soon, each seat would be occupied by a well-fed, pampered body, one that had never known labor or serious pain. Wealth diffused stress the way umbrellas shed rain, showering it on the people beneath them, whose job it was to support the canopy at all costs, at any cost, for life.

Those people were not invited to experience rain.

Celine staged the white umbrella on the guest of honor's chair and went back to her table to make sure the pieces were prepared for the hired dancers. The ice wall dripped behind her. She was seized with a sudden desire to press her tongue to it, then her face, just to know what it was really like.

Celine had never tasted ice. Most people never even saw it in real life. They had ice on television, but it was just blocks of Bakelite painted with pale blue glycerin. The power grid drip was too weak and slow to make frozen water at home; even if it was possible, a tiny chip of ice was not the same thing as this monolith that loomed over the whole arrangement. Celine could see the individual shrink-wrapped Prada and Balenciaga jewelry boxes floating within the glossy ice. The logos on the packaging looked wavy and distorted through sixteen inches of frozen water. Spigots in the ceiling were programmed to spray body-temperature rain on command in a pattern that complemented the evening's agenda. Celine eyed the angle of the nozzle over her head, trying to guess when she should make herself scarce to avoid getting soaked.

"Excuse me," someone said, caressing the small of her back.

Celine recoiled.

"Not at all," she said. A trademark: even startled, she had perfect manners.

"Are you with Broussard's?" He was tall and wore a deep blue suit, the color of simulated whale hide. His azure hair was naturally silvered around his widow's peak and his eyes shimmered like a specialty tech display.

"Yes."

The miniature camera on his lapel blinked at her. He wore no jewelry, and his skin was flawless, as though grafted over his skeleton. Poreless, but his complexion was rich and plump with vitamins. Celine realized she was looking into the face of the of Henry Weiss-Broms, the son of the richest man in the world.

She turned to collect the pair of barbed umbrellas and offered them like a deadly bouquet.

"I can show you how to open them," she said. "The tips are hand-filed and very sharp."

"Cork," he noted.

"Synthetic. It's just a protective measure."

He shook his head; it didn't matter. "How did you get here?" he asked.

"I hired a van."

"When are they coming back?"

"I wanted to stay for the chocolate," she said, feeling childish. "And I wanted to see the rain."

"So, after."

Although she could hear some clinking from the direction of the galley kitchen, nobody was nearby. They were all alone at the wall of ice: the quadrillionaire and the umbrella maker.

"I will give you a year's worth of chocolate if you can arrange to have the van come before the rain begins."

It was a fortune. Celine was grateful for the gift of preternatural composure.

"But I will miss the dancers," she said. Both of them ignored the fact that she hadn't been invited, wasn't staff, and could be removed from the premises at his whim. She was the only artist of her kind: a species of one. There were plenty of nouveau-riche billionaires and trillionaires out there who would have paid for her art with their firstborns' blood. She kept this in mind as she began to push her luck. "I don't know if I want that much chocolate. What would I do with it? I might get tired of it after a month."

"You could sell it. High grade isn't available—most places," he said, tactful. He was a good negotiator, and his expression was unnervingly gentle. "You go to all the rain parties. You'll miss an hour of this one."

"But what an hour," she said.

His eyes flickered blue with temper. Then the silver rings around his irises clarified as the pixels in them resolved.

"Time is the only commodity I acknowledge," he said.

"I don't want something that lasts for a year," Celine said, pursing her lips. "I want to see rain."

He placed his hand against a frozen block and drew his fingers over its flank. "You know all about rain," he said. "What do you know about ice?"

She shrugged.

"Do you know what water used to taste like, before? It was like vegetable juice and flower petals, filtered through fine charcoal," he said. "The minerals in the earth gave each spring a signature flavor, finer than an elite champagne and impossible to synthesize."

She could tell *spring* meant something other than the season but did not ask what it was.

"I drink factory water, like everyone," she said.

He took her hand, made a cuff around her wrist, and pressed her palm to the ice. Shocked, she would have jerked back, but his grip was like steel. In an instant, her skin was numb, and the hand she used to hold her artisan's razor was useless.

"We talk about the power of water," he said, "but ice is more powerful. Collecting the purest water, containing it, transporting it, and preserving it is beyond what most people can envision. They drink boiled runoff from plastic bottles."

The nerve endings in her hands started to burn with over-stimulation. She did not dare flinch or struggle. She stared at her hand, splayed like a cuttlefish on the blasted-smooth block. Her nail beds were pale purple.

"Are you offering me ice?" she said, forcing herself to smile.

He relinquished her hand and watched as she slipped it under her blouse to reanimate against her warm belly.

"Your own glacier. Like I have in each of my homes. Real water, prehistoric."

She considered. "You would bring this to me?"

"Delivered. Not with your friend's van, my personal courier service."

"You can't use this courier for your errand today?"

He smiled. "Five years of chocolate and your own small iceberg. My final offer."

"When do you need us?"

Satisfied at winning her over, he gathered the bundled umbrellas.

"After everyone is seated and the preliminary toast is poured, there will be a dance. The dancers have two cues, identical movements. Each time, all twenty dancers open their umbrellas and create a shield around my father's chair. The second time they do this, the rain will begin. As the rain starts, I need you and your friend to load a box of packing materials on your catering cart and remove it for me."

Celine squeezed her tingling fingers into a fist. Her vision wavered, as though she was one of the inert gift boxes, waiting to be released.

"What do you mean?"

"Get rid of it. Burn the box. Drop it into a septic tank. I never want to see it again." He stepped back with his armload of umbrellas. He looked pleased: He knew he'd gotten the better end of the deal. As soon as he was gone, Celine flexed her fingers and then tapped Paul's code into her device.

Come early.

Why u OK

I got a wooden nickel, she wrote. He put a thumbs up on the message, and she knew he was turning the key even as he put the phone on the passenger seat. He would be downstairs at the loading dock in less than ten minutes. She could always trust Paul: he never went far.

☂

Laszlo and Henry's father Robert Weiss retained the breadth and heartiness of a much younger man, but, even from across the room, Celine could see he was fading. The manicured hand that clutched his crystal highball trembled when he raised it to drink. He seemed clamped to the chair on the dais, stiff with the effort of not shaking. Injections eased most neurological symptoms, but there were some things even money couldn't solve. The man was old, he was sick, he was rich. He leaned back in his padded throne, not bothering to conceal his look of tired disdain as he confronted the three hundred people who had gathered to retire him.

When the dancers came in, Henry and his half-brother Laszlo rose to their feet. As the rest of the guests followed suit, a throbbing bass line pulsed through the speakers in the walls, and the floor sparkled with an LED display of falling rain. The pattern changed from translucent bubbles to green ones, then faded to a rich, velvety shade of red. The dancers fanned out into two lines, pirouetted around one another, and sashayed to the beat. Umbrellas popped open in sync, prompting an enthusiastic riffle of applause from the audience. The dancers twirled, then clustered in a tight formation around the throne on the platform. Their umbrellas spun hypnotically, then snapped shut, revealing Robert glowering in the center. His expression was unchanged and malevolent; his hand was a claw around his glass. The dancers' bright face paint and glittering costumes were stretched tight, a pantomime of glee.

Celine, on cue, edged around the tables and chairs, sidestepping guests who had taken to their feet to cheer on the performers. She went into the far corner of the kitchen, suddenly nervous, wondering what she had agreed to. Nobody was here; the catering staff clustered around the portholes, watching the rain fall on their guests. Unable to concentrate, she fidgeted near the pastry racks. What had Henry Weiss-Broms told her? The cart would be ready, and all she had to do was take it down to the loading dock for Paul.

She checked her messages. Nothing yet, but she knew he would be there. The music continued. Two of the caterers had their devices out, surreptitiously filming the dance. This was forbidden; the excesses of the ice-drinking class were protected from criticism, outcry, the press. Even the security streams were off for a couple of hours, guaranteeing the privilege of privacy.

That is why Celine did not see the death itself; she only heard the screams. As she rushed to the kitchen window to see what had happened, she was shoved back by the swinging doors. Two dancers in rain-dappled encasement costumes dragged a sodden body in a crumpled, soaking-wet suit.

Rainwater mixed with vivid blood that oozed from puncture wounds that pitted the corpse's torso as its lungs seeped lilac fluid into its dress shirt.

Robert's face was like wax, his features displaced as though smeared by a giant's thumb. His ears, Celine noticed, were full of blood that ran down his neck in rivulets and pooled inside his collar.

The dancers flopped his body onto a plastic sheet and rolled it up, then folded the loose ends around the head and feet so it looked like a chrysalis harboring a malevolent larva. Then, they shoved the whole package into the long pasteboard carton Celine had used to package the party umbrellas.

It was over in an instant. The killers rolled Celine's creaky cart toward the service elevator and then disappeared, shedding their costumes as they dashed out of the kitchen and back through the rain and into the frenzied crowd. She could not have identified them if she'd wanted to.

She thought of the ice blocks Henry offered her and felt a craving for chocolate—her accomplice's payment, five years of sweetness, night-dark and acidic as blood.

7

YOCHANNA WAS TRYING to balance the Brooklyn Urban Bird Society's ledger. The numbers glitched in front of her tired eyes. The smoke from the tent fires outside leaked into the office, bringing the stink of chemical cinders with it. The smell made her feel prickly, as though she'd swallowed a tablespoon of coffee grounds.

It was hard to add up something that wasn't there; most of the nonprofit's work was done by volunteers, hoping to earn points towards their annual civic contribution quota. Yochanna had once caught one of them in the supply closet, sneaking a box of silver-edged member stickers into his bag. Those sold on the black market for ridiculously high prices, sometimes even higher than an annual membership fee. Yochanna had heard about people adding them to swag bags or distributing them at rain parties as favors. You could get counterfeits, of course, but the real ones had serial numbers and the difference was easy to spot. After Yochanna reported the attempted theft, the stickers were kept in a locked case in the supply closet, next to the coffee. They'd also instituted a bag check policy. Nothing was exempt from search. In fact, she was sure her container of pistachios was lighter than it had been when she left work last Friday. She suspected Mitch: he never kept his hands to himself.

It was simple math, just in and out and filling in the blanks with the same information as last time, but she struggled to make the numbers match. She saved her own timesheet for last, reluctant to look at how little she'd made. Her paycheck was not enough for anything; taxes took out close to half, and she paid for insurance on top of that. She missed a day last week when she was too sad to get out of bed and now she regretted it, looking at the piddly sum marked on her income sheet. Another three-figure paycheck, always a day late. Her anxiety started to bubble through the muscles in her lower back. The *hours* field blinked at her, its pixels a soothing grassy green.

If she missed a rent payment, she'd be evicted.

If she had no permanent address, she would be ineligible for income and benefits.

She would be sitting on the pavement in no time, holding a beggar's sign of her own.

The smoke stink from outside was sour and clotted. Unable to focus, she pushed her seat back and searched for a roll of adhesive in her desk. If there was a crack in the windowsill, she could patch it. Stress dragged its nails over her nerve endings. Old claw marks raised welts that she could feel through her clothes in a pattern like an ampule rash. She traced her fingers over the backs of her arms, resisting the urge to press into her skin again. Her jaw ached from trying to clamp the smell out of her head, so she took a painkiller, chewing it so it would work faster.

Mitch loitered in his office, a steaming cup of coffee at his elbow. He was engrossed by something on his screen and ignored Yochanna as she scuttled from room to room, spraying disinfectant in the air and inspecting the vents for fungus or mold.

"I'm sure it's nothing," he said hazily when she asked him for the fourth time whether something might have died in the walls or if the smoke was bothering him.

"New construction shouldn't have these problems," she said.

"Of course," he said, but he wasn't paying attention.

The bathroom down the hall smelled better than her work space; plus, it had a lock on the door. She sat on the toilet tank with her feet on the lowered seat and tried to identify a source of tolerable air. Even here, she couldn't escape the stink. She bent down to examine the rubber sealant around the rim of the sink pedestal and noticed that one edge was delicately rippled, like the creases in a newborn's elbow. She slid down for a closer look and ran her finger across the seam, feeling the irregularity in the artificially soft caulk. When she dug her nail into it, a nearly invisible line appeared, then resolved. She gouged it again, trying to coax out the wrinkles that only she could see.

In the other room, on the far side of the glass, the sirens still howled. She didn't move from her place on the floor. Her knees were cold from the tiles. A few more minutes of scratching and the sealant would be smooth and her brain could relax, this small corner of the universe restored to its ideal condition.

She slumped on now-numb knees beside the sink, digging at a grain of dirt she wasn't completely sure was visible to the eye.

Bill collectors, debt agencies—every emergency sounded the same to Yochanna. The tops of her feet began to tingle with pins and needles. She sat up. Her vision sparkled, then resolved as the capillaries in her head refilled. She touched her forehead, feeling a surge of nausea. Her throat spasmed several times and she leaned over, clutching her stomach as though kicked. Her skull felt stuffed with cotton. She stuck out her tongue and disgorged a milk-colored clot the size of a bottle cap. It stuck to the basin, its bright stratum of mucus glistening like gelatin. She put her finger into her throat. All she felt was the slimy tunnel of her neck, the dark hole at her center that led to nothing.

What was wrong with her? She rinsed the gooey lump into the drain, grateful that it vanished without staining the white porcelain. As she watched it swirl down the tube, she realized it was the first thing her body had secreted in many weeks.

Her period was late.

This wasn't a first; lose enough weight or stop sleeping, and the body's rhythms change, too. In the past, she'd blasted her natural cycles out of their rotation with stress or diet change and thought nothing of it. If she didn't bleed, so what? Tampons were expensive and she had more important things to do—like staying up late painting, mixing powders, and wondering why she wasn't happy yet.

She counted backward, trying to guess how many days it had been. Three weeks? A month. Six weeks. Who knew. She closed her eyes and felt a stirring, deep inside, as though a school of tiny fish flickered in the sea south of her stomach. She was becoming more horribly certain by the minute. She could sense the magnitude of the wave inside her and knew it was not yet at its peak;

it was the beginning of something that could not be stopped or turned away. She was *with child,* the cells embedded in her uterus asserting themselves in every action she took. She put her hands over her belly and imagined what might be happening inside—as though her organs were drifting around inside, deciding where they were going to reattach.

"We are so fucked," she whispered to the empty bathroom stall. The baseboard was covered in dust; dust she could breathe, full of chemicals that could be passed on to a baby. The tiles were greasy. She hid her hands in her shirt; she felt the same sensation when she pricked herself with a dirty needle, a syringe that came from God-knows-where that bit her when she carelessly put her hand on a public bench without first checking for sharps. She'd stared at the red dot on her finger and wondered if she'd feel a virus rooting in her, if it would hijack her system the way fear did, infiltrating her nerves and veins and turning her skin the wrong color. She listened to her body, hoping it would give some sign of whether she should be afraid or not. The chlorine-scented steam filled her nose.

Whether she kept the pregnancy or not, she was entering a period when she had to make decisions for two beings. For now, she was not thinking only of herself.

"They haven't put the fire out yet," Mitch said as he passed her at her desk a few minutes later, briefcase in hand. His tie was loosened, as though the foul fumes from the burning encampment finally slipped in the window to choke him. His sleeves were still rolled up. "This stinks. Take a half day. I'm working from home."

He slipped out the door before she could ask any questions. As she dumped her cold coffee down the disposal, she supposed she had nothing to say to him. She knew where this pregnancy came from and she knew, in a common sense way, that keeping it—not that she wanted to—would only multiply her troubles.

The guppy-bubble feeling shimmered inside her again. She was likely past the six-week licensing period for pregnancy; an unlicensed one came with extra paperwork and, inevitably, a compulsory abortion. Yochanna knew her tiny studio would never pass the child safety inspection. After one look at her bank account, even the most softhearted case worker would deny her application, frowning at the unchecked boxes on the review form. Income? Low. Domestic space? Polluted. Vermin? Yes. Intimate support? None. Responsible party? The rapist who employed her. Supplies and registry? Non-existent. Babies were expensive; even with federal assistance, it was impossible not to work. And mothering was more than a full time job.

She went through the motions of closing up. The monitors shut down with a tinny chime. The sirens outside were dulled now, and she barely heard them, as though this disaster was happening to someone else, in another place entirely. She slid the silicone screen across the single window; a silhouette was printed on it, to prevent real birds from colliding with the glass, though birds rarely flew this far from the shrinking green spaces or the parks, where it was easy to scrounge a free meal from the popcorn-eating tourists.

Leaving work, she walked in the wrong direction, too jittery to remember which way the maternity management center was until she'd gone several blocks uptown. Though she'd lived in New York for years, she felt utterly lost in what felt like new and bewildering terrain. The indeterminate colors of the concrete, which she collected for powders and home-boiled ink, flitted past her eyes like minnows. She was a stranger to herself and to this city. She turned back toward the Brooklyn Bridge and nearly collided with a raspy man in a frayed blue work uniform.

"Got a lighter?" he asked. The LED units around his coverall seams were half dead, and the front panel was smeared with tarry soot that matched the black stains on his palms. She wasn't wearing her blockers and she could see and hear him—the smoky note in his voice, the red lines around his eyes. She smiled at him, an apology for having too much of the wrong things. His teeth were stained black when he showed them in return.

She didn't have a spark setup, but if she did, she would have given it to him. Even her ratty sweater could have been his. In this moment, she had nothing except a ruined future to offer. Everything she owned that she hadn't made herself was worthless. Only her love of colors and ink was priceless. Irreplaceable.

Devotion was what made life worthwhile, Yochanna thought. The creative process was transubstantiation, just as monks undertook all those centuries ago when they scraped sheepskin into translucent panes of vellum and covered them with the hundred secret little leering faces that peeked like opossums out of the dense foliage of the illuminations' holy garden. Bending over their work, Yochanna had once felt the invisible hand that shaped words from inky brambles and turned leather into the holy word. Flesh from flesh and soul from soul. When those marks were made, they could not be undone, she thought, and maybe all of life, like art, was layers of mistakes that curled around one another like overgrown cables or hothouse vines that depended more on one another than the structure far beneath them, so entwined nobody knew the error from the forms that had produced it, supported it, and finally concealed its origins.

This moment was her life, and she could craft it as she wished. She boarded the crosstown bus feeling as though she had ascended to the corroded cross on the steeple of St. Paul's, so stark against the metal sky; so temporarily fixed, in a perch high out of reach.

8

IN THE ELEVATOR, Celine averted her eyes from the bundle that contained Robert Weiss' body, which was shrouded in an opaque plastic sheet and hastily stuffed into a long plywood crate. The descent through the air-conditioned building took longer than she remembered. Each time the cable clanked or she caught a whiff of the offices, her throat tightened; by the time the service car settled at the loading dock, she was strangling with anxiety.

As he'd promised, Paul was waiting for her. After one look at her panicked face, he lifted the lid of the coffin, grunted, and resealed it without a word before he threw the van's doors open and shoved the box inside, working faster alone than if she interfered. He hustled Celine into the passenger side and coaxed the van toward the Queens-Midtown tunnel.

She twisted to look behind them at the loading dock, wondering if there was still time to ditch the coffin on the ramp. It was too late. They had been seen. A group of people, shouting, pointing. A figure broke off, sprinted after the van, and launched himself at the vehicle. His landing was a detonation that sparked the adrenaline in Celine's veins. The stranger bounced off the side panel, but Celine got a look at him before he staggered back into the writhing crowd. He was masked and his eyes were covered with germ shields—a sick person. Gloved hands raked his cloth-covered cheeks. She slapped the dashboard as though it was an ignition.

"Drive," she shrieked.

Paul's foot hit the pedal and the momentum threw Celine back in her seat as they careened along an alley, taking a hard turn out into the street. The coffin in the back smashed against the van's walls, then flailed loosely on the metal bed as Paul rounded a second corner. Celine seemed to hear the corpse scrabbling along the floor, clawing its way toward the cab. Although the bulkhead was a thick shield, Celine knew anything could come through the mesh—an ice pick, a bullet, a wire. She seemed to smell its sweetly rancid breath and hear its ragged, anxious gasps. She was afraid to turn and look, as though that would bring the danger even closer.

"Faster," she screamed at Paul. Her plan had already turned on them, spiraling out of control. Her body surged with adrenaline and she began to rock in her seat, caught in an animal panic.

The long minutes under the high rises that filled the East River district only amplified Celine's anxiety. Guilt settled in her stomach like a block of ice. The darkness, threaded with lines of electronic guideposts, compressed around them while traffic stacked around the van on both sides, the red lights forming an impenetrable shield.

Paul yanked the wheel left, then right. There was nothing to restrain the box's movement in the back. The van's bed was slick metal, no handles, a container that could be pressure-washed clean in an instant. The box floundered sideways as they took another sharp turn. Celine heard the pressboard fracture. She clutched at her seatbelt, the window, desperate to escape into a world that somehow made sense. Her hands did not know what to do and darted like birds seeking safety. The thrashing sounds in the back made her heart do terrified backflips.

She rolled her window down to ease her nausea. Paul sped into a commuter tunnel and zipped around the buses and bicycles, leaning on his horn when the traffic congealed at the intersections. They went around the column at the base of the Brooklyn Bridge and Celine heard the box in the back hit the wall again, harder than before and the impact was a soft bomb in her ears. She heard the arms and skull collide with the metal bulkhead and the corpse's helpless velocity as it rolled across the rubber mat and lay inert, without breathing, undoubtedly dead.

Celine reached across the gear box and put her hand on Paul's arm. His skin was damp and blazing hot with a feverish temper she'd never felt before. Although he drove with his usual precision, his movements were jerky and rough.

"Five minutes," she said, to steady herself.

"Two," he said, and gunned the engine. The van shuddered and dove down another alley, going the wrong way past a line of pressboard collectors on bicycles loaded with tall stacks of battered panels that teetered on their handlebars. They rang their warning bells as the van passed them, shouting at Paul and slapping the sides of the van as it passed them. A hand clung to Celine's window for an instant, then vanished as the body was flung free and lost in a heap of garbage. The raw music of the bells receded, fading down the alley as Paul made the final turn and swung the van into its parking spot between the dumpster and the surveillance battery station behind Celine's studio.

The headlights touched the soft fog of grit that engulfed them. He snapped the motor off and they sat in silence, listening to the engine tick. The van stank of mustard and rot. Paul reached down next to his seat and grasped the tire iron he kept rolled in a towel. Celine wondered what kind of mess Robert Weiss had made in the back.

She shook her head at Paul—it was silent in the cab, even her ragged breathing was subdued. He frowned. The tire iron lolled in his grip, a misshapen pipe with a wicked, scarred lug at one end. The towel Paul wrapped it in was pale pink and printed with orange-centered daisies, faded from wear and time, with a few black grease stains.

Celine knew Paul as a precise man, imposing but never violent. She needed him; he enabled her to survive. Since they'd met, he was the one who moved her umbrellas, pushed the cart, carried the loads of materials between the van and the shop, swept the studio, and repaired the space, mending the damage that was inevitable in the city's borderline toxic environment. Wires frizzled, paste sheeting melted, pipes burst, windows got broken, and vermin proliferated in the walls. The clean-coat trucks that drove through the streets weekly, spraying antibiotics and chlorine in the air, couldn't fit through the alley, which became a repository for copper pellets and tumbleweeds of electric lint. Now, she saw as though for the first time the scars across the backs of his hands and the ball bearing-smooth muscles in his massive forearms. He was as tough and unsparing as the tool he picked up by its crooked stem. She wondered what else he was capable of.

"What's one more?" he whispered. He opened his door before she could respond.

She heard him slip around to the back of the van. The hinge on the back hatch squeaked as he cracked it open. She twisted in her seat to look over her shoulder into the dark cave behind her.

Paul was a silhouette, his features erased by the LED illuminators that tinted the alleyway a murky olive. His arm was cocked, the tire iron poised by his ear. He leaned into the gap over the battered coffin and the body sprawled across its now-ruined lid. A few loose bolts rolled on the mat, next to an overturned bucket.

A device, flung free from the body's pockets, blipped in the corner. Paul poked it with the tire iron, then flipped it out of the van onto the pavement. He smashed its screen with a single piston-like movement of his foot. The broken case wheezed a pathetic, final electronic whine and then split in half when he stomped it a second time. He kicked half of it into the sewer grate and the other half under the dumpster.

"Who's this?" he asked Celine, gesturing to the coffin. Its lid was loose. Robert flopped half-out. An arm covered his face and his legs and pelvis were twisted.

"I made a mistake," she said. "I said we could transport it."

"Make it disappear?"

"Henry said he'd give us a glacier," she said. It sounded foolish when she said it out loud, a child's lie. The *us* slipped out; it was Celine who was promised ice. Henry hadn't offered anything to Paul.

"We should get rid of it now," he said. "This is only going to get worse."

"How?" she whispered.

"I'm not going back to prison."

She hadn't known that her solid, soft-spoken friend was a convict. Few people survived the work camps and carceral programs in the western desert.

He said, "You won't like it there, either. If I break this thing's face some, it will look like a mugging. Like it drowned in its own blood. We can leave it in another district."

"Don't you know who this is?" she asked.

"I don't want to know. I want to wake up tomorrow like none of this happened."

"You can't—" Celine began, but as she said it, she knew the words were wrong. Paul *could* smash Robert Weiss' face to unidentifiable fragments. He even wanted to. But there were people walking at the near end of the alley. A surveillance drone could fly over at any moment. This familiar space was more open than she'd thought; they weren't safe here. Or any place.

She said, "First, we take the box inside."

He lowered the iron and shrugged. She knew how quick he could be, even if he seemed languid; he sometimes snapped into motion with a fluidity that frightened her. He wouldn't wait to ask for her permission.

Paul draped a polyurethane tarp over the corpse in the back with the same efficiency he used to clear the clutter that washed up around the doorways. This body too was all just so much trash. The sheeting crinkled as Paul tucked Robert Weiss back into his box, then levered them both onto the cart with the rubber wheels.

Celine darted around to the studio's back door to key her passcode into the access pad. Her hands were sweating and her finger slid across the sensor, leaving a greasy smear that confused the optic scanner inside.

"It's me," she muttered, trying again. The robot beeped in protest, then acquiesced. She heard the bolt retract and snapped the handle and with Paul and the cart right behind her, on her heels, she stepped through the door and into the familiar silence of the place she made umbrellas.

In here, the low ceiling was painted a pale, liquid aquamarine to remind Celine of the rain as she worked. Tubs of panels and pre-cut gores absorbed the sound in the space and soaked up the clatter of Paul's cart and the ambient rush in the street outside. The heaps of fabrics were somber in their boxes: gray, white splattered with metallic webs, a dull red the color of a fresh scar, black. How had she accumulated so many of them, over the years? They were arranged in strata, the fashions and whims of the upper class overlaying one another like dynasties in a catacomb. Dim lights pulsed from the corners, casting a gray light that turned the room to static. Whatever happened in this studio, nobody would see it: nobody would hear.

The floor was sticky. Her toe dislodged a plastic-headed drafting pin which she picked up and jabbed into the silicon mat on the sewing table. The long-legged work stool she'd inherited from her mother and grandmother was still pushed back, waiting for her to return. Then, she patted the mat.

With a nod, Paul drew the cart up next to her, retracted the tarp, and levered the coffin onto the razor-scarred surface. They pulled back the sheet, then the splintering lid.

Robert flopped gracelessly on his back. His limbs lolled on the silicone. His rain-spattered face was slack and androgynous, the open mouth a blank space that wheezed as Paul loosened the sheeting from his shoulders. Celine saw in the darkness the shining, uneven teeth and bloodied gums. A fleck of glitter from the rain party adhered to his cheek. One eye socket was swollen. A marble-sized lump on his forehead, filled with chartreuse-colored fluid, seemed to throb with a pulse that wasn't there. His tongue probed from his lips, as if testing to see if the coast was clear.

"You didn't think this through," Paul growled.

She shook her head, ashamed. The fact of the body loomed large in her mind. Robert still looked partially animated to her, as though at any moment he would sit up and lunge across her drafting table.

Even dead, he was heavy. Meaty. How stupid she had been to accept Henry's offer. Vanishing as a living person in New York was hard enough; making a dead one evaporate would be impossible. Corpses stank. They took up space. The means of disappearing them drew as much attention as hiding them did. Everywhere you went, there were cameras, or people streaming content, or police, or strangers eager to report alarming activity. In smuggling Robert out of the building, she had created an unsolvable problem for herself.

"What do I do?" she asked her friend.

Paul's frown deepened. One of his hands stroked the smooth exterior of the coffin, as though assessing its flammability. Celine watched him anxiously as he calculated their options.

"I don't need to know how he got in the box," Paul finally said. "What's done can't be reversed. But it seems to me that if you took a bum deal, you need to return this man to his family and break the agreement."

"Go back to zero?" She imagined the iceberg Henry offered, glinting like a massive diamond on a pedestal. She had never tasted clear, glacial water and when she imagined its flavor, her veins twitched like thirsty worms under her skin. Her whole body yearned for it—concentrated centuries of rain frozen in time, to be sipped, slurped, consumed. She looked down at Robert's corpse again. His skin was smooth and pliable from a lifetime of being immersed in and imbibing clean water. Her own skin felt like a stifling suit of dust.

Paul said, "Whatever he offered you, I can say it's not worth it. A pact with the devil is poison."

"But I'm thirsty," she said.

"We're all thirsty," Paul snorted. "I'd rather eat soot than be some ice-drinker's fall guy. The body goes back to its family and you tell Henry you changed your mind."

"Is that the only way?"

He fixed her with a gimlet eye. "Half-measures avail us nothing," he recited. "You want to give in to temptation, be my guest. But I won't help you move this thing unless it's to take it back to Henry."

She noted again the solid muscles in his face and the scar along the side of his neck. He may have dealt in flowers, but the greater part of him was more than comfortable with danger. He was more than she'd assumed, and while the shadows in his past frightened her, she knew him as a trusted friend.

In this situation, he was her only one.

"Henry wouldn't be in the city," she said. "They have that acreage out west, the place they call Otzara. People say he stays there all the time."

"That's where we'll go, then."

"Paul, it's far away. I've made umbrellas for these people for years and even then, I've hardly learned anything about them except that they like shantung silk and custom screen prints. I don't know where their garden is, or how to get there. I've never even been out of the city."

"I have," he said. "You made a deal with Henry, and now I'll make a deal with you. We will return Robert's body to Otzara, and you will be free. OK? You gave me my fresh start once, didn't you? It's right that I repay you by doing the same."

Celine nodded. She didn't know how they would find their way out of New York, much less transport a coffin into the wild lands beyond the city, but Paul's certitude convinced her it wasn't impossible. He was determined, and she made up her mind to at least give the plan a try. As he said, it was better than incarceration; the new prisons were offshore processing plants that churned the thickened, saline sea water for minerals. In these labor camps, the convicted shipped containers of silicone and waste to the logic-chip manufacturers in Taiwan Bay. Most people sprouted layers of bilious subcutaneous tumors within a few months; holes in the atmosphere rotated over the farms, cooking the sea and the rafts of trash the prisoners picked through in their search for credit zero. The tumors pushed up through the epidermis and made people's skin look like bubble wrap. Celine shuddered, imagining the festering heat of the sun in the Gulf.

"We'll do it your way." She dug her stolen piece of chocolate cake out of her purse. It was only a little battered and still wrapped in the bamboo fiber napkin stamped with the rain party's foil crest.

"You took that?" Paul asked, his eyes drifting to the treat. She snuck a bite into his mouth and then into her own; their tooth marks overlapped.

The sticky sponge adhered to her tongue and to the roof of her mouth; its flavor was as black as hell and overwhelmed her senses.

"If we won't get the glacier ice, we may as well enjoy the chocolate," she said.

"They eat this every day?" Paul blanched and spat the dark fragments toward the glossy trash chute bolted to the studio wall. He wiped his tongue with his sleeve, over and over, like a cat convinced he would never be clean. "No wonder they're like that."

"No, it's good," Celine said. She swallowed. The bittersweetness moved through the tunnel of her body and its secret rivers and hidden springs. She was already folding the napkin, then folding it again, smaller and smaller, into a shape the size of a seed that she could bury in herself, a seed that knew how to wait forever for rain.

The Battery

9

LASZLO'S PRESS RELEASE came through the Weiss Executive Center's wire at 18:29, 31 seconds before the evening telecast. Henry scanned the text, noting its familiar, commercial tone—his half-brother's trademark. Its encoded serial strip was the pale pink of a lab rat's irritated eyes. C-level code, for distribution only to Henry in his glass cube of an office, high above the Manhattan haze. The family's publicist would see to the public narrative of Robert's death. The story should be believable, simple, and in the end—forgettable.

Not that there was anything wrong with erasure, Henry thought, pushing his neon-azure toupee a little closer to his hairline. A bulletin from the Weiss family could drive the market up, end a foreign war, or devastate real estate prices. Laszlo, for example, wasn't above peppering the news with speculation, then hedging against it to collect a market windfall. When you owned a major media conglomerate, the world was your microphone. Networks didn't bother to run publicity from the Weisses through a claim checker. The truth was like everything else and could be manufactured, bought, and traded. All facts belonged to the ice-drinking class; everyone else picked up their scraps and recycled their quotes until speculation became certainty. Every word the ice-drinkers uttered was currency unto itself. The fraction of a minute that Henry held the press release, he possessed a wealth of information. As they invented the truth, the Weisses knew more than anyone else on earth; they had the pleasure of breaking the story, however distorted, to an audience who could not stop consuming it.

The telecast jingle erupted from the screen on Henry's wall and he settled back to watch it, one in an audience of millions. Seven optical turrets orbited the host's elaborate chair as the stage lights dimmed, while the green backdrop fluttered in the generator's sudden breeze. Tinted overhead lights rotated in their ports. They tended to overdo things, Henry thought. Still, he leaned forward, eager to hear how the official story would land.

The Next 2 News host's expression was fixed in a mask of professional friendliness. The first lens extended an inch from the camera casing, catching a thread of green light from the ceiling gels. The host lifted the corners of their mouth into their signature grin and launched into the script that scrolled out of the prompter.

"Did you kill yourself this week? Me neither!" they squawked. One hand clawed a flirtatious high-five toward the lens. "Suicide is for quitters!"

The exclamation points in the script were large and red. Henry followed along with the press release in his lap, noting the places where the host stumbled. It wasn't a hard job, but still. Errors. This host parroted their lines without comprehending the words. Henry sighed. He and Laszlo should have bought a showrunner who at least knew how to read.

"Now, we have some drama-rama from on high," the host said. "America's favorite number one sugar daddy Robert Weiss was stabbed to death by—a ninja death squad. Are you for real? Killed on his actual stinking *birthday*. Now that's what I call Next 2 News!"

Patriarch was a publicist word. The host glossed over it, probably not even sure what it meant. Why couldn't these people just make things easy? The average Next 2 News viewer was borderline illiterate. Long words confused them; they used GIFs and memes to share information. Nobody said *infiltrate* or *assassinate*, even when that's what had happened. If this telecaster could have spoken in emojis, they would have. Henry suspected it would have been better for ratings.

"The suspects are being tracked via police tech as we speak and law enforcement is confident that the criminals will be captured within hours. Here's the reveal: the killers are haute couture creator Celine Broussard and an unidentified male-bodied accomplice. Gotta love a fast takedown! Let's check out the leaked video."

The host swiveled on their stool, turning to the blank green wall where CGI waterfalls oozed cotton candy pink ropes of three-dimensional flow. The curtains of the waterfall parted, revealing a square of shaky cell phone footage shot through the porthole window of a commercial galley kitchen. This was a hot item, proprietary and released to Next 2 News as an exclusive. At Henry's command, the Weiss' personal PR firm had spent the last hours scrubbing those same videos from the web, confiscating devices and their stored data, and blacklisting the caterers who recorded them. The family kept total control of the narrative, always.

Through the steady haze of artificial rain, sturdy figures dressed in shiny costumes pirouetted around a throne that held a stiff, regal figure: Robert Weiss. A spotlight floated over him. His expression was puckered and disapproving as he gazed out at his guests. The strobe turned the dancing bodies to silhouettes. Umbrellas popped open, sending a speckle of rain over the porthole glass. Then, a dramatic splatter of blood that coated the round pane in the kitchen door; the scattering guests; and two stony figures, standing over the body, leaning with their full weight on the barbed points of their custom umbrellas. The videos showed how the dancers made a protective ring around the murder, shielding the audience but not the stunned people in the kitchen. Even with the killers' outlines blurred by both water and digital manipulation, their intent was clear.

There was a clatter as the person filming fumbled their phone, then a scream: the rain obscured the edges of Robert's body as it spasmed. The lights turned red, then white, then gray. Nobody had a face. When the host whipped back to the camera, the video disappeared and was replaced by an image of golden donor stickers.

"The Weiss family is offering $100 million to anyone who has information leading to an arrest," the host babbled. The optic swivel nodded, which was the cue to pivot to the weather. Henry watched as the host slid out of the anchor seat and minced toward the wings. The segment was over; they would have time to hoover a few bumps in their dressing room and prep for the next bout of headlines.

Henry disconnected the show and lazed among the cushions of his office couch, massaging his cheeks with his chilly fingertips. He and Laszlo had gotten rid of Robert. Next, they'd dispose of Celine. His dermal filler hardened in a ridge along his eye that itched at night. Allergic reaction. It wouldn't be guilt. He had unambiguous feelings about what he had done, or what he was about to do. Henry hated Robert and never cared about the umbrella maker; the only thing he loved was Otzara, and he was one step closer to being with it and in it all the time.

The whole setup was bemusingly simple. Murder was one of the oldest stories in the world—easy to understand, easy to sell. People had always killed one another for every imaginable reason. Greed, fear, lust, boredom. By the time the umbrella maker was caught, they'd manage to make her guilt seem obvious, a foregone conclusion.

The details of the publicist's story were irrelevant—Henry knew the average person was only peripherally invested in his father's murder, but the point was to convince, not captivate. Masterminding the killing had been easy. Controlling the media fallout only needed time and attention.

Murders happened every day. Just not to rain party people.

Thinking ahead, Henry knew the next update would be the police bulletin announcing the accused killers' arrest. Maybe a tasteful shot of the dead quadrillionaire in his golden years, standing at the center of his family in a posed photo portrait. Once Celine was caught by the authorities, she'd be incarcerated and condemned. The media might run footage of her impassioned denials. Then, the family's public statement on her eventual execution. As Henry considered what he was getting away with, he felt a tiny burst of dopamine. The well-oiled machine of his brain pumped its pleasure centers to capacity.

It wasn't too early to celebrate, he thought.

The first granular line of pale yellow powder lay on his sinuses like a gentle cloud, tainting his bloodstream and turning to a mustard paste that dripped down his throat. This was the high end stuff; it was cut with saffron, each vivid stamen harvested by hands in the lily fields that belonged to Integrated Vietnam. The pollen was supposed to make the high last longer, but Henry didn't wait for his sensation levels to dip between bumps. He ran his swollen tongue over his rubbery soft palate and bent his head to the mirrored compact for another taste.

When the dazzling lights behind his eyes subsided, Henry slouched in his favorite chair and put his feet on the stuffed-rhino ottoman whose tail he'd decorated with a sardonic silk ribbon. The jelly in his scalp itched, but the Viet-108 dulled the frazzled edges of his corporeal senses. This body was a wig, he thought, sloughed off in a moment.

He held the celluloid news strip up to his office's vanity lights and eyeballed the code on the press' feed tip. It was an hour old now. In another few minutes, the corn sugar fiber would degrade into a thread of foam. Henry had enough time to pop a picture of it and send it through the encoded filter app on his device. A private line—essential for ice-drinkers. Another reason to love this kind of power. The celluloid curled on the table, melting.

The word is out. Cops should have the collar in a day.

Laszlo's response percolated on Henry's device. *Our agreement was that you get rid of the obstacles and I get the chairman position.*

Majority shareholder, not the chair. Henry bent over the table again, sucked up another bump, and tapped his iridescent proto-claws on the mirror. Henry knew his half-brother would bite on the generous offer of exposure, the kind that only the conglomerate owners commanded at will. Majority shares in the family corporation should have been snapped up immediately. But Laszlo would want more. In fact, Henry was counting on it. The fabricated murder scandal would drive stock prices up, since controversy was news and everyone wanted clicks. Analytics. Every second that Laszlo debated with himself was another million down the tubes. Henry found a dot of saffron on the rim of his nostril, picked it free, and pressed it to the dried-out receptors on his tongue. Laszlo's response, when it came, was short.

We'll do it your way. Load the portfolio now, divest when you take the chair.

Deal.

Laszlo was so easy to manipulate, Henry thought. He was the opposite of Otzara—instead of growth, he was a human sinkhole, always sucking up more than his share, greedy to acquire and consolidate the next company. Henry swiped the screen and the messages vanished into the ether, pixels vaporized by a data-destroying code.

He planned to go far beyond his half-brother's plot to corner the remaining clean resources their leaking planet had to offer. Laszlo was ever-ready to drive prices up and collect the profits. His plan was to crash the international markets and wash commodities into the negative. Henry, on the other hand, intended to watch the world burn and bubble into nothingness outside the borders of his garden. His so-called divestment was akin to sweeping a tray clear. This first murder set the table. Then, the global accident could finally start to happen.

He clacked his acrylic tips against the vial of Viet-108 flakes and contemplated the spin of this story, the angle of its ricochet.

The saffron in his bloodstream conspired with the lazy prattle from the screens that scrolled across his office ceiling. Henry sensed reality ebbing from him and gave himself to its wicked tide, letting his body float loose among the scurf of his imagination.

10

The maternity management center was at the edge of Battery Park, in the dark ruler between the crowd-control gates and the segment of ornate metal fence left over from the last mayor's urban beautification project. Yochanna cut through the concrete plaza and dodged around the statue in the center, its silhouette distorted by the thick cloud of ionic dust that settled on the cooling metal and landed in the bronze giant's outstretched hand and the folds of its tunic. She skirted the security beams and moved across the park's desolate face, keeping to the welcoming pools of shadow that ringed the park. Chilled-gas lighting tubes installed at intervals emitted a high-pitched, repellent hum designed to prevent people from lingering; a skeeterish tone penetrated the air, clinging to Yochanna's ears.

At the center of the square, a ten-by-ten square of brickwork was marked off with two-inch chrome spikes that protruded like fangs from the ground. A round red placard indicated a Free Speech Zone. Yochanna avoided it. The bricks were stained with blood, lachrymator, and paintball jets that police used to mark protesters' clothing, making it impossible for them to vanish once they left the space. Cameras mounted on the fence were trained on the brick square, recording whatever stepped into their electronic sights.

Although the park was power-washed nightly, a fresh tag adorned the pavement: *Watch Yourself.* Yochanna stepped over it, heading for the far end, out of the cold rows of light. In an hour, the second-shift city maintenance trucks would rumble through the streets, spraying copper pellets and sweeping the gutters bare of the loose detritus that accumulated in every crack. There was never a sleeping eye in New York; Yochanna knew that her invisibility was conditional. There would be cameras in the clinic, her name in a database. After she went in, there was no hiding from anyone the kind of trouble she was in. The cells developing inside her would reveal anything and everything that went into her system.

The waiting room at the maternity management center was full of agitated bodies—people waiting to hear which way their luck would go. Yochanna gave her ID to the agent at the desk, submitted to a quick cheek swab and temperature check, and was given a number. The only available chair was in the corner. As she walked toward it, she smelled why nobody else wanted to sit there; the person in the next seat was pungent with the possum-piss smell of dirty pants and rot. Yochanna's first impression was of illness, a bubble gum pink sweatshirt covered in stains, and pants that were so filthy they did not have a color anymore. It was too late to change direction and nowhere else to put herself, so Yochanna marched toward the unoccupied spot, hoping it wasn't as bad as her nose was telling her. The top of the person's head was shiny-bald, but a ring of strawberry blonde hair crackled like straws on their shoulders. Mangled feet puffed through the ruined loops of their sandals. Blisters of yellow mange crusted on their exposed skin. Nobody would leave a child with this person. They looked like a giant toddler, in need of care themselves.

A revolving globe projected images of starving infants with lesions clinging monkey-like to emaciated mothers. Ribbons of white milk covered them, resolving into the maternity management slogan Yochanna had heard every day of her life: *Plan a Better Future.* Termination was normal, she told herself. Many of the people she'd gone to school with had at least one, especially if they were repro-attracted.

The liquid eyes of the babies on the screen made Yochanna queasy. She took shallow breaths through her mouth, trying not to inhale the rancid odor of the person beside her. Nobody spoke above a murmur except the welcoming agents at the check-in desk.

Staring at the battered lounger benches and sticky toys that cluttered the waiting room, Yochanna still told herself the jigging shrimp in her uterus was an anxious delusion. Part of her didn't believe she *could* get pregnant, even though all the signs were there. Egg plus sperm equals cells, which eventually equals fetus, which tends to yield baby. Mitch had subjected her to the formula and now she was going to get the results.

She fidgeted in her seat until finally, a woman in a staid twinset came to get her. As she waved Yochanna through the door, she tucked her lapels closer to her neck, concealing a tiny button with a silver eye printed on it. She took Yochanna into a private office down the hall from the exam rooms. The desk was covered in pamphlets in multiple languages; they had titles like "What Are My Options?" and "Your Body, Your Abortion." Yochanna sat down, feeling as though she was about to have her fortune read. Her future was in one of those pamphlets. The maternity agent composed her expression into one of professional compassion and gave Yochanna a gentle but serious smile.

"I need you to piss for me," she said.

"Really?" Yochanna blurted.

"Your swab gave you a positive. We need to confirm it with a urine sample," she said, as though consoling Yochanna. She must do this same performance a hundred times a day. Her tone was tender, aggrieved. Yochanna felt sorry for her, giving bad news to people who cried or were angry or scared or unbalanced.

The transmitter mounted at the edge of the ventilation grid blipped. She reached for one of the brochures, which showed a picture of a beautiful girl looking out a window, one hand covering her cheek.

"We can discuss your next steps now, if you want."

"What do you mean, next steps?"

She looked at Yochanna, stunned. "For termination, of course," she said. "We should schedule you while you're still in the first trimester."

"I don't have enough health points," Yochanna said.

The agent sank back in her chair, looking dubious.

Yochanna was too young, obviously incompetent; Yochanna could see it on her face.

"Wow," the agent said. "Ideally, sexually active people maintain a reserve for situations like these."

"I wasn't 'sexually active,'" Yochanna said. She was sexually acted *on,* which wasn't the same thing. She wanted to tell the woman about the mental health module she spent her points on and how it was supposed to help with her stress, which was partially caused by Mitch, but the words died on her lips. She ironed her grimace out flat into a painful, polite smile.

"You *do* know how pregnancy is initiated?" the agent said to Yochanna.

"Yes, but I don't have points either way. My plan resets on the fifth of next month."

Briskly, the woman cleared the pamphlets from the desk and laid them aside with a huff. She opened her scheduler case and rotated the disks, aligning the dates as they blinked up in red and pink holographic squares. After a moment, she frowned.

"The first appointment we would have for you after your reset is in four weeks. That puts you solidly in the second trimester, which is a little more costly in terms of your health plan. If you can do your urine sample today and get on the calendar, I will be able to waive the fee for the missing maternity license."

Her expression was sly. The license was expensive—a couple hundred points—and it was for people who had the luxury of anticipating their pregnancies. You needed a license to conceive, receive prenatal care, deliver in a hospital, and even register the baby. Unlicensed babies belonged to no one; they were basically born to be landfillers, living outside the system, without access to sterilized water or vaccines. Without a license, termination wasn't covered by insurance—and neither were any other pregnancy-related services. Certainly, it was essential for anyone who took their bodily autonomy seriously. If you wanted a choice, you had to pay for it. Or plan for it. Yochanna looked down at her hands, which were silently clawing at the front of her skirt.

She was unfit.

When had this started? She thought back—Mitch in his office, Mitch in the storage closet, Mitch by the coffee maker. She knew that, at conception, the fertilized ovum was the size of the dot a pencil makes on a pristine piece of paper. Before it was anything, it was next to nothing: all potential, a universe in a grain of sand. Yochanna's ovum was lush with the complex codes and proteins that spiral into strings of DNA and form new life. It contained everything her body would ever know.

By the time the termination appointment came, the fetus inside Yochanna would be growing ovaries of its own, packed tight as a pomegranate with millions of primitive eggs. Assuming this fetus lived to reproduce, one of those surviving eggs would become her child. Yochanna's hands sensed a flutter beneath her skin. She calculated. For a few months, the proto-ovum within the baby inside her linked two generations. As she became a mother, she was becoming a grandmother, too, feeding each egg on her blood and amniotic fluid.

"In four weeks, I'll be able to feel it turning over," Yochanna said.

"You likely feel it now," the agent said. "The swab darkened very quickly. You may be as far as 16 weeks already. Or else it could be twins."

"That's impossible."

The woman shrugged. She heard the denials all day, the tears. The tests didn't lie. She said, "Can't you get a points advance? We have a purchase program through the clinic."

"How much?" Yochanna asked.

"Let's see." The agent consulted the calendar again. "For two thousand points, we could get you in tomorrow."

"Two thousand?" It was more than Yochanna's monthly salary.

The agent clicked the calendar shut and slid it aside. She folded her hands on the desk, making an arrow of her interlaced fingers.

"Listen," she said. "Strike the word 'impossible' from your vocabulary. Everything you have said is impossible is happening. So, you see, it is possible. It is real. Join the rest of us in the real world and deal with this."

"I am dealing with it."

"You'll have to. Third-trimester terminations are challenging. To put it mildly."

Yochanna pushed back in her chair. She felt lightheaded, nauseous. The movement under her palms suddenly ceased, and all she could feel was her heartbeat throbbing in the artery that ran along her belly. The small creature seemed to be holding its breath, waiting for her to make a decision.

"Okay," she said. "I'll get the two thousand from the father."

The agent slid an empty cup toward her. "I'm glad you made the right decision. The sample area is around the corner at the end of the hall. I'll put you on the schedule for tomorrow and we can get you back to your regular life as quickly as possible."

"Plan a better future," Yochanna said.

"The only choice is to do what's right," the woman recited in response. She watched Yochanna pick up the cup. By the time

Yochanna reached the door, the agent's eyes had slid back to the calendar and the floating pink squares that blipped and rotated in the projected ether of the glowing field. Each one of them was a little life, a life within a life, a path not taken.

Yochanna backed into the hall holding the cup as the rosy kaleidoscope shimmered over the woman's face, a fractured rainbow that represented hope, disappointment—beginnings and ends.

Squatting in the restroom, Yochanna felt liquid leave her in a stream hot as shame. Her sample stank of condensed acids. It sizzled in the bowl, splashed into the collection cup, and stained the basin orange. The tank burbled as it processed the leftovers and pushed them through to the septic system. The same fluids she drank, boiled, and cleaned herself with had filtered through the kidneys of millions of strangers. New York was a perfect, stagnant pond that turned its own moisture to good use. Strange to think that long ago, they'd built huge seawalls and retaining structures for the hurricanes that didn't come and floods that failed to fill the streets. Instead, this part of the world was stricken with drought. Subterranean irrigation, artificial clouds, and aerial misting drones kept things growing—to a point. But without rain, without the wild water produced through the climate's natural systems, everyone was essentially drinking their own sweat. She hit the flush button, acknowledging one more tiny contribution to the artificial ecosystem that trapped them all.

Her urine was the color and clarity of a Brazilian yellow topaz. She capped the container and slid it into the metal door in the wall near the cleansing station. A faint click on the other side of the wall told her that the sample had been captured and would be processed momentarily. The agent had said, maybe twins.

That meant twice the license fee, twice the points. She'd given Yochanna a deal on this termination—a two-for-one deal, if the test results were accurate. Or maybe she offered that to everyone. It seemed unlikely that the scabrous creature in the waiting room would have enough points saved for a conveniently timed abortion. But what did Yochanna know? Nothing, or she wouldn't be in this horrific situation.

She needed two thousand points to get it taken care of by tomorrow, and that meant she was going to have to steal. When she walked out of the clinic, it was still third shift. A bevy of starlings clustered near the subway gates, picking popcorn off the pavement. She skirted a body sleeping beside a dumpster, legs stretched onto the pavement like a mechanic investigating the undercarriage of a van. As she passed, the body jerked, then rolled over and vanished beneath the dumpster's metal lip.

The office was empty, lights dimmed. Her foot knocked against the trash hamper as she came in, making a hollow clang. She held her breath, but she was all alone here. Mitch's office was just as he'd left it—door open, images of flying grackles on the wall, bureaucratic clutter across the desk. Only the darkening windows suggested that they were done for the day. The scent of encampment smoke lingered delicately in the air with a fragile note of jasmine oil and human shit. The purifiers would eradicate it by morning.

The supply closet yawned open when she turned its handle. The darkness inside seemed to suck her into its hideous mouth. For a moment she was blind, but as her eyes adjusted to the dark, she perceived the dim edges and corners of the small anteroom. A broom leaned in one corner and the ancient floor tiles were so worn that Yochanna could feel the rough texture through her soles. Crates lined one wall. The ceiling was low, with a single dead LED dangling from the rafters like a shredded nerve.

The safe was next to the cartons of coffee—a stodgy, old-fashioned box with a passcode panel on its front. Yochanna took a narrow, serrated file from her tote. She used this one to scrape filings off industrial surfaces, collecting a dank, green oily crust that stained her ink-making pots near-black. It was a crude tool, but it would have to work; only Mitch had the combination to this door. She hissed as she levered the file into the safe and felt along its edge for the bolt that would release the lock. With a gentle touch, she pried open the pins along the seam until the passcode panel popped open with a squirt of static electricity.

There were more gold and silver stickers in the locker than Yochanna remembered. She meant to sneak only a few, at first, but as she counted them out she found herself thinking of Mitch and all he owed her. Yochanna reviewed her morning routine. Door, lock, coffee, screen, boss. She handled the stack of grant proposals, with their vapid, bureaucratic titles in bold: *Not All Songbirds, Watching Native Singers in Brooklyn, Urban Appetites and Foraging.* She was already coming in early, working half an hour in the mornings, off the clock. Over the past three years, that added up to almost a thousand unpaid labor hours—not to mention the extras Mitch extorted from her body. She calculated that more than half a year's wages were packed into those undocumented hours. Nobody was keeping track except for Yochanna. She took the entire box of stickers out of the safe and shut the security door, then clicked the blue moon in the passcode's upper right corner.

She was tired of doing the right thing. This theft felt like a small repayment for the many services she'd rendered; nobody would know how little was left over except her and Mitch, and what was he going to do? Swag meant nothing to him; they got new shipments of it any time there was a fundraising drive. He probably wouldn't even notice.

But he'd notice a pregnancy. Yochanna patted the lump in her tote bag and backed out of the closet. Now that she had paid herself, she considered herself and Mitch square.

She closed up the office again, repeating the ritual of shutting off lights and securing the entry door. She slid her blockers over her eyes. Once she'd found a black market dealer to exchange the sparkling stickers, she would have enough points to terminate a nursery's worth of babies. She would be able to afford to control what happened to her body, and when, beyond what grew in it or how it labored. Now, she had stolen back her time. She walked toward the transit station feeling rich beyond her wildest dreams— the wealth of autonomy, decisions, peace.

11

THE SCREENS ALONG the pedestrian tunnel lit up one at a time as Yochanna passed them, sensing her movement. The flickering lights dizzied her. Her blockers made the signs difficult to read, fading the neon lettering and inserting a layer of calming static between her and the unbearable disorder of Manhattan.

It might have looked like a city, but Yochanna knew New York was a metal merry-go-round. To get on, you had to jump at the exact right instant and get a sure grip on the rusted sun-warm steel tubes; if you matched the speed of the turning disc, the momentum magically lifted you from the packed playground dirt onto the serrated platform that could shred you like a block of probiotic cheese. You flew so fast in the city that your stomach traveled up your gullet into your throat, your brain knocked against the bones of your skull, and the fluid in your ears churned until you couldn't stand up straight, but in the heady moments when you clung to those carousel bars, nothing else mattered.

She knew that after New York, nothing could ever be the same. The lights were dull outside the city, the people less beautiful, and the world turned slowly. Other places are boring; they're full of people who dream of Manhattan.

After she'd come to the city from Georgetown, Yochanna had seen other people try to hold on longer than they should. It only ever ended badly. They were the ones who failed to feel the wheel's lethal power, the way it could suck you under its steel lip and hold you there, dragging you until you were broken. Sometimes, people got to come back—but only if they'd left at the right time, the first time. Yochanna would hold on as long as she could. She had hunkered down in her dead-end job with her powders and paints and hoped the city would have mercy and leave her alone.

The pregnancy, however, changed things. It destabilized her tenuous position and exposed her to New York's ravenousness. She sensed the metal edge whirring closer; even the subway sounded like an abattoir. This was a dangerous place to try living; it wasn't made to be welcoming, or built to be safe.

Yochanna knew that beneath its mesmerizing exterior, the city was a sickening, exhilarating whirl that turned everything outside itself to blurry stripes. The trick with New York was timing when to jump clear, far out past the beaten ring into the gravel scrub. You left the bright avenues, the faces. You surrendered your place on the wheel and flew out and hit your knees and finally, when it was done, your body was just a body, acclimated to the pedestrian velocity of the earth.

The Next 2 News host's bleach-brilliant, trademarked grin slicked across the screens as Yochanna made her way toward the train. The host's eyelashes, glued into sharp points that were each tipped with a rhinestone, fluttered like passing train lights.

They spoke in letters that bubbled at the bottom of the screen. "Next 2 News has an exclusive update on the murder of quadrillionaire Robert Weiss. Let's see those mugshots again!"

A grainy image captioned "Celine Broussard" popped onto the screen. It was a tasteful shot from a cultural feature, stuck next to a shadowy male silhouette marked "unidentified killer." Computer– generated blood spatters appeared, saturating the graphic until it was solid neon red. A twirling police siren flashed in each corner.

The murderers, the inflatable headline announced, had hiding places all over New York, from the Lower East Side to the outskirts of Harlem, where the kudzu swallowed buildings long-abandoned to rats. Keep watching. Next 2 News would have breaking updates as law enforcement worked to find whatever mutual aid network was hiding the perpetrators. They could film police brutality all they wanted. Didn't change a thing. This is America! Ask not!

The host smiled as they vogued for the camera, pretending to drown in their own blood for an audience they could neither see nor hear. Yochanna kept walking, trying to ignore the rippling tech banner that bombarded her with its images. The graphics tracked alongside her as she turned a corner.

Just as abruptly as the city sucked you in, it could be finished with you, too. There were no soft landing places in New York. When you were out, you're *out*. Yochanna was in real trouble, but all the same, she was no fool. She still had a grip on the city's metal bars. She refused to become one of the people who rode for a single revolution and then returned to insignificance and darkness. For now, her New York sparkled; it enthralled her.

Through a gravel-scarred silicone window in the pedestrian tunnel, she spotted the transit sign, dented and discolored and nearly obscured by a neon yellow ribbon of caution tape. She boarded the first bus that stopped and made her way to a seat. Her stomach lurched. The bus shuddered as though taking a deep breath and then dove below the streets into the vapor choked tunnel that connected the terminal district to Tribeca. She needed to find a dealer, and Soho seemed like a good place to start.

The dust was thick underground and imbued with invisible metal particles that short circuited cheaper devices; the new, name brand ones were supposed to be dust-proof, but as Yochanna glanced at the other passengers, she saw that the screens in other people's hands flickered and winked out as the air muffled their mini conductors. In a moment, the only light was the dim pink glow of the overhead tubes. They ran on static electricity; if the bus stopped, its motor would glitch out in a minute or so. Down here was a dead zone. Only the high, irregular whine of the driver's radio connected them to the world on the surface.

Yochanna's blockers sputtered as a mustard-tinted fog seeped through the bus' vents and filled the air with the acidulous scent of copper. She pushed the now-useless device up on her forehead and leaned against the window, although its antibacterial film was long-gone. Pitted plastic pebbled against her forehead as she peered into the dusk. The curved concrete wall of the transit tunnel was like the hide of an elephant she'd seen in an image, vast and misshapen. The graffiti artists practiced on these walls, but at close range all Yochanna could make out was a line here, a curve there. The images vanished as soon as she focused her eyes on them. Still, she tried to piece together the tags into words, warnings, names. A repeating arc of red paint swizzled past the window like the tail of a crimson rocket as the bus rattled down the slipstream toward the west side of the park.

Once she cashed out the stickers, her account would be flush. She'd never had so much at once in her life—enough for anything she could possibly need. She was used to pecking away at her debt, which seemed to quadruple with every payment. There was an exchange on practically every corner, willing to cash in non-standardized paychecks, pawn electronics, and offer a high-interest advance when you'd gone over your limit. She could pass by them now, knowing she was safe from ever having to use their predatory services.

She was walking around with over a million in value on her person, though you'd never know it from her stained shoes and tattered tote bag. She had saved up for three months for her blocker glasses, which weren't even Apfel, just a knockoff brand from one of the pop-up marts. The strap on her bag was wearing out. At home, a rat had climbed in her window, stinking of the Gowanus Canal, and chewed through every pair of her shoes in a terrible frenzy. But money could fix those problems, and she'd stolen enough to live on for years. With the stickers, she could get medical care, order takeout noodles, watch a new Skin Series episode, and buy a pair of decent boots. She'd make rent. She could travel. Pay off her student debt. Walk away from Mitch and his sour spunk and wandering hands. Buy broadsheets instead of making messes in the sink. Store her collection of powders in clean ampoules instead of salvaged street baggies.

On her way home, she'd buy herself a real, fresh bouquet and a new coat, with a lining thick enough to get her through the February storms. A whole ream of paper made from botanical fibers for her powders, her art project. She could finally have the shiny bracelet she'd coveted, with a charm on it. Her eyes unfocused. She'd get a year-long transit pass instead of scratching to pay for a two-hour ticket. She would saturate each sheet of paper with ink and transform it from a blank rectangle to a picture of the inside of her heart. She would become a real artist, making the leap to independence with the stolen currency. She'd sit on her bed and finally experience the relief the mental health module promised, stress melting down her shoulders like wings. She would have *enough*. She had never known what that felt like until this moment. Her stomach rolled over and ruffled its feathers, like a pigeon bathing in a puddle.

It was the kind of transformation that only happened in fairy tales. Now, it was happening to Yochanna. The life she'd always imagined herself in was the opposite of the place where she was now—in the dank tunnels under the Financial District, jostling along a track that hadn't been improved since the mid-2000s.

The faint, rosy light of the carriage made the other passengers look younger and sweeter than they probably were. When Yochanna caught a glimpse of her reflection in the window, she saw that she was actually *glowing,* the way pregnancy is said to imbue a halo around someone who is gestating. Her cheeks were pink, as though permanently post-coital. A bead of sweat congealed on her neck and wandered down inside her collar. Her body felt like it was filling out, as though her cells were plumping up like pillows of sweet ricotta-filled ravioli immersed in hot water. She was floating, swollen, into the next phase of her life.

Though Yochanna knew not to stare at others without her blockers on, she stole a glance at the young man across from her. It was so dark that the only proof of his existence were the curved lines of light that stuck to the ridges of his naked face. A pair of glasses hung around his neck, their lenses inoperative. His cheekbones and full lips were illuminated, while his eyes were sunken into shadows, forming a neon death mask that bared its teeth when it realized it had caught Yochanna's attention. Before Yochanna could avert her eyes and pretend she'd never looked, the boy slithered into the seat next to her. His breath was warm against her neck.

"Aww, don't do that," he said, as she scooted away, one hand on her blockers. "What's your name?"

"Candace," she lied.

"That's cute, what kind of name is that?"

"I don't know."

He leaned closer. His breath was warm, or maybe it was the interior of the bus, charged with static and the ionic dust that clouded the overhead tubes. The hand that groped for her hip moved lazily, as though stunned. She pushed it away and watched it clamber back over his lap, the seats, a lustful spider looking for a place to rest.

"You get high?" he asked.

"I don't have anything." She was afraid to take her eyes off this stranger. If they were above ground, she could slide between the other passengers or find a seat closer to the driver; she might make a fuss, or get off at the next stop. She was used to being shouted at by men, but Mitch was the only one who pawed her. She tightened her grip on her bag.

He said, "Look." He reached into his pocket and extracted a small, folded packet. A magazine model vamped on the label, which looked home-printed, not mass-produced. He opened it enough for Yochanna to peek inside; a few pellets slushed around in a pinch of off-white powder. He extracted a pill and placed it in the center of his palm. It was stamped with a brilliant yellow flower that glittered as he tilted his hand toward Yochanna, tempting her.

"What is it?"

"Lotta things," he said. His shoulder was against hers.

Yochanna glanced at the bodies around them, but the other passengers weren't looking. They kept their eyes glued to their devices, ears plugged. The ratty posters on the bus ceiling gazed down at her like the angels in Michaelangelo's friezes. *Help*, she thought. He was bigger, heavier, likely faster. She smelled the tang of citrus spray and mold on his skin, and she wondered how many of those pellets he'd already eaten.

"Fennies?" she guessed, stalling.

He nodded. "With some Ee-85, too. It's not strong. Gives you trails."

"Ee makes me sick," she said.

"That's the point. See stuff, puke a little. Get out of yourself."

His lips grazed her ear and she pressed herself against the window, putting another inch of space between them. Busy with the packet, his hands were docile, occupied. The bus hit a road tie on the tunnel track and the stranger clutched the pellets. The loose pill vanished into his lap and he jerked away from Yochanna, patting his clothes.

She saw it before he did. The vivid lily stamp sparkled from the floor and in spite of herself, she nudged him, pointed. He snatched it up and blew on it, as though that was enough to make it palatable.

"You should have this one, since you found it," he said, offering it again.

"What's the flower for? There's sensiva in it?"

He snorted. "Stupid. It's the source. Everything good runs through the flower shop."

She shifted in her seat. The air in the bus seemed to thrum around them, as though the particles magnetized to their skin. Her knee was drawn toward his, stuck. The physical contact made him straighten up and his hands were momentarily still on the packet, the stained front of his shirt.

"Everything?" she asked.

"Anything you can think of," he said. His eyes flitted over the people in the nearby seats. He lowered his voice and muttered against her cheek, the black market goods that he claimed to plug. He told her what he'd heard maybe came from the florist in Tribeca. Collagen. Drugs. Knockoff liquor that tasted like the real thing. Dry ice. Nerve injections. Value chips, untraceable. You name it, it went out the back door at this spot. At least, that's what his friend Fish said.

"Plus flowers," he added, with a flourish, as though producing a real bouquet. Bragging.

"That's the only thing I want," she said.

He grinned. "Place over off the park with a green sign over the door. Maybe I'll see you again sometime."

The bus emerged from the guts of the transit tubes and the silver threads of the commuter bridge ran along next to the windows, cables absorbing the static in the air and dispelling the deadening ions as the tube gasses pulsed and evaporated and the artificial heart-colored shine was replaced with the wan, amber daylight that revealed the stranger as not even a man, just a boy with a fistful of pellets and ketchup on his chin. Yochanna pulled the cord for the first stop and slipped off the bus before he could decide to follow her. She didn't need him anymore. She could find her own way. She spotted the green awning down the block and pulled her blockers down over her eyes. If the florist's was the place for contraband, she would go there.

She set off with the single-mindedness of a subway car, jittering forward on an electrified track.

12

IN HIS THIRTY-ODD years of criminality, Paul had experienced plenty of close calls, but never a bust. After his only period of incarceration, he was mindful, always erring on the side of caution. He knew that longevity, in a criminal's line of work, was not a matter of chance but the outcome of taking the utmost care with every detail of his enterprises.

He left Celine and Robert's corpse in her studio and went to the front of Broussard's to pull the buckets into the shop, lower the awning, and switch off the business lights. Body or no body, he knew that survival was dependent in part on routine. The strongest defense in any questionable situation was to come through clean, and the best way to look clean was to be clean.

While he was dimming the cold case tubes, a girl carrying a canvas tote bag paused in the entry, removed her bulky blocker glasses, and started to inch around the display of LED-dotted house cactuses. She clutched the handle of her tote as though afraid someone would snatch it off her shoulder—such a ratty thing, the strap practically worn through, the bottom panel balding and partly blackened from resting on the ground, the circular crest faded to indecipherability.

She came to the counter and leaned toward Paul, although they were the only two people in the shop and the neon out front blinked *closed*. Paul noticed that she was holding an unbent paper clip. As she spoke, she jammed it into the surface of the counter and gouged a half-inch mark into its face; a small heap of aqua-blue shavings piled up by her hand. She looked as though she'd happily take a scratch out of Paul while she was at it.

She said, "I heard you could do off-market exchanges here."

"I don't know what that is." He spread his hands. People came through with all kinds of trash. He wasn't a pawn shop, he told them, but he had seen every flavor of human greed in this place, all kinds of desperation splashed here among the flowers. He noted the girl's steady, color-stained fingers.

"You want a bouquet, I'll make one, but that's all I have for you," Paul said.

"I heard you had other things, for the right price."

She didn't look like a pro, which was a mixed blessing, Paul knew. He couldn't tell if she was a thief or not, but her caution made him nervous. Fencing paid big; the risk wasn't something Paul took on lightly. Take a bad shipment and you'd have so many pigs down your neck, you'd look like a sausage stuffer. First-timers got away with more, but Paul was a veteran offender. Many of the men he'd been imprisoned with were caught because they didn't know what to do with what they had; they were greedy, unreliable, and demanding. They didn't keep their mouths shut. Even in solitary, they bragged to the floor and the zinging walls about their exploits. Confession was the worst sin, in Paul's opinion; it was digging your grave with your own mouth. In less than a day, this girl might be sitting in an interrogation room, and what was she going to say?

"What else did you want?" he asked.

"To trade these for whatever they're worth. Today." She opened the tote bag and in its stained belly, Paul saw the unmistakable glint of donor stickers. Fistfuls of them, a fortune of printed celluloid. Each one was engraved with a proprietary, secure microchip that could override values in any system. They didn't come cheap.

Paul paused. This was a true underworld request.

"We closed half an hour ago," he said. He should finish sweeping, refill the buckets, and weed out the withered stock. Go back to Celine and the mess she'd made in the back. Robert Weiss wasn't going to be any less dead after Paul's closing routine; ritual, he'd found, cleared his mind. It presented him with the answers he needed, as though they sprouted in the pee-paw gravel alongside the dud amaryllis. The girl stuck her lip out a little further and refused to budge.

"I can wait," she said.

"If you're going to stick around, turn off your data."

She fished her device out of the unraveling tote and powered it down, then did the same with her blockers. It made her safer, temporarily invisible from the ubiquitous security scanners. Paul watched her slide the now-dead tech back into her bag, revealing another peek at the packets of stickers.

"I'll wait in the back," she said. "Or I can sit at the counter, anywhere out of the way."

"You stay where I can see you. Don't touch anything."

She edged around the corner of the register and past him, settling on the high stool in the corner, behind a potted palm. She was so still that in a moment, Paul forgot she was there. He puttered around the store, plucking stems from the bouquets and deadheading flowers that were past their prime. The broken bulb in the back corner still flashed in an irregular pattern, and he noted it, thinking of the replacement he stashed in the shop's supply closet. It was a moment's work. He stepped into the small space, out of sight, and found the black comm box mounted to the wall. He tapped a few keys and entered a short code, jamming the data to a single line, as he always did when conducting business. His pulse upticked just slightly. Opportunities like an unattended girl—carrying a glacier's worth of stolen stickers, no less—didn't appear out of thin air without strings attached.

This whole thing was too easy.

Paul frowned. Bait, and he'd been on the verge of taking it.

He peeked around the supply closet's door, taking a closer look at the girl. He wondered what else was in that tote, under her skirt, or hiding in her shoes. He'd been foolish not to search her when she insisted on staying put. She had a bland quality that made him forget her as soon as he looked the other way. Her expressionlessness captivated him. She was a blank slate, perfectly symmetrical. Hair parted in the middle. Her skin was the same even shade all over, without a single blemish or freckle. Looking at her was like shaking hands with someone and realizing that they had no fingerprints. He wasn't able to recall what she looked like the moment after she was out of his sight.

She did not look like someone who needed currency. She looked like a spy. Whoever hired her planned on getting their money's worth.

Paul felt his stomach sprout whiskers. He went to the front door and double-locked it. The metal grate rolled down until it was flush with the cement, turning the flower shop into a cage. The only way out now was through the sterile room, which led to the studio and its side door, which opened onto the loading dock that accessed the high, narrow, windowless alley that bled into the back end of Carroll Street.

The girl wouldn't know that; she could not hear Celine's anxious keening in the back room or the van's running engine. And, by the same token, nobody but Celine would hear this girl scream when Paul took the next necessary steps.

He was not sure how he would do the girl in—throttled, maybe. Broken neck. But the planning didn't matter. The only thing Paul knew was that he intended to come through this in one piece. He gave the grate a jiggle and heard its reassuring clank. Locked in.

But the girl had heard the grate latch, too. He didn't notice her footsteps until she was nearly on top of him. She passed him in a blur, leaping over a row of flower buckets and clearing them with the agility of a sparrow. Paul was too startled to grab her, although her skirt's hem whisked within inches of him. Her speed stirred up the blossoms and combined their perfumes into a heady mix. Paul heard her shoes scuffle on the tiles of the clean room, then fists pounding against the corrugated back door. The bolt rattled;

she abandoned it as Paul followed her. He was on her heels as she darted down the darkened hall toward the studio. She stopped dead in the doorway. Beyond her, Paul could see Celine's wide eyes as she bent over the body, trying to cover it with a bolt of cloth.

Robert Weiss had rolled part way off the drafting table, one leg draped across a hamper of unsewn gores. His lifeless limbs entwined with Celine's. The strange girl took in the inert mass of Robert's body and the horrible, wrong angle of his neck. Robert Weiss' face was violet; the frail veins in his cheeks had exploded into florid chrysanthemums. The skin of his neck bulged on both sides of his collar. His shirt-front seemed to convulse, though he was not breathing.

Paul was nearly on top of the girl when she turned abruptly, as though to escape back down the hallway. Her eyes met Paul's with a petrified expression. Her mouth hinged open in a silent shriek, but he covered her mouth and clasped her against his chest. She was light as a pigeon; as she struggled, he felt he grasped a fledgling in his arms. Paul tightened his grip on the girl and carried her into the studio, kicking the door closed behind him.

The girl scrambled against Paul's arms, hindered by her grip on her filthy bag. As she thrashed, Paul grabbed her by the shirt, spun her around, and slammed his fist into her face like a piston—hard, twice, *pop pop*. Her nose burst into a bloody rose under his knuckles and she slumped to the floor. Paul looked over his shoulder at Celine, who stared at him, stunned, but didn't say a word.

Paul retrieved the tire iron from the lower rack of the cart and stood beside the table. Prone, the girl seemed helpless—but that could change in an instant. Consciousness brought out the worst in people. You never knew who someone was until they were awake.

Celine nudged the stranger's limp shoulder with tentative fingers. The girl's facial muscles fluttered and her tongue reappeared in the corner of her mouth and gave a sentient twitch. Her unbruised eye began to vibrate in its socket as it tracked under the closed lid, then flickered open. Saliva congealed on her lips. Her nose was already discolored, cheeks bloated.

"Get a gel pack," Celine said. "I keep pain relief units in the kitchen."

Paul shook his head. "It's a waste."

He leaned over the girl and watched her eyes open, consciousness wavering in her uneven, dilated eyes. The girl's left pupil expanded, sucking in the light before it shrank to a pin prick and focused on Paul's face. Paul felt it analyze his features before rolling away to investigate the details of the room. He raised the tire iron. The girl's hands began to twitch, then frantically skittered to the edges of the table.

"Don't move," Celine cautioned, and the hands froze, rigid claws.

"Where's my bag," the girl muttered. Her face was a crime scene. Her battered nose oozed thick rivulets of blood that clogged her breathing, coated her chin, and dribbled down into the gutters of her ears. She turned her head to the side to spit a red mouthful onto the drafting table.

"First things first," Paul said. He gripped her wrist, pinning it to the table, and brought the tire iron down gently so it rested on the back of the immobilized elbow. "You tell us who you are and why you came in the shop or I'll break every bone in your arm."

She stiffened, as though electrified.

"Don't," she said. "I'm nobody. Yochanna Rother."

"Who sent you?" Paul asked. "If you're lying, I'll bleed you out on this floor, right now."

"I came for myself," she whimpered.

He patted Yochanna's elbow with the tire iron. She flinched and began to cry.

"I need my hand," she said.

Paul felt his own fingers begin to tingle. The fragile filaments under the skin prickled and he imagined what it would feel like, to have a hand that was a baggie of broken bones and torn veins. Repairing that kind of damage would be impossible, even with mass-graft electro treatments.

Her hand, pink and perfect, flexed into a useless fist and then stretched out like a starfish, looking for an escape. There was none.

"Just tell us," Celine said. "We don't want to hurt you. We only want to know."

"I heard you could exchange my stickers here," the girl said. "I'm sorry I saw the dead man. I didn't mean to. I just want to go home—please, I need a termination. I'm not doing this for anyone else."

"Where'd you get the swag?" he asked.

"I stole from my work and someone said the florist could help me get a fresh start. Please. I need my hand back, can I have my hand now, please?"

She was beginning to babble and a string of blood-tinged drool ran from the corner of her mouth, making a pink line on her skin. She was sweating so intensely that Paul could see the outline of her shape on the table, each leg and even her hair making a damp shadow of itself. As her nose bled, a pool of mucus and drool condensed into droplets on the silicone. Her perspiration smelled like smoke and crushed pigment. For an instant, he wanted to bite into her and let her body's flavors mingle on his tongue.

He raised the iron again.

Then, a weight hung on his elbow, as though his arm was suddenly made of stone.

"Don't," Celine said. She clung to him, swinging. Her toes dusted the studio floor. "She's pregnant. It's wrong."

"Could be a lie. You want to find out what prison's like?"

"She's not lying."

He fought the urge to shake her off. Celine had been his path back to life, once upon a time. The shop, its flowers, his soft bed indoors, a good reputation, and income all flowed from his patron. She had never sought to control or even guide him, before now. Did he owe her? He might say so. He put the iron aside on the table.

"I'm going to let you go," he told the girl. "Don't move."

"I need to throw up."

Celine moved a bin close to the table and the girl sat up and vomited into it. Her hands retracted into the folds of her skirt, hiding from Paul. The soft, worn tote bag splayed on the table beside her, guts inside out. The bent paperclip shimmered amidst a splatter of colored powders that were already beginning to mix into a nonsense shade of puce. A clamshell case slid out and spilled the stickers onto the mat. They caught the subdued light of the studio, exposing the authenticity dots on the corners of the bronze-stenciled chip inside. It was a heap of tiny black market gems, and even though he'd seen a glimpse of it before, the sheer value of the pile took Paul's breath away. *Ice money.*

As Yochanna wiped her mouth, Paul took a longer look at her, this totally unremarkable person who contained so many golden surprises.

"She needs first aid," Celine said, shoving the soiled liner into a discreet corner to spare them all from the stink of stomach acid. She glanced at the contents of the bin and shuddered. There was nothing in this girl's digestion, just regurgitated soylent and darkened flakes of swallowed blood. Pregnancy made people sick, sometimes for weeks. There was no explanation for the mysterious grip a baby could get on a person's guts. Or their heart, Paul thought. It was already working on Celine.

"I told you we didn't have to keep her alive," he said.

"One body is hard enough to get rid of," Celine told him. "This one used to be the richest man in the world. How long do you think we have before his sons figure out that we still have him with us?"

"An hour, maybe."

"Less," croaked Yochanna. She held up her reactivated device in a quavering hand. "The murder footage hit the stream. They're saying—the telecast says you two killed him."

13

CELINE'S THROAT SEIZED as she absorbed Yochanna's news. She supposed she was in shock. Her ears felt as though they were packed with spools of cotton. She heard the vibration in the overhead filament light and the way it wove between the voices in the room, a fabric of tones and texture that deadened meaning. Each sound had its unique weft, loops, sizzles. The darkest rumble was resonant and smoky and was punctuation to the higher tones, which played around each other and made a single, indecipherable thread. She shook her head, trying to clear her eardrums.

Next to the drafting table, Robert Weiss' silent corpse sagged in the wreckage of his coffin. The tarp covered his head, but the rest of him lay in a contorted heap.

"I want to go home," Yochanna whined. She propped herself up on one elbow in the corner where she'd wilted against the crates of scraps. Her eyes were darkening into bruised rings from where Paul had hit her. Her voice rasped with a touch of vocal fry as delicate but persistent as a strip of sharkskin. She was young. And belligerent.

"This isn't my fault," she said.

Paul growled. "You're not going anywhere."

"We are out of time, Paul," Celine said. His head turned reflexively at the rounded, bell-like notes of culture in her voice. Once upon a time, Celine's type was called *a voice for radio*, because no matter what it said, you couldn't help but lean toward the transmitter, and try to catch each honeyed, irresistible syllable. In the old days, everyone strove to inject this magical quality into their voices; telecast hosts used to sound like someone you *wanted* to listen to. Now, all audio material was digitized and run through encryption programs until the voice came out robotic and anonymous. Accessible, but inhuman, too. Humanity was always the first thing to go, under fascism. The voice of her grandmother, humming in the kitchen. Then, beauty.

Celine missed it.

She said, "You can stay if you want, but I need to get out before I'm arrested. You said the best way was to return the body, so that is what I will do. They didn't name you. Or this girl."

Yochanna slid off the long-legged table. She cradled her forearm against her chest. "How long will it take them to make the connection? They know 'Celine.' Surveillance will have hundreds of hours of footage of you two together. And me, I'm here, which is enough to make me an accessory."

Celine noted the tire iron in Paul's hand. If he threw it, he would hit one of them; blood was easy to identify and trace, much easier than facial identification. She took a calculated step back.

"And what about *him*," Yochanna continued, pointing to the long, narrow pasteboard coffin on the floor. The flimsy panels were battered and beginning to splinter at the corner. The lid was bashed in, as though someone had stepped through it like the skin of a drum. Through the hole, Celine could see a shred of dark, expensive fabric—a lush blend of natural fibers, wool and cotton. It was tinted authentic indigo, not like the colorburst dyes used to produce ordinary clothes.

For a moment, Celine had the sense of staring at the naked night sky through shreds of cirrus cloud. As a child, she had once been far enough away from the city's ambient light that she could sense the presence of the stars. That indigo night, she'd stared into the gash between the clouds as though she could have flown through it—her first time seeing the sky, which she realized was not an empty bowl that sat over the earth, containing it, but a portal to a place beyond their scummy, browning planet. There was something else out there, where disarmed satellites shot blank signals into space and refracted ancient light beams back to the ground, seeking receivers that were long since dismantled or destroyed.

A mangled hand drooped over the side of the broken box, its snapped wrist emerging from a designer pinstripe sleeve. Celine could make out the monogram *W* on the platinum and pearlescent cufflink; it was the same shade as his torpid skin. It wore a watch worth several generations of wealth. Yet, none of them had even touched its solid-ruby band. Was that not proof of their innocence?

"I'll carry him," Paul said.

"It'll slow you down," Celine ventured, knowing it wasn't a choice. They couldn't afford to leave anything behind.

Paul shook his head. "The girl will slow us down. This man doesn't talk and he doesn't have any opinions. Always bring your proof with you. Understand? If we abandon it, they'll find a way to show we killed him. And then it won't matter what we say."

Celine snapped, "We need to leave now or we won't make it far at all. The news is out which means the police are next. This is only getting worse."

"Her, too," said Paul, pointing to the girl.

Yochanna stuttered, "It was a misunderstanding—I'm not even supposed to be here. I have nothing to do with it."

Paul grunted. "The only reason you're alive right now is that you have nothing to do with it. We can't let you go, and if you try to run, I'll break your skull in half. Those are my terms. Take it or leave it. Nobody is going to let you explain yourself to the cops."

Where had Paul learned such things? The girl's already strained face seemed to stretch to its tearing point. Celine edged toward her and grasped her arm. To her surprise, the other woman leaned against her. The gentle pressure felt good. She felt sorry for Yochanna, pregnant and bleeding from the nose. Getting help from people was difficult these days. When someone was in enough trouble they would listen to anyone, even a murder suspect.

Yochanna was fidgeting, plucking a loose thread in Celine's patchwork shawl. Celine extricated the loose thread from her fingers, whipped a bolt of fabric from the wall racks, and dragged it onto the drafting table. She sliced a few yards free and nodded to Paul, who knelt, broke the last bits of sealant from the coffin lid, and seized Robert Weiss' body by the arms.

Standing, they looked like grotesque tango partners. Paul dragged the corpse out of the wreckage of the box and hugged it to his chest. Its feet dragged on the floor and its luxurious suit rumpled against Paul's rough coveralls. The bloodstain that puckered Robert's creamy shirt looked like a vermilion sun whose rays diffused from the puncture wound in the center the combed cotton. Blood pooled by his belt and in the cradle of the coffin there was some standing liquid that the air blackened as the platelets cooled and settled outside their master's body.

Robert Weiss had never lifted anything heavier than a silk necktie in his long and privileged life. He was needle-thin and his skin was pale and slick as tofu. He was twice Celine's age but looked sixty-five himself—vitamins, clean water, skin smoothing treatments.

Paul's dark, scarred hands clasped the body's waist. Its head lolled against his neck. Even dead, Robert's expression had not changed and he still looked implacable and impossible to please. One marbled eye was open; the other was a glassy slit. The rich never aged. They simply decayed.

Paul laid him on the canvas yardage and watched as Celine whip-stitched the fabric into a long, loose tube around the dead man.

"We could leave him in the alley," the girl said. She edged away from the two friends—the rain artist kneeling by the makeshift stretcher, and the brutally formed man who stood silently beside her as she worked. "Without his clothes. Or burn him in the box."

"You don't know what you're talking about," Paul said. He drove his boot through one of the sides of the coffin, forcing it flat, then stomped the others down. "Hand me that can by your elbow."

The stink of turpentine made Celine's nose wrinkle as Paul poured it over the carton. When he was done, he tossed the can aside and wiped his hands on his clothes, leaving an amber stain.

"We will take the subway to the Upper West Side, then look for a loose PATH car to go further north. We need to go before we lose any more time."

He bent, shouldered the shrouded corpse, and nodded at the women.

Celine picked up the splintered panels gingerly and followed Paul as he moved toward the hallway. The door swung open and, after glancing left and right, he signaled that it was clear. They carried the ruined box a short distance to the dumpster, then dropped each piece in, followed by an emergency blister pack that ignited the contents of the metal box and cast a deep chocolate glow as the pasteboard burned.

Yochanna stared into the dumpster's innards until Celine appeared at the threshold. Her balaclava covered her face and she touched Yochanna's hands, deciding how to comfort her. If they were going, they had to move together. No escapes. No last minute changes.

Celine knew how girls could be; she'd been a girl herself, once, believing she had powers that excused her from the laws of gravity, the state, and her the body itself—its aging and frailty, its agonizing dependence on other people's tenderness. She used to be young, but now she was wise. She felt it was an even-handed trade. She would not go back, even if she could.

Celine sensed the permanence of the choices she was making, from the smoking dumpster to the handful of needles and thread she stuffed into her bag as she took a final look at the shop that bore her family name. She opened her black umbrella, making herself invisible from above, and followed Paul. She was ready to disappear, and the decision filled her with grief. Yochanna could not have understood the enormity of this loss; she was too young to believe that you could not un-see your fate, once it had looked you in the eye. Overwhelming or not, this was the time to go. Every minute brought their hunters closer. They were entering a period of extreme risk, with survival odds slimmer than an eel-skin glove.

The box and its bloody contents hung over Celine's head like a nightmare. Then, she blinked, and the world clicked back into its mechanism and continued as though it was an ordinary Thursday evening. The trains still rattled under her feet. Yellow dust coated the night sky, falling in gentle veils. With a scrape and a sigh, Paul settled the body on his shoulder. They began to walk toward the end of the alley, watching the pastel lights zip back and forth in the narrow gap that connected them to the rest of the Lower East Side.

They had to go on. There was no choice but to try.

One hundred percent of zero is nothing, Celine reminded herself.

Yochanna's hand was in Celine's. The girl still needed medicine for her pain, Celine thought. They said willow took the sting away. Or calendula, or oats, these plants that persisted from another time, each carrying a promise in their fragile leaves.

I can fix you.

I'll help you.

You're loved.

14

At the end of the alley, Paul palmed his device, shading it with his free hand so the dim screen wouldn't attract any sensors. The same metal particles that clogged wireless receivers worked perfectly for shortwave transmissions. The grid on the screen rotated, showing a textured grid that moved like a porous, fist-sized cloud. The magnetic dust generated by the clean-up copper was a gentle, passive conductor for radio signals. Each dot in the map's cloud was generated by a microscopic transmitter concealed in the city's crevices. The map in Paul's hand pulsed in time with the district's heartbeat, from the gated storefronts vibrating as the subway coursed beneath them to billboard awnings—huge, slick, graphic—the filaments in their banners bulging like eyeballs about to rupture, filling in a wind that raced over the steel and concrete security fences, making the transmitters shiver.

Celine and Yochanna huddled close to him, forming a tight cluster with a tiny map at its center. A yellow flare marked their destination: the train station two blocks away. Carrying Robert's swaddled body, they hastened between the artificial shadows. The map's dots moved in tandem, tracing the trio with the smoothness of a dream. As they came to the transit gate, their map's yellow marker sputtered and doubled in size.

This was it.

Although Celine was born inside the city and had few memories outside its limits, her heart began to pound as Paul guided them toward the gullet of the subway. He ran ahead of her and Yochanna Robert Weiss draped over his shoulders like a muffler. The girl was next, trailing along with her tote clutched in both hands. Her shoes were silent on the pavement, as though their soles were quilted silk. Celine was last, slowed down by a chill of anxiety.

She was afraid to look left or right as they darted into the entrance of the Wall Street train station. The daytime crush of people had faded to a trickle of between-shift workers, people heading home or away. Every commuter was loaded down, holding dingy shopping bags, sacks that dripped broth from poorly packed lunches, trash salvaged for reuse, and rolling luggage cases that functioned as portable pop-up shops. A puddle of soup glimmered on the top steps, so curry-rich that for an instant Celine thought it was a neon spill and dodged to go around it. She closed her charcoal-satin umbrella and hooked its bamboo handle over her wrist as they entered the filthy tunnel. Her umbrella hardly attracted attention on the street—few people even knew what the avant-garde accessory was—but down here, under the watchful eyes of the transit authority cameras, any difference might be a liability.

"This way," Paul said. His free hand clamped onto Celine and Yochanna. Shackled together by his iron grip, they picked their way down the stairs, keeping close to the wall. The security cameras down here were crusted with chemical runoff and damaged by vandals. Celine glanced up at the shotgun-barrel casing of one camera, flinching as she realized she was caught in its sights. Even with her face and hair covered, there were other ways for them to identify you. From your gait pattern to the rings of your iris, every fact about your body could betray you. That was why some people wore special blockers that obscured ocular data or coated their clothes in a reflective spray that made the fabric slippery and harder to digitize. Fingerprints, device IP—your uniqueness could be used against you to rip your privacy away and reveal you to prying or seeking eyes. But Celine had never been a criminal before, or ever coveted something that was not hers; she was not a law-breaker, she had never learned how to conceal herself from justice, legitimate or not.

Yochanna, sensing her tension, murmured a few indecipherable words of comfort. Celine glanced up again as the girl pulled her down the stairs. The camera was broken. Its polymer shield was spray-painted black and someone had smashed its primary lens with something blunt, leaving a deep pit in the center of the glass. A red bulb throbbed feebly in the darkness like a dying predator's heart.

At the turnstile, Paul hissed and brought the others closer. While a group of shrieking boys in PVC-leather mini skirts stamped their incandescent boots in rhythm with the song playing in their earbuds, Celine and her friends slipped down the stairs to the boarding area reserved for the 4 train.

New York was too vast to leave in an hour, even under conventional circumstances. Many times, Celine had waited on a platform for long periods, breathing the stuffy, too-warm, copper-scented air through her filtration mask. The subways were always late; it seemed like a line went inactive for repairs every six months, then immediately broke down after re-opening.

The system itself deteriorated into a series of commercial fragments, covering short distances between stops that nobody used. Two transit monopolies edged out the municipal cars, installing tracks that were an inch narrower or weren't compatible with the green energy rail, which only delayed things further. There were three 4 trains and none of them ran on time or in the same direction. Celine worried for a moment that her group would have to linger and watch the ever-inaccurate stop clock count down to a train that wouldn't arrive.

Even underground, she knew they were not unobserved. Her pulse thrummed through her neck. She felt her common sense unraveling. Down here, anyone could be a spy or an undercover cop. She had never felt so unsafe before in her own city, never looked over her shoulder and wondered whether a stranger was holding a stun gas detonator or a two-way radio. She felt anxiety claw at her trachea. Her feet itched, as if urging her to run. Commuters packed close around her, creating a barrier or a cage, she could not distinguish which.

She couldn't stand it anymore—desperately needed to hide. She opened her umbrella and propped it on her shoulder, shielding her face. Her mother had been superstitious about umbrellas, saying it was bad luck to open one indoors, worse than breaking a mirror. The black satin panels were stitched double-thick, with a hand-waxed canvas layer in between them. Celine did not know if it was enough to provide any protection. Heat-tracing sensors could stencil your silhouette through an atmospheric veil. The idiosyncratic movements of your smallest facial muscles were stored in the surveillance database, in case you transgressed.

Even the closeness of other people down here, the way their breath filled the space and the way their eyes touched every part of her body and clothes, was a reminder that nothing was private or kept for yourself. As the world was divided into percents, the non-wealthy were left to scrap among themselves.

Although New York had once been bordered by broad-banked rivers, the canals and beds were decades dry and filled with concrete and turned into more real estate. Each inch of ground was packed, measured, weighed, assessed, and fought over. The air belonged to the wealthy and their private and commissioned police forces. Celine had flown once or twice and knew how small the world looked from above. No wonder the ice-drinkers liked it this way. While they commanded the air, the rest of humanity waited on the train platform along with Celine, whose worry wrapped around her heart like a strand of florist's wire that pulled tighter with each passing breath.

From the time Celine could walk, her mother taught her that she had to be ready to leave at any time, at short notice. She was raised to believe that mistakes became part of who you were because they informed your future. Like opening an umbrella in the house. Putting the wrong shoe on first. Not repeating a certain prayer or numeric code at exactly the right time. She drummed it into Celine. You missed one step and the opportunity you wanted went to someone who was maybe less deserving but better prepared. Being on time was a survival skill.

Celine's mother was always sweaty and short-tempered when her daughter was young. She suffered from chronic frustration. She was fed up with Celine, who took too long at anything, whether it was climbing into the dining seats, unloading the groceries, getting ready for bed, finishing meals, or dressing herself. Even as she tried to keep up, Celine knew she was a disappointment. The only way to be on time was to be early, anticipate the next move, and do what was expected before it was ever even expressed.

If you could see the future, you might be prepared.

Not that the Broussard's ever were.

Standing on the subway platform, Celine shifted from foot to foot. She could see the station clock re-fracturing itself as each second elapsed. As the numerals clicked into new shapes, she felt sweat soak her waistband and the patch between her shoulders. Time was passing. The trains came every two minutes, with a fraction of a minute saved for boarding. The seconds trickled by. She sensed she was already late.

"We can't stay here," she whispered. The clock over the platform rearranged its pixels in meaningless patterns. A covert-type camera, flush with the station's stained, nicotine-colored tiles, blinked over the entrance of the train tunnel. Its glazed lens flickered, gathering information.

She sensed the first tremor of current in the air as the rail conduits picked up the charge of the distant train. The transit information display generated an image of a bouncing red apple with a golden numeral "4" inscribed on its skin. The apple rolled to one side of the board and blinked. The other passengers began to crowd closer and gather near the steel girders that marked the charge pads that aligned with the train car doors. Celine felt the surge of human bodies on both sides of her and reached out instinctively for Yochanna so they would not be separated. She could see Paul and his burden further down the platform, so tall that his head was clearly visible above the clusters of commuters. She felt her mother's old frustration coursing through her body like mercury. It pulsed in her capillaries and made the overworked tendons in her wrists throb.

The concrete under her feet vibrated as the 4 approached. The transit tunnel extruded a tremendous bubble of stale air, followed instantly by the train's gleaming face. As the doors slid open, Celine took a few shuffling steps forward into the nearest car. Her hand was clamped around Yochanna's as people surrounded them like wads of damp excelsior. Celine felt the connection between her own fingers and the girl's, their heartbeats momentarily synced through their interlinked flesh.

"We will ride four stops and then move to our own transport," Paul whispered in Celine's ear. "A friend of mine told me about an offline LIRR track in the Metro-North section."

Celine nodded. She did not ask how he knew, or if it was safe: it didn't matter. Their only hope was to leave New York with their evidence and hope that Henry would call off the search. Celine squeezed Yochanna's hand and sidled closer to Paul, until they were smashed against one another in the crowded plastic-lined pod.

The doors suctioned closed and the advertising banners on the floor, walls, and ceiling began their animated dance. Celine read their promises with skepticism. *New teeth delivered to your door. Wipe away debt with a year on our data server farm. Eat more hormones and labor happier.* She knew there was no better world ahead for anyone on the train.

She glanced around at the bent, dark heads. One man was wrapped in layers of plastic, voluminous as a jellyfish. The passenger beside him leaned on the shimmering pillow of his costume, a strand of drool seeping from slackened lips and leaving a sticky trail. Two girls played a compact game that emitted bursts of candy-sweet sounds. A man whose hair was matted into a single beaver-tail dreadlock poked a meat kabob between the bars of the rolling cage clamped between his knees. Inside, two juvenile raccoons scrabbled over one another, seized the morsel, and began to fight over it. Sounds of conflict filled the car as the train lurched around a corner to the next platform. Some people were live-capping the raccoon fight with their cameras. Celine caught a stray lens flare as someone's curved optic captured the space and transmitted it to social media. She shielded her face—too late. She turned toward Paul and buried her head against his chest to hide from any unwanted observers.

They stopped at Gotham Parkway, Banksy Block, and American Dream and each time the doors hissed open Celine held her breath. Through the flux of boarding and disembarking, she huddled closer to Paul and Yochanna, making a protective circle around their shrouded cargo. Yochanna's fingers were clammy in hers. This close to her companions, she could smell the oil in Paul's clothes and the dry shampoo dusting Yochanna's shoulders. Robert Weiss emitted the delicate scent of seared salmon steaks and cultured butter as his cells decomposed, jellying into a rich, putrescent paste that spread like an oil stain over the soft face of his whip-stitched shroud.

Their final stop came. Paul tugged Celine's sleeve.

He said, "Take the gondola waiting by the west down-ramp. It's supposed to be marked. We'll know it when we see it."

When the doors opened, the other passengers dodged around them and filtered into the station, bodies mixing in an indiscernible pattern. Celine and her friends hung back until they were the only ones left in the car, packed in a snug cluster in one corner like a stubborn collagen polyp, unwilling to detach from the wall of some unlucky bastard's liver. Celine peeked through the plastic panes at the strangers dispersing on the platform. The door would only be open for another eight seconds, but she could not bring herself to leave the safety of the train.

The station was too exposed; then, it reverberated with the rhythm of boots.

Squeezing Yochanna's hand, Celine felt its rough nail beds and the fear that heated it to sizzling, so hot that Celine's own palm started to sweat. The girl clung to her, eyes tracking over the scuffed windows as a phalanx of police lined the track.

The officers' black visors absorbed light, transferring data to the ear and mouth pieces inside. The ceramic plates under their full body armored uniforms seemed to vibrate with power. Each uniform was scored with thin blue lines that glittered when the officer moved. Nothing short of a shrapnel pressure bomb would slow them down. Each suit was invisible to surveillance, with a gloss that repelled sensors.

Like everyone, Celine watched the protest footage on television, where cops mangled Free Speech applicants and journalists without mercy or restraint. Their weapons could emit sound like a sonar cannon and break the bones in your legs and arms; they could shock you with enough voltage to make your cardiac organs hesitate in your chest; they could bludgeon you with their cattle prod batons.

Paul's chest vibrated in a deep, inaudible growl. Yochanna whimpered.

The west stairs out of the subway station were within sight: twenty running paces. But that was on the other side of the line of police, who were so close to the train car that Celine could see the conductive webbing etched in their uniforms' panels.

The lieutenant's monitor yapped, "You have the right to remain silent."

There were no other rights.

"Celine Broussard, you are ordered to surrender yourself to the custody of the state."

Hearing the cop shout her name swamped Celine's bloodstream with adrenaline. Her scalp stung so intensely that she felt as if her eardrums had been skewered with needles. Her hold on Yochanna's fingers took on a robotic rigor not unlike her mother's insensate grip. The west stairs out of the subway station were within sight: twenty running paces. But that was on the other side of the line of police, who were so close to the train car that Celine could see the conductive webbing etched in their uniforms' panels.

The lieutenant stepped into the doorway and pointed his baton at Celine.

"Surrender," he intoned.

Celine felt Paul shift beside her. Even with Robert's body on his back, he appeared undiminished, unaffected by the fear that seized Celine. He straightened and seemed to expand in size until he filled the car, swelling with a fury she had never seen before.

"Three, two, one," he muttered, and as he reached the final count he reached out and gently shoved the officer back into the doorway of the car. The man stumbled, but before he could step free, the subway doors slammed closed on his body. His baton clanged to the floor and rolled under the seats. Powerful hydraulics clamped his arms against his sides and trapped him, half on the platform and half inside the train. He made a strangled sound, more in surprise than pain, as the relentless pressure of the doors' lips scraped against his uniform's plates. One of the other cops seized him by the helmet and pulled it back, trying to drag him free. Celine glimpsed a button-sized square of dark skin under the lieutenant's chin as his head tilted up.

The train jolted forward. For an instant, the armored figure thrashed in space as the car sped toward the tunnel and its next destination. One arm was flung free by the train's momentum and jerked loose before it bounced off a caution sign and slapped the outside of the door.

In half a breath, the train car reached the end of the platform and entered the narrow transfer port. The lieutenant's suit was indestructible. The human inside was not. He was smeared against the train's windows and instantly crushed against the inches-away wall of the tube. From his naked strip of exposed throat came a spurt of purplish blood and spinal fluid as his lolling skull snapped into the gap between the subway and its commuter casing. The rest of him bulged in its ceramic carapace, which was suddenly a disjointed jumble of limbs only held together by its uniform's teflon lining. The train halted and downvibed its engine to neutral in response to the crash.

That moment of hesitation was their only chance. Paul crashed against the door panels and shoved aside the cop's bloated, broken body, forcing the suction to relinquish its hold just long enough for the two women to squeeze onto the concrete catwalk and run for the west stairs.

They dodged into the ascent corridor and then to the top of the down-ramp, pursued by the pounding boots behind them and the shouts to stop. As they turned the first corner, one of the police fired a sonar shot at them. It ricocheted off the wall, smashing a cat-sized crater into the aging tiles. A rubber bullet bounced off Robert Weiss and winged the side of Yochanna's head, tearing a skidmark of tender skin from her temple. She slapped her hand over the wound and stumbled, but Celine, now possessed with the fury of her perpetually-late mother, dragged Yochanna to her feet and pulled her to the bottom of the ramp. The police came careening after them, the clatter of their uniforms echoing off the walls like the rigid prongs of a processor.

There was no gondola waiting.

Paul swore.

"Keep running," he huffed. Celine followed him to the end of the ramp and into the service tunnel that ran alongside the train tracks. It was a lightless sinkhole; within a few steps, she was blind as a mole. She fumbled along, listening to the gravel under her feet. She kept one hand linked to Yochanna's and the other on the crumbling partition that separated their escape route from the transit shaft that led to the world above and the trouble they were in. She was certain they were entering a pit, following a path to nowhere. Ahead, she could hear Paul's labored breathing.

"Left," he told her, and she obeyed the sound of his voice. The black air pressed in on her until she felt it squeezing her skull. The tunnel was a quiet place. Without the constant symphony of traffic and construction, her ears rang—hypersensitive, combing the air for any industrial clang that resonated with the sounds of home. She closed her eyes: in the theater of her mind, the cop's screams became frantic and the arm flailed from its shattered socket. When she opened her eyes again, she could still see the blank, bright dots of the pure, naked skin at the base of his throat. Celine seemed to see again how the hydraulics drove the rubber edge guard into him and locked before the train blasted forward on its magnetic track. His body, smashed between the train and its casing, was rigid with pressure. The sensors in the door did not perceive his armor and chopped shut forcefully. She could not un-hear his scream.

A soft pop pushed the darkness back as Paul broke the bladder on a light pack. The gentle, marine glow of the jellyfish protein inside it drew Celine out of her nightmare. They were in a small, empty chamber lined with concrete blocks and a gravel floor. A length of dry pipe dangled from the ceiling like a mummified snake.

"They'll have your sample now," Paul said to Yochanna, whose cheek was seeping blood between her fingers. The light pack's wan glow revealed her face floating in the darkness, a nervous planet unsure of its own orbit.

Celine sighed. "Yours, too. We're all known."

He sat back against the wall and closed his eyes. The untidy bundle on the ground had a dent in it from the bullet, and Celine thought that, if Robert Weiss were not already dead, the shot would certainly have done him in.

"Killing a cop is a capital offense," Paul said quietly.

"How long were you in?" Yochanna asked.

Paul glanced at Celine, looked away. "There's no way to measure time there except to count the suicides. They don't kill us in that system, we kill ourselves."

"What did you do?"

"I hurt somebody's feelings," he said, and folded his arms across his chest, refusing to say more. He leaned back against the bare walls, which were unadorned by the near-ubiquitous graffiti of the surface world. Gray grooves and textured mortar reminded Celine of the bald face of the moon, pitted and scarred by falling stars.

"There's nothing here," Yochanna said.

"It's underground," Paul said. "They won't find us. Not right away."

"What about him?" Yochanna asked. She nudged the body, which moldered in its canvas bag.

"Won't find *him* either."

He extracted a pocket knife from his coveralls and handed it to Celine. His finger traced an invisible line halfway up his forearm. She unfolded the blade and snicked its point through the rough denax, cutting away the cuff and a section of sleeve. He caught the cut end as it dangled loose and collected it with his free hand, then took the knife back. With the shred wrapped around his mouth and nose, only his eyes were visible. His breath condensed in a wet spot in the center of the improvised mask.

Even with the thick bandage in place, Celine saw how his steps slowed as he approached the corpse. Hours after death, it was putrefying in its own husk, releasing foul gasses that would only attract searchers. Paul bent down and grasped it by its shroud, then dragged it clear of the tunnel walls and out of the sand.

Kneeling over Robert, Paul peeled back its suit jacket and gently popped open the buttons on its shirt. The smell was immediate and toxic. A dry paroxysm heaved through Paul. He shook his head and took out his knife again, blade hovering over the bloated abdomen. Celine watched as Paul lowered the point toward the vital organs, his free hand palpating the hard skin as though picking a lock. Whatever he was looking for in Robert refused to give itself up.

"Are you going to return him in pieces?" Celine asked.

"We should just leave him here," Yochanna said. "Bury him where nobody will find him. It's easier than—whatever Paul's doing."

Paul probed the corpse's ribs, which protruded like flabby wings under the skin. He slid the knife in and jiggled it between the slots of cartilage. The skin, which had in life been marinated in shea butter, caviar, fatty beluga cream, and every hydrating compound under the sun, was soft; Robert's bones, however, resisted Paul's first efforts.

A rib cracked as Paul jammed the blade deeper. Then, Celine heard the stifled gasp of the punctured lung deflating. She closed her eyes and gulped back a wave of stomach acid. When she opened them again, Paul had turned the body on its side and was stabbing deep holes in its back side. Black gel ran from the wounds into the ground, which drank the liquid greedily. The knife made vents that leaked sulphuretted hydrogen; the stench worsened and drove Celine and Yochanna back with their hands clamped over noses and mouths.

Yet, soon the body was relaxing into the gravel as though sleeping; the apparent rigor mortis was released in the form of blood and bloat, and the discolored skin slackened over the bones that Paul snapped as he compressed the body into a small heap of human-shaped segments.

Yochanna had taken refuge further down the tunnel and was sitting on top of a concrete slab, legs drawn up by her face, clutching her tote bag. She wore her blockers, as though to spare herself the sight of Paul as he packed the corpse into the length of the hastily deconstructed shroud. Now, Robert Weiss could be lifted like a piece of luggage. The stained yardage was sinister in its compactness, as though the efficient-looking package held a bomb that might detonate at any moment.

"Nobody will believe we didn't do that to him," Yochanna said.

Paul ignored her and turned to Celine, who was picking a loose grain of mica out of her shoe tread.

"He's our proof," he reminded her. "You said the son wanted him delivered."

Celine said, "I was supposed to remove a box."

"In exchange for chocolate."

"And ice," she said. She remembered with regret her self of the afternoon and the greed that had made her negotiate with Henry Weiss-Broms for more chocolate, real ice. His eyes had flickered as if lit by faulty fuses. She realized that he had never intended to pay her; a false promise was all he had needed to achieve his ends. This was how the ultra-wealthy got rich and stayed that way. By lying. By leaving their invoices unfulfilled. Somewhere in the Weiss-Broms holdings was a chip from an iceberg that was rightfully Celine's. She had nothing beyond a verbal contract—and a body—that proved the deal had ever existed.

Her neck began to tingle as she considered the stories she'd heard about criminals who wronged the ice-drinkers. They suffered in ways that surpassed Celine's worst nightmares. She shivered.

She wasn't alone in her fear. Celine reached her hands out toward Paul and Yochanna and felt their garments. Her fingertips worried over the prickles of dry grit that stuck like small burrs to the cloth. Listening to Paul and Yochanna's voices, she detected a tremor of anxiety in each of them as they argued about whether to leave Robert. Safety in one moment was not security in the next, and the accident in the subway had sealed that avenue of escape. The transit stations would be crawling, and soon the more intrepid searchers might follow their tracks into the tunnels. Going back now meant they would be arrested on detection; there would be no moment with the press and likely no trial. Cop killers didn't get second chances. With the body in tow, their only choice was to keep going and hope to find a way out that was not through.

They had reached the borders of the known world, here in the underground. Beyond here, she guessed, was the abyss—a disordered wilderness that ate civilization in greedy bites. She shuddered and put her free hand in Paul's. They were entering the belly of the earth, the place that was the origin of all things.

Somewhere in the distance, she sensed a reservoir of ice waiting for her.

The Meadowlands

15

Two tumblers of acetylene into the evening, the leafy borders of Otzara took on the texture of graying digital snow. In Henry's parlor in the cedar plank teahouse, the tasseled loungers and hassocks seemed lazily charged, as though their rows of twisted fringe might begin to writhe and frazzle toward the ceiling vents. He tapped another bump of hydrolyzed pollen into the nail curve on the back of his pinky. The granules were aromatic. They coated his throat with the familiar flavor of dissolution. Strong stuff, it congested Henry and turned his throat into an uptown sewage pipe that spewed flower-flush and toxins.

The pollen was all-wild, not synthetic. Technicians plucked it from the panniers of overloaded bumblebees and processed it into a mild psychedelic. When Henry sucked it into his sinuses, he felt like a bee himself, his thoughts a whirring hive, each with their own frequency and frenetic, bow-legged dance. His mind pulsed with colors as the substance touched his pleasure-centers. He could see his plan unfolding its bloody petals, drawing him in with a sense of inevitability.

Now that their father was gone, Henry would ensure that Otzara was the only place that experienced rain—no more rain parties, no more sharing. He would shut off the water that cascaded onto the shoulders of the nouveau-riche pretenders who had buttered up his foolish father, hoping for rewards in the form of ice and fruit. The markets would crash and cities turn to dust while the farms stalled out and produced nothing but husks. His land alone would be fertile—a true treasure, untouched by the corruption of the world.

The acetylene fogged his vision, but he could make out the lines of his own highly contoured face in the mirror by his chaise. Without his signature neon wig, his head looked lopsided. His silk turban slipped over one ear and began slithering down toward the ruffled collar of his robe.

He should not have answered the commlink's summons, but the blinking blue light on the console drew him in. He hovered over the speaker with his hands splayed on either side of it, watching the light flick on and off. Then, he pressed the access switch and sank onto a nearby chair. He fumbled with the silk wrap self-consciously, even though the caller was audio-only—listening, unable to see him.

"The media is recycling the story about the rain artist," Laszlo's voice said. His sonorous, moneyed tones made Henry fidget even harder. His self-important half-brother sounded so much like their father sometimes. Robert's false generosities put the family's land at stake; Henry shivered with suppressed rage as he remembered the greed on Robert's face, his pleasure in withholding anything you showed desire for. Robert had loved the rain parties because they were an excuse to show his wealth. He squeezed the clouds for grand and inconsequential reasons, and the rain he paid for soaked into the shoes of the fools who danced around him.

Well, soon those would be over. The family—and their resources—would withdraw from the world at large. It gave Henry great pleasure to know the earth could not live without him, that he held the parts of it that were essential for survival.

He said, "Have the syndicate run Celine's mugshot again. Co-conspirators beware."

"Downgraded, then assigned to a debt farm."

The debt farms were a slow death, under the aegis of respectable incarceration. Most people developed epidermal cancers that leached into the bone within a few months in the sun. The cure was chemical drains and medication; the Weisses owned the only offshore clinics that serviced the farms. Survival-only services. A single bone fracture could wipe out a year's worth of a prisoner's HealthGo points and—adding to the sentence—put the injured person's debt-earn on hold. Six weeks off to heal that bone and they'd go back to the plant with a bigger balance than before. It was a cycle of misery that spiraled into ruin. If the inmate perished before serving their term, their family members could be indentured onto the sentence. Whole lineages died out on the garbage rafts, paying into the clinics for treatment they needed to prolong their torture. In the end, someone always owed Henry's family. The Weisses were at the bottom line of most transactions, collecting contractual fees.

"What about the other one? The younger woman?" Henry asked.

In the pause that followed, he detected a faint, electronic keening in the commlink's transmission frequency. Bugged. He shouldn't have been surprised. Of course Laszlo Weiss-Broms would archive their conversations. Henry inserted an acrylic claw into the chamber of his ear and jiggled the modified stirrup inside. The whine subsided, but Henry found himself suddenly stymied. His lips felt dry, as though he was out on the processing raft himself, scorching under the cancerous sun.

"Lost her."

"What do you mean?" Henry stuttered. "They're all gone?"

"Nothing is ever gone," Laszlo said. His voice oozed from the speaker and spilled over the silicate chaise and the Moroccan-weave carpet. It filled Henry's teahouse like a steady drip of stevia-syrup. The voice was slippery and unbearably saccarine—sugared on both sides, Robert might have said. He always found creative ways to mock his sons. Ever a wag.

"Gone is not real," Henry agreed. They both knew there was nothing their family could not obtain, if they wanted it. Horses in what was left of Russia laid down their lives so that the Weisses could have better glue in their shoe-soles. The guts of the planet were rearranged in a quest for high-clarity sapphires to ornament the handles of their smaller jets' bathroom spigots. Henry himself had sunk a substantial amount of cash into engineering a prototype for a rain machine. Rain on demand—more valuable than an archangel's tears. If the Weiss-Bromses wanted to find three fugitives, they would be detected no matter where they'd gone to earth.

"The police traced them into the subway, but it was too removed from the charge tower to give clean data. They vanished. Of course, we are deploying better spyware. More searchers. It shouldn't be much longer," Laszlo said.

"Have they found our father yet?" Henry asked.

Another pause and a transmission whine that sent Henry's hands back to his ears. His silk turban slipped off completely, leaving his head unprotected. His scalp prickled as his nerve endings vibrated in sync with the transmission's inaudible hertz range. His body could hear it, even if the ultrasonics were beyond the capacity of the natural human senses.

"No."

Henry ventured, "But why wouldn't they leave the body?"

"My team's suggestion is to make out that this senseless, violent act was coordinated by terrorists, who wish to make a political statement. To deny my family our last rites, when our tradition asserts the body must be buried within twenty-four hours, is an act of hatred. Any thinking person can see that these people targeted us because of our faith. They killed him on Thursday. Now it is Friday, after sunset. They are holding the body hostage."

"Terrible," Henry whispered. He knew the story was shaky at best. There was no evidence that suggested this crime was planned by an outsider, or that the motive was terrorism; the falsified sources the half-brothers hired to alert the media was merely capitalizing on a media opportunity—high profile, high risk, and inevitably low return. Yes, Robert's body remained unburied. But couldn't that seem incidental, and not by design?

"You doubted we were capable of orchestrating this," Laszlo gloated.

Henry demurred. He'd been confident in the murder, but their alibi was weak. A closer look at the evidence would show that this woman—Broussard—whose name was tied to the crime seemed to have no true connection to it. Her presence was a coincidence. Even a thorough scan of the umbrella studio would turn up nothing but fabric and thread. Useless. Their private detective told Henry the preliminary search turned up so little that they didn't even bother to burn the place afterward. Their squad rifled through the boxes and left the tiny room untouched, a partially constructed canopy still pinned to the drawing board. It was Henry's belief that anyone had the capacity to become a criminal, especially given the fluid laws around ownership and civilian autonomy. But the umbrella maker? There was no obvious motive. Her livelihood was courting the wealthy, making favors for their parties. Even desperate people knew not to bite the hands that fed them.

Which made her hard to frame. But where there was a will, the Weisses would do it.

Henry said, "If you think the public will believe that, put some budget into it. Have the broadcast emphasize that the old man's killer is an enemy of the faithful. Anti-theism is radical, antisocial. They're not to be portrayed as heroes."

"Our father, the victim—the martyr," Laszlo agreed, musing. "We mourn with an empty coffin. We have no body to bury and the twenty-four hours have elapsed. This is a spiritual affront to us, and the terrorists did it deliberately to violate our tradition."

"Monstrous," Henry said. Hearing his half-brother invoke the holy traditions doubled his queasiness. He sank deeper into the chaise's velour arms. His head throbbed with sonar pulses.

Laszlo said, "We will persecute these criminals with the full range of our powers. It is only just. Quote me on that. 'It is only just.' And we'll hope they don't bring the corpse back at all. Let the whole thing sink into the sludge."

Henry wheezed his assent as the commlink disconnected. He seized the length of silk which lay limply on his shoulders and balled it up in his trembling fists. Laszlo Weiss-Broms was not making a request. It was an order, shared unilaterally from the position of majority shareholder. Henry did not enjoy being spoken down to from the top of a pyramid of analytics-driving bricks. The fact that each layer of the story Laszlo constructed was false, and so distorted that might have been better just to dispense with the lie, made Henry sick. It would not be the first—or even the biggest—lie they had ever told together. But spin was one thing and outright untruth was another, requiring a degree of rationalization that was physically painful for him.

He was grateful that this would be over soon. His brother's half of what they shared would be ashes and dust—and Otzara would be green and fresh as ever, unendingly verdant.

Henry reached for the acetylene decanter and poured another tumbler, this time to the brim. In another era, he thought, truth was an unmalleable thing. Humans gave up their lives to protect it. And now, here was the species, with more sensors, spyware, and synthesis capabilities than ever, knowing less than before. They had no idea what was worth defending.

Henry placed his hand in the delicate curve of his cranial plate. In the glass next to the acetylene, his stage denture floated in a blue whitening fluid. A pair of neon eyelashes adhered to the edge of the tumbler. Without these things, Henry knew he was unrecognizable; his public face was a truth people only knew because they'd been taught to know it. The family's giant eye gazed over everyone, and nothing could be hidden from it for long.

Once upon a time, Henry thought, humans imagined a future where everyone was safe. Instead, it became a place with more conveniences and less curiosity. We dreamed of this future because we thought it would be a place where we could be better—better off, better people. Perhaps it still existed. More likely, it was a falsehood used to sell new products.

Henry eased himself out of his chair and stood in the frame of the teahouse's sliding paper door. A bat flitted across the garden outside, drawing the red dot of a motion sensor to its brown, mammalian body before vanishing into the dark.

Their father was dead. Soon enough, he'd have Laszlo's half of the empire and the garden all to himself.

He took an unsteady step out toward the night. His feet scuffed on the paving stones, which were still settling into their places. Each of the twenty-six massive stones was as broad as Henry's arms could reach and many inches thick. They were partner-stones, which meant they had been broken from the same original slab in whatever canyon the masons had discovered them. At one point, they had been conjoined and presented a unified face to the sun, the heat, the dust. Now, they were arranged like crime scene victims in a crisp, soothing presentation.

It soothed Henry to think of their brokenness. A pinch here, a pebble there—Otzara was brought together into a smooth, well-defined illusion of wholeness. Each plant and handful of soil and stone was harvested from another place, but at first glance, it looked like something that had always been here. Only when you cared for it did you begin to see its joints and fractures.

In a matter of days, Henry thought with a smile, it would be the sole reserve of livable space on earth.

16

At first, Yochanna was afraid to go deeper into the tunnel. Stalagmites coated in copper-colored slime dribbled across the rough ceiling, piping greenish drain water down from the landfill above them. A metal trapdoor that provided minimal cover over the tunnel entrance seemed to shrink, then vanish into the earthen walls as they left the transit center and the upper world behind. She hoped they were walking toward what Paul said might be a way out. It was safer than the surface—as far as Yochanna could tell, there were no drones here, no police—but as they wended their way through the curving channels, she wondered what might be waiting around each twist in the road.

As they edged forward, every fiber of Yochanna's body felt electrified by detail. The sandy soil under her feet gave way to smooth tiles made of stamped clay. Concrete was replaced by sod, and even the smell of the tunnel changed as she walked, becoming softer, dank, organic. The air was warm and slightly rotten, as though she inhaled the sleeping breath of some distant earthen giant.

The gravel faded into sand, becoming something different. Yochanna could feel the soft glaze and scraped grout that joined each slab through her soles. It was like walking across a burnished ballroom floor—a phenomenon she had only ever seen in the more romantic Skin Series episodes, where heroines twirled over polished marble to the strains of electro-pop of the previous millennium. If Celine and Paul had not been with her, she would have stopped to kneel down and examine the handiwork of the brickmakers.

She was surprised, most of all, by the amount of light they had down here, a warm, flickering light emitted by amber bubbles without a filament or fuse. They drew her like a human moth deeper into the labyrinth. She sensed the human touch in the floor and the rivets of the welded ribs that created a delicate scaffold around them. The metal was one she hadn't seen before, but the smiths cut botanical whimsies and curlicues into the fan-shaped brackets, giving the sense that they were walking not through an underground tunnel but down a sunlit forest path, through a grove of trees who bore glowing, golden apples. These lamps dangled just out of reach, but Yochanna noticed the breath-ripples in the glass and the gentle discolorations in its schmelze. They were not produced, but blown by people—people, who had once breathed.

As she followed the others, Yochanna's sense of foreboding faded. She tugged her face wrappings away from her mouth and nose. The air was clear down here, with a sharp note of water that shocked Yochanna. She expected decay, but instead it was fresh—not like city air at all.

She glanced at Celine, whose eyes shone like elevator buttons over her mask. The older woman clung to Paul with both hands, too nervous to look anywhere except directly ahead. Yet, even wrapped up, Yochanna could tell that some of the details were seeping through the other woman's veil. The lamp light caught the light hairs on Celine's brow and softened the anxious lines around her eyes and made her look brighter, younger. The leafy shadows caressed Paul's shoulders, which seemed to relax as they walked. The ramp's slope was gentle enough that she didn't notice a downgrade, but the temperature cooled to a subterranean springtime.

They passed through an arch of packed mica chips that glittered like fallen stars. Distracted, Yochanna glanced up and stumbled as her toe caught against an invisible stone. She tripped and slid into the shallow trench that ran alongside the path, landing in a spray of dust that blinded her and filled her mouth.

The body she landed on was fragrant and squealed violently on impact. Together, they stumbled against the wall of the trench, with Yochanna doing her best to fend off the invisible slaps and feeble punches that came out of the darkness. As her eyes adjusted, she saw that the person was even smaller than she'd guessed. Their face was blanched of color and their head bobbled on an albino stamen inside the broad cupola of their synthetic ruff. Their cheeks were the same texture as a block of unpressed tofu patty. Yochanna felt that her hands might penetrate the soggy skin and sink into it. Their shrunken limbs and the potpourri of unfamiliar smells that wafted from their body alarmed her. Their panicked squeaks reminded Yochanna of the Gowanus Canal rats that wrestled under her window at night.

Then, she heard a snarl overhead. She and her adversary were both lifted out of the trench and dumped back on the walkway. Yochanna scrabbled free, and Paul—the giant, the criminal—took over.

"It's a landfiller," Celine murmured.

"You must go see Sant-Dagda," the stranger gasped.

"I must do nothing," Paul said. His hold on the stranger's neck looked potentially lethal; his mitts pressed into the fragile skin of their throat. Yochanna felt a sympathetic twinge in her arm where Paul grabbed her earlier. She knew the sensation of those hands; they clamped onto her like iron.

"We welcome you," the stranger stuttered, back-pedaling. "Forgive my antagonisms. I feared you were invaders."

Paul grunted, but opened his fingers. The person stepped clear, smoothing the rumpled layers of their collar. The lamps softened their haggard features and revealed the detail in the rich brocade of their garments, each one stitched with miniature figures that cavorted in a nonsensical tapestry. In this light, they looked less pasty than Yochanna's first impression. The tall columns beside them seemed to sway gently in the lamps' glimmer, like saplings caught by a gentle summer breeze.

"Sant-Dagda embraces you," the stranger gulped. "Whatever brings you here, know that you are not alone. Many people seek our refuge. We invite you to leave your burdens from Up Above and enter a new communion with the earth."

"I'll keep my burdens, thanks," Paul said, tightening his grip on Robert Weiss.

The stranger's voice was pinched as an unfed stomach and their eyes glistened at the corners with unshed tears. Yochanna rubbed the side of her head, where one lucky punch had landed. If the stranger were as big as Paul—or even Celine—Yochanna might still be in that trench.

"Follow me," the stranger said.

Yochanna glanced at her companions. Paul shifted from foot to foot, deciding.

"Mark which way we come," he muttered to the others. "If we need to double back, we can thread back through the subway tunnel. Hopefully, they'll show us a better way through."

"I don't like it," Celine said.

"Would you rather fight a cop or a couple of these weaklings?" he asked.

Celine caught Yochanna's eye and shivered, wrapping her arms around herself although the air was warm and soft as ever. A sweet smell wafted from the stranger—violets. Despite her misgivings, Yochanna felt herself leaning toward the landfiller, sniffing the foreign aroma and wishing she could finger the illustrations on their robe. She wanted to ask them about the tunnels, how they were constructed. Who made the glass and formed the clay into petals? Who hammered the struts together to lift the roof of the tunnel and separated the segments into roads? How long had they been down here, making magic in the dark? Her own experiments with paints and powders seemed childish in comparison with the nuance and control in the art that surrounded them. The stranger would know all about ink, Yochanna guessed.

"Let's go," she said, plucking at Celine's sleeve. "Even if they can't help us, it's better than trying to hide in the city."

Celine sighed. "I miss the sky," was all she said.

The stranger beckoned them deeper into the labyrinth. It grew brighter; without the anxiety of being lost, Yochanna could look around her, marveling at the complexity of the secret colony.

The stranger walked with the intensity of a guided missile. Yochanna skipped, then jogged, trying to catch up. A moment's hesitation would be all it took to get lost down here, and although she was not especially scared of the dark, she was afraid to be separated from her friends. She looked from side to side, snapping up colors and images, but did not dare to stop and really see.

However, when the stranger led them past a wall of vines, Yochanna could not resist. She fell a step or two behind the group. The vines were threaded along hair-thin cables riveted to the ceiling and the floor. Sconces hid the metal eyes at either end, making it look as though the plants cascaded from the buttresses, falling like water toward the ornate mosaic under Yochanna's feet. The thousands of leaves were close and dense, but a pale lilac light pulsed behind them, feeding the plants on ultraviolet rays. As Yochanna drew closer, she noticed that the leaves themselves were an enriched, royal purple. It was the same color as the screen-print of her school's crest on her tote bag, the same color as the darkest shadows underneath the Verrazano-Narrows Overbridge. It was a shade that sucked in light, collecting every beam into its lavish folds.

Yochanna slid her hands among the leaves. Their coolness was astonishing; it rushed up her arms, as though her hands were immersed in water, not growing things. Each leaf seemed to be patterned like celluloid lace. Fine, silver pinpricks decorated them and reflected back the purple light at Yochanna.

She pressed closer and felt the leaves brush against the fronts of her legs and belly and chest. Soon, she was up to her shoulders, reaching for the wall that she was sure must be on the other side of the vines. Her fingertips groped through the air. Her face entered the leaves and she closed her eyes. Then, contact.

She traced her hands across the rough texture of the supporting wall. It seemed to be a single, massive slab of stone, without seams or cracks. As Yochanna leaned into the trellis, she opened her eyes and peeked through the dense stems. The stone was the blue of the thin membrane on the inside of a broken pigeon egg, the color the medieval monks used for the Madonna's holy robes. Yochanna tilted her face and peered up the sheer expanse of granite. What she saw made her gasp with delight.

Starting at the top of the stone, delicate shadows cascaded in shades of amethyst and orchid. At first, they seemed haphazard—reflections of the dark, heart shaped leaves that shielded every inch of the wall. But as Yochanna looked more closely, she began to recognize pairs of short parallel lines and clusters of cuts that resolved before her eyes into letters. Words. The scrolling vines rippled as she reached for the inscriptions etched into the granite page. Her hands traced each letter, feeling the scabbed edges where a chisel and mallet had fastidiously tapped out shards of living stone. The negative spaces were half a knuckle deep and as Yochanna explored them with her hands she felt a ripple of serene power coursing through her hands, up to her shoulders and into her heart, a steady pulse that seemed to push its way into her across the centuries. She seemed to hear the words as she touched them, although the language was too old for her to understand.

She drifted over the syllables and phrases, feeling their meaning as concretely as the granite under her palms.

When Paul appeared at her back, she sensed him as an extension of the carvings. His brutality made sense here and his rough-hewn edges expressed a sensitivity she hadn't noticed before. He was a freak in their world on the surface, but down here in the succulent shadows of the vines he reminded Yochanna of a gargoyle leering from an ancient temple's niche. His flat forehead and heavy jaw thickened as he peeked between the leaves. Yochanna heard a gentle rumble leave his throat; it sent icicles through her skin. Gargoyles were supposed to be protectors, but who could tell at this proximity if one wanted to maim you or save you? His breath touched Yochanna's shoulder as he leaned past her and looked through the cables at the wall.

"What is it?" he asked.

She guided his gaze upward and watched his lips move as he tried to make sense of the work, this graven illumination and its ecstatic hieroglyphics. A monkey swung from the crossbar of a tree on one side, while higher up three men in robes much like the pallid stranger's sculled across a fluid line of letters whose message so insistent that the sailors nearly capsized amid their waves and peaks.

Overhead, a pigeon carried a sprig of yarrow toward a dark circle—Yochanna thought it was the sun, but when she looked closer she saw that its rays pointed inward. It was a black hole that drained to the edges of the wall, collecting beads of rain and ushering them to a row of skeletons who nuzzled one another as they slept. The pipeline was marked with flowers, reminding Yochanna of the Roman custom of pouring perfumes inside the coffins of the dead. Once, people shared luscious wines with their loved one's sarcophagus. It was unthinkable now, to sprinkle even a handful of raindrops on something that ceased to breathe, generate value, or revive to return the favor. Rain was priceless; someone like Yochanna would never feel its tiny fingers on her face. She gazed at the skeletons' interlaced phalanges and tilted skulls. They received the rain with ease, as though it meant nothing.

Yochanna leaned forward to see the bottom edge of the image. To her surprise, there was more—another world that scrolled below her sight line and into a lower level of the mine.

The whole slab was marked with these words and images. They were not in a tunnel at all, but standing inside a living manuscript. The landfillers lived in the pages of a holy book.

If Paul had not pulled her back, she would have cleared the vines and shimmied down the granite face with her fingers jammed into the letters. But he was faster than she was, and so strong—she barely got one shoe through the barrier before he seized her by the waist and dragged her, cursing and thrashing, out of the heady foliage and back onto the path.

"Nope," he said, and clutching her to his chest, carried her back down the ramp.

"The temple of Sant-Dagda," the landfiller said. They tugged back the curtain of vines and in a moment Yochanna was through, on the other side of the story, in the sacred hall of the land beneath the earth.

17

THE FETUS INSIDE Yochanna fluttered as she followed Paul through the curtain of vines into the cave where Sant-Dagda waited. This chamber was carpeted with an iridescent, fibrous lichen that dampened Yochanna's footsteps and made her feel like she was walking on a cloud. The lacy, greenish plant filled the air with a woody fragrance. Heaps of the plant matter shaped into large nests cushioned the floor; Yochanna noticed figures sprawled on them, in sleep or contemplation.

At the center of the room, under a cascade of stalactites, a throne jutted from the earth like a clay toadstool, fed by the water that filtered through the pumice columns above it. The stones overhead caught and softened the light. Yochanna saw that the stalactite had carvings on it too, with interlaced runes marked around its core. It was expressed in combinations of snowflakes, featherless ravens with outstretched wings, a coyote holding his own tongue—not a language she understood, but one she sensed in the deepest parts of herself. Her eye traced the beasts and shapes to the apex of the stone, then followed its point to the massive throne beneath.

At first, she mistook Sant-Dagda for a junk-pile. The land-fillers' god was huge, bigger even than Paul, and covered in a carapace of armor that cascaded off his body to the vegetation on the floor. His legs were pillars that seemed to be as broad as the columns overhead. The greaves of his armor were blackened at the edges and unctuous as a cockroach's wings. He squatted on his toadstool under the heap of protective plates, hands on the knobs of his knees and a murky expression on his face. A puff of air escaped from his lips as Yochanna and her friends gathered around the throne. His eyes slid over her body with a heat she knew all too well.

"From Up Above," their pale guide said, sweeping their arm wide in a curtsey. "They were in the Freida Mine and consented to our welcome."

Sant-Dagda grunted. "Displacement is a sin," he said. His voice was higher than Yochanna expected, sibilant. "You are welcome in the Gaspar Colony. All may contribute. None shall be denied free use of their offerings."

"But we are empty-handed," Celine said.

"You are not without your gifts," the god retorted. "Join my table, and sample what Gaspar has to offer."

His mealy eyes sought Yochanna. She slipped in beside Paul, wishing she could disappear into his bulk. The ravenous glint in Sant-Dagda's eyes frightened her; it was at odds with the beauty of the creations around them. How could such elegance and craftsmanship, the hallmark of humanity, have been created under this man's avaricious gaze? She noted the crude shape of his epaulets, which jutted out so far that he looked as if he was carrying his own head on a tarnished platter. Stringy hair coiled around his ears; the creases of his face were gray, giving him the appearance of a ravenous ghost. His chest rose and fell in hoarse gasps, laboring to lift the heavy plates of armor. He was truly a giant.

Suddenly, a spangle of dew fell from the ceiling and struck the tip of the monster's bare nose. He blinked and winced—a smile packed with rotting teeth that wobbled in his crimson gums. He tilted his head back to catch another droplet on his tongue.

"You see?" he crowed. "We have rain here, too. There is nothing the surface can withhold from Sant-Dagda's whim. Our power is limited only by the planet's generosity."

Yochanna shivered. She watched from the corner of her eye as two big-headed, bony strangers doddered from the beds of lichen. They moved with such aching slowness that she could almost hear their bones creak. Even in a place of so much abundance, she could see that they were malnourished. Their shoulders protruded like doorknobs under their rich, flapping robes. The bones of their throats—knotted trachea, bulging vertebrae—seemed to float under the surface of their bloodless skin. They leaned on one another for balance and as they came closer, Yochanna saw that the rivets in their skulls were nearly transparent. The purple lightning bolts in their cranial veins shocked her. Were these the people who had created such delicate craftwork? She thought of the flowers etched into each clay tile and the ripples in the lampglass. She assumed they were a symbol of plenitude—after all, art was made of time and talent, the two essential ingredients of luxury. Now, she wondered what their creations meant to them.

One of them wheezed, "The honor of satisfaction in our guests."

The other rubbed his hands together, perused the three visitors, and nodded. A flicker of black tongue darted into the corner of his mouth. His eyes sharpened, suddenly intent, and Yochanna realized that it was not fear that made his stare so beady, but hunger.

He said, "May this be your homecoming to Gaspar. At Sant-Dagda's table, you will offer and be offered. Come with me."

Yochanna glanced at the clay throne and the heap of divine rubbish moldering on its seat. Sant-Dagda's head lolled to one side. He seemed to have fallen asleep; a pearly bead of saliva drizzled down his chin. His breastplate vibrated gently as the lungs within them pumped out a filthy-sounding snore.

The landfiller beckoned to them, finger placed to lips.

Yochanna slipped her hand around Celine's waist as they were guided from the throne room. A granite bust with blank eyes and a broken muzzle stared at her from its post by the door. It was a genderless face, neither male nor female, wreathed in vines. Its missing nose was a jagged cavity. The succulent leaves of its crown were tattered at their edges, as uneven as the edges of the face's snout. The fury in its carved expression shocked Yochanna. She considered the power behind the blunt impact that had cracked the stone so deeply and split the forehead and crown into a deep, malevolent scowl. In the pupil-less eyes, Yochanna sensed a warning.

Watch yourself, the blind face said.

Yochanna shuddered, holding tightly to Celine as they slipped through the door and followed their guide into the dusky-lit cavern of the mine. The light from the throbbing worm-lamps took on a sickly cast and leached the color out of Celine's patchwork shawl. Yochanna wished she could burrow into the fabric and hide in its folds. Over Celine's shoulder, Yochanna could see the blue minerals sparkling in the basalt slabs that lined the tunnel. Once, this had all been metal and stars; now, they were tucked into the earth's fallopian tubes, waiting to see what was on the other end of being born.

In the beginning, as the planet cooled its molten face, the steam and smoke made a swirling mantle that turned into miles of clouds, which poured their water into the newly formed basins of basalt and granite and the long scar on the earth that would become the Pacific. The moon was born out of that gash and flung into space to orbit the new planet like a lost calf; the breach that used to be the moon swelled from a lake to a sea to an ocean that moved in response to its silver child.

The Pacific was warm then, warmer than Yochanna's body, and each rainstorm prompted more clouds of steam from the sea, a cycle of rain that drenched the stone and washed salts and minerals out of the rock into the ocean, enriching it. She learned in school that a human body amounts to a bucket of water and a handful of vitamins, and the earth began the same way, washed and washed with the warm saline storms that made the world into a fertile basin that could hold and sustain and nourish life. In class, the teacher told her to imagine her pelvis as a bowl, to be tilted without spilling; a salty sea that had its own waves and tides and a similar mineral composition to the sun-heated shallow tide pools that were all that was left of the edges of the Pacific. These pools became a microcosm of life as the budding cells nestled against their mother's tissue. Each one contained the seeds of a body, a family, a history.

Yochanna walked along behind the others, counting the tunnels that branched off to the other parts of the mine—some dark, some lit with phosphorescent globes. Whales were a fairy tale, but Yochanna remembered that the curl of one's tail contained uncountable generations of its ancestors, the cetaceans that leapt from the water toward the distant stars, the parents and grand-parents who sang to the moon and remembered its original name.

The amniotic fluid that pulsed around Yochanna's growing pregnancy was rich in carbohydrates and protein, a soup like the bathtub temperature waters of her native planet in its first million years, at the very beginning, babies making babies, salt and rain and heat and steam combining to make the rich contours the trio now crossed on foot.

They rounded a turn and came to a high slick wall of obsidi-an. Beyond it, a meadow of moss opened its blind star-lilies toward the cave's roof, hoping to pull some sustenance from its reflective light. The black glass was so sharply polished that from the ridge of the walkway, Yochanna felt that she was looking at an island floating in a midnight sea. Once, the whole planet had been like this—Yochanna could see how the artificial sky reached down to the pool that surrounded the moss and sucked the moisture from it and prepared to return that same ocean to the thirsty plants.

A rushing sound pressed against her ears. The wind? Instinctively, she turned her cheek toward it, hoping to feel its breath. This place had seemed so magical at first, but now she found herself missing the surface and its lights, smells, and sounds. She missed the dusty flurries of the city and the fried-potato stink of bus exhaust. When she stroked the obsidian barricade, she felt as though she was touching the frozen, black flank of an ancient leviathan. Its chill transferred through her hand. She withdrew it quickly, slipped it back among Celine's wraps.

"Don't do that again," Celine muttered. Her fingers—stubby, strong—squeezed Yochanna's for a moment, forcing the cold out of them.

Their guide led them around the wall and to the edge of the water. It was not a pool, as Yochanna thought, but a deep basin cut into troughs. People dressed in soggy rags squatted at the crystalline edge, their clothes so darkened by water that they were difficult to see unless a flash of skin or face flickered from the layers. A hand attached to a thin wrist shot from a sleeve, plunged into the murk, and extracted a massive, wriggling fish with golden-slimed scales. It was as long as Paul's arm and thrashed so powerfully that two workers had to hold it to the slick black stone to expose its glimmering belly. A curved scar on its dorsal vent was newly healed and ran the length of its body. Under the scar was a bulging lump so large it slid under the skin to the hard side of the ground and rested there. Noodly whiskers lined the fish's gasping mouth. Its gills were red as gaping wounds.

The person who'd caught the fish inserted two bony fingers into the gills, hooked them open, and immobilized the fish's slick head against the stones. A sharp metal hook flashed over the sturgeon's body as its muscles bunched with the effort to escape. The tip of the hook found the healed edge of the vent and peeled it open. Yochanna saw an exposed pink slice of flesh, throbbing like a third set of gills and lined with white fatty tissue and a layer of thick, tangerine-colored mucus. The knife pulled the fish's belly skin back as if peeling a latex glove off a hand and the glossy flesh resolved into a pouch stuffed with spawn the color of a Chinatown sunset.

With a few precise slashes, the worker opened the pouch and squeezed its hoard into a shallow blown-glass dish. A loop of pinkish intestine spurted from the cut, its kink dark with un-released refuse. The fish's eyes were gray, sightless marbles in its head; they rolled uselessly, perceiving a world that meant nothing to it but darkness, suffocation, and pain.

Yochanna felt a spasm of sympathy in her abdomen as the worker pressed their palm across the cut, smearing out the last drop-lets of eggs. The lining of the pouch, empty and lonesome-looking, was flaccid and translucent. The fish herself appeared deflated. Tight hands clasped its fins. A damp patch of slime and water stained the stones under its body.

The harvested roe amounted to a few spoonfuls. The worker smeared it against the side of the dish, dabbed the golden pearls with one finger, then rubbed it over their graying gums.

"Salty," they announced. They pursed their lips and sucked in their cheeks, tasting the stray flavors of the stolen roe. "Stitch it up."

The person holding the fish's head tugged a curved needle threaded with a strand of thick, waxed fiber through the sliced body. With one hand, they carefully tucked the pouch back into the struggling fish's cavity; the other deftly repaired the vent. When they were done, a new, evil-looking wound lay next to the seam of the previous cut.

Yochanna saw how the fish, despite its size, would only tolerate a few harvests before its belly was in shreds. Four more? Five? It ovulated faster than its scales could close over the twine, and each operation perforated through layers of skin that turned to hard scar and made it progressively harder to swim, to twitch the tail, to move and eat and breathe. Even a healthy animal could only heal so many times. Had it not been so productive, it would not suffer like this.

"It doesn't pay to taste good," Paul said.

"The harvest is for Sant-Dagda," the person with the bowl said. Their arms were so emaciated that the flesh lay flat to their bones. The tendons in their desiccated face tightened, making their cloudy eyeballs bulge even further from their sockets. Their mouth seemed to gape, and for an instant, Yochanna saw the sturgeon's own suffering in the stranger's expression. "God eats first, and we are satisfied with his leavings."

Paul grunted. "Pure protein, caviar is. Almost enough to keep you going."

"I'm not eating that," Yochanna whispered, though she was aware of a gnawing hunger gathering inside her like a distant and threatening cloud.

"It's all they have, except for what they can grow," Celine said. "Look at these people. They're starving."

Yochanna scanned the faces of the other workers, some of whom were so thin that they seemed to be nothing but a heap of rags with glistening eyes. Their clothes, she realized, were even more richly embroidered than Celine's. The stitching was smaller than grains of pollen and as delicate as dust. The glass bowl of roe, crafted by hands as bony as the ones that cupped its silky riches; the curved needle and metal gut-hook were made, too, forged under the earth by master craftsmen. These people were ornamented in finery that even people like the Weisses could barely dream of—yet, their fragile skin and drawn cheeks were proof of worse conditions than unhoused scarecrows who begged for scratch and slept in doorways.

"You will sit at Sant-Dagda's table," the worker said. They pursed their cracked, splitting lips. "We are God's meat. May you be satisfied, for you are what you eat."

18

Sant-Dagda's teeth were capped in silver and sharper than a sturgeon knife. The slab of polished metal that ran the length of the god's eating-room was covered in cups, salvers, bowls, and plates, but Yochanna could not seem to taste anything. She was fascinated by the gaping, needled maw of the chieftain. Sant-Dagda ate from a chalice the size of his own helmet, scraping and slurping from its broad, dented lip. He seemed incapable of distinguishing between flavors, textures, or even dishes; he dumped the crackle-cups into his personal tureen and drank the mixture greedily.

Yochanna's stomach rumbled with hunger but when she reached for the nearest plate, nausea closed her throat. Celine nudged her. *Manners.* Yochanna picked up a blown glass egg-cup, hoping that the clear substance it contained was only water.

Instead, a saline, aseptic burn assaulted her nostrils. She pushed the cup away and held her breath, hoping her nose would forget the smell of fetid vinegar and let her eat a little. She scanned the table—more of a trough, she thought, oriented to pour itself toward their host.

Paul knelt across from her on a pile of cushions with Robert Weiss's body tucked beside him. He picked at some type of crunchy-fried fungus that was combed to look like an electrified beehive. His look of distrust suggested it tasted even worse than it looked. Celine was to her right, tutting as she took miniscule sips of a glowing soup.

After a moment, Yochanna realized that the other woman was not drinking at all, but only touching the bowl to her lips. It was a convincing performance, though Dagda ate with such gusto that he was oblivious to his guests or their appetites.

He flashed his teeth in Yochanna's direction. That same unsettling, greedy expression crossed his face, breaking into a rapacious leer as he leaned toward her.

"A delicacy," he said. "I've not seen one like you since I named this place Gaspar."

Yochanna shoved back her disgust and forced herself to smile.

"When was that?" she asked.

"We do not measure time by the sun here. Or the stars. It is not like Up Above," he said. The tureen lolled in his lap. A smear of pulp glistened on his incisor, which he sucked meditatively, as if remembering the skies of long ago.

"Time underground is eternal. It is why Gaspar will live forever."

"You don't have clocks?" Yochanna said. "Hours and minutes?"

She heard a delicate rustle and glanced over her shoulder. The pale, big-headed people who slept in piles around Dagda's toadstool slumped against the chamber's walls. They shifted as they listened—in protest or approbation, it was impossible to say. Maybe they were waiting for their turn at the trough, Yochanna thought. Her ill feeling doubled up—they were starving, and she could not eat a single bite.

"You're of age," the god smirked. "The clocks we have here are inside the women. Men like me hold power, but women—yes. Women can do something even this god cannot. They hold time."

Paul stiffened. He still held the rigid beehive of back-combed fungus but his eyes were riveted on the carving knife set beside his place. Celine put her soup down with a flourish.

"Those clocks stop after a while," she said primly. "And they run down without nutrients. How long can a malnourished woman keep menstruating? I think it sounds barbaric."

Again, Yochanna heard thick rustling at the edges of the room, as though the walls themselves were whispering. Sant-Dagda clicked the brazen castanets of his metal fangs a few times, then bared their shiny points at Celine. She met his mechanical grin with a look that would strip the sullen layers of lead off Lady Liberty.

"Tick, tock," he gloated. A tumor-spotted hand fanned over the table. He plucked up a few more skewers of unknown meat, then slopped them into his personal bowl and swirled its juices into a mealy slush.

Yochanna bit her tongue to push back the surge that splashed into the back of her throat. She reached blindly for the nearest bowl and tried to pantomime interest in the hideous banquet and the dozens of sickening delicacies laid out before her. The pot she picked up was heavy and full of something stewed. The clay was warm against her palms, the temperature of a body. When she lifted the ridged, oval lid, it released a column of steam and spices that reminded her of the rug in Mitch's office. It was a salty, pickled smell—the smell of tender, unwashed flesh festering under synthetic fibers where the crease of the thigh rubbed against the edge of the pubis and its sebaceous rind of hairs. This time, she had to cover her mouth as she dropped the lid back into place and leaned back from the table. Her stomach heaved with an audible retch.

Dagda giggled. He dipped a hand into his tureen and smeared the mess across his dangling tongue. Sickness shot through Yochanna, from the backs of her legs to the goosebumps on her scalp. She reached for the edge of the table, but somehow she was tilting sideways in her seat and could not stay upright. One hand gripped the side of her bench, but the other collided with the vile-smelling urn and knocked it over. Its lid rolled to Paul's end of the table and off the edge, landing with a popping sound. The pot slopped dark, rich soup across the other dishes. It rolled toward Yochanna and collided with a stout carafe of foamy sponge. The clay wall cracked and the pot collapsed and released its foul contents onto Yochanna's plate.

"Help yourself," Sant-Dagda said.

Yochanna wedged herself against the table. The broth seeped around the edge of her plate. It was the color of the half-boiled tube steaks the vendors sold in Brooklyn and dotted with thick clots of gelatin the size of candied eggs. She was sure this was a nightmare, and just as the fluid reached her, she would wake up in her own bed, thirsty and disoriented, and get a glass of water and wait for her pulse to subside. But no. At the deepest part of the messy puddle—something more. A larger embolus floated with the other bits, its round bulk catching the shine of the worm-lamps and the glow reflected from the vined ceiling. The curve of it was familiar to Yochanna, and she stared at it in fascination as its parts and facets gelled before her watering eyes. She saw the bulbous melon and puckered spinal column. Parboiled nubs protruded like miniscule flippers from its chubby trunk. The digestive line was visible through the jellied skin, which was a pink sauce barely contained in the bubble of the fragile epidermis. Rays of capillaries, baked red by the heated pot, lined the blind burrs of the fetus' eyes. It had no mouth, no teeth, and its nose was melted and boneless as a root. It had no face and no soul, no guts and no skull, but Yochanna saw what it might have been and fell right onto the floor.

She must have tried to scream, because when she uncovered her mouth, she was sick—on herself, the table. The vomit missed Celine, who jumped up and whipped her shawl around herself. Yochanna was on her hands and knees, heaving as though her body would turn inside out. She would have done anything to be alone, but she could not escape her nausea or the hard fact of her body. The tiny mandrake on the table rebuked her with its salamander limbs and bulging forehead. Just the thought of its molten tissues floating in a bowl made Yochanna retch and she could not seem to turn her mind away from it. Her body lurched and mewled on the banquet floor, while Dagda howled at her—the free show, the freak, the fool.

Celine picked up her plate and smashed it on the table.

"Can't you see she's unwell?" she shouted at Sant-Dagda. His giggles were obscenely high-pitched. They bubbled from his lips between bites of caviar and sliced yucca root.

"I see that she's productive," he snickered. "You may be past your prime, but every creature has its season."

Celine threw the plate at him, but the disc clanged harmlessly off his armor. He continued to stuff himself as though nothing had happened. Yochanna clung to the leg of her seat, hoping to regain her sense of balance. Her stomach was empty, but ripples of nausea kept rolling through her. She focused on the edge of Celine's cape and tried to make herself believe the whole world was a bolt of silk brocade. Wouldn't that be better? A smattering of flowers covered the rigid gold cloth, each petal outlined in brown pin-stitches so small they looked machine-generated. The flowers were no bigger than the nail on Yochanna's pinky, but they were each painted a shade of pale lilac that made them seem to glow against the fabric, rippling in an invisible wind. If Yochanna looked closely enough, her body and its problems felt far away—not the first time she had resorted to this trick of mind, but the first time she had left her body for a place as beautiful as this.

Sant-Dagda's voice came floating over the embroidered hills and needled Yochanna's ears. In an instant, she was back on her knees, rancid saliva running in a necklace from her mouth. How long had she been gone? Paul was easing his way toward the head of the table, carving knife in his hand. He lunged at the putrid god with a clatter of dishes.

From her place on the floor, Yochanna watched the bright barb of the knife jab toward Dagda's face. She closed her eyes when Celine shrieked, and when she opened them again she saw that Dagda was on his feet, a wicked giant twice Paul's size. He crushed the smaller man against the table with one armored hand, leaning on him so hard that Yochanna could see Paul's ribs bowing out between the iron fingers. The carving knife protruded from Dagda's teeth, caught between his silver-capped incisors.

"I'll eat you one bite at a time," the god slavered. His chin was dark with blood and rich sauces. He pressed against Paul's sternum until he gasped with pain. Yochanna could hear Paul's bones creaking as he strained to breathe.

"The next time you see my table, you will be on it."

Sant-Dagda beckoned to a corner of the room, and three weaklings hobbled toward him. They clutched one another with skeletal hands.

"Take them to the scullery," Dagda said. His fangs dripped buttery pus onto his breastplate. His subjects clutched at Paul and eased his wheezing body to the floor. They tugged at his clothes, dragging him across the polished granite floor. Yochanna felt rigid fingers grasp her shoulder. She was too sick to resist them and soon she was half-crawling, half-stumbling through the tunnel to the antechamber, then through a passage that was thick with moss.

A sickly wind blew past them as they lurched along. Yochanna reached out and grabbed the nearest solid warm body. Even in the darkness, she knew him by his wheezing; she held onto Paul so tightly that she could feel the ligaments in his forearm pop. He didn't flinch, gave no sign of pain. Celine edged closer to them both, until they were one solid lump of anxiety: a six-footed, three-headed heavy-breathing beast dragging a broken umbrella and a lifeless, stinking garment bag.

19

THE PLACE KNOWN as the scullery was lined with decaying heads and saturated with the rancid smell of thickening fluids and crisping marrow. Celine curled in a heap with the girl. Paul's breath came thick and ragged from his bruised and beaten lungs. They huddled together, crowded into the corner of the rough-hewn prison with Robert Weiss' corpse.

Celine felt the uneven ridges of the floor through the dried fibers strewn across the stones. She'd had such confidence in Paul's strength, but here in the bowels of Gaspar, Celine felt as though the world was topsy-turvy. She had always thought of Paul as too big to be harmed, too solid—but the giant Dagda made him look like a baby doll, weak and floppy. In the iron claws, Paul became fragile. Mortal, even. His powers were surmounted by a greater evil than she could have imagined when they first entered the decommissioned subway line.

He moaned when she leaned against him.

"Three broken," he whispered. His hand probed the side of his torso.

"Is there a puncture?" Celine asked.

She knelt beside him to feel the wounded ribs. If the cartilage snapped and drove the bone into his lungs, he would drown in his own blood. Maybe Dagda's grip had only fractured a few bones. She found herself hoping for lesser injuries, the kind that ached and disfigured you but left you breathing. If they were on the surface, Paul would be hospitalized by now and inching head-first into the scanner tube's purple spectrum light. A beady-eyed arthroscope the size of a single thread could repair his damaged cells from inside with invisible medical stents. Within a week, his side would be good as new.

But they were not on the surface; they were a mile or more under New York City, so deeply out of data range that even the Weisses couldn't find them. Celine felt a twinge of homesickness for the city above. The darkness in their cell made her wish she could trade the sickening death she was sure Sant-Dagda intended for them for the constant surveillance. Like everyone else, she lived in fear of the police and the violence of the state—but in this moment, with the breath of their bobble-headed captors on their very necks, she would have welcomed the ordinarily terrifying peal of a crowd dispersal siren. She would turn herself in this time, without resistance. A cell above ground was better than this windowless, lightless, hopeless tomb that held them in its belly.

She stroked Paul's forehead until, restless, he pushed her hand away. He turned on his uninjured side and she heard the breath come out of him in a silken rush. He was hurt but not on his way to dying. As long as he was alive, they still had a chance.

"Try to sleep," he said. His voice came soft and slow. "There's nothing to do but fight now, and you can't fight if you're tired and hungry. One is manageable. Both, impossible. Close your eyes."

Celine curled up between him and the girl. When she blinked, the prison was the same color as the insides of her eyelids. The scratchy covering on the floor felt like reeds or twigs, and she was grateful that she was temporarily blind. Having sat at Dagda's table, she knew that sight and taste were not necessarily a gift; sometimes, her senses could turn on her, betray her with their wiles.

She held up her hand in front of her face and brought the fingertips close, until she felt them brush the ends of her eyelashes. Nothing. Her body was indistinguishable from the darkness. As she lay there listening to Paul's labored breaths, she felt her other senses switch on one at a time, like the lights in a house where a family of women is waking up to finish sewing an order of umbrellas for a bridal party—all in white, the satin panels catching the buttery tones of the focus bulbs and turning the blank field of fabric to yards of burnished gold. It was not a frequent memory for Celine, but for a moment she could hear her mother and grandmother's near-identical voices as they swapped threads and pins across the drafting table, gossiping about whether this marriage would be the one that lasted.

"Don't sew a curse in, this time," her mother used to say; Helen would only cackle gaily, affixing Broussard's trademark red stitch to the apex of the stem. There was no curse, they reassured Celine. People cursed themselves with bad actions. But when

Celine looked at her own decisions, she could not pick out the single choice that led her here. She wiggled her fingers and tried to make their outlines resolve in front of her face.

The girl—she had a name. Yochanna. She still smelled of ick and rancid perspiration. Celine didn't need to see Yochanna to envision her waxen face or the thin, wavy strands glued to her forehead by sweat. The stink of stomach acid made Celine wrinkle her nose, but underneath it, she could smell an animal warmth. Something was cooking in there—something like the half-formed lump that moldered on Dagda's banquet trough. The thin veneer of bile on Yochanna's breath thickened as she turned toward Celine. A tentative touch on the shoulder, then a caustic puff on Celine's cheek.

"They're going to eat us," she whispered.

"Probably."

The girl was quiet for a moment. Then, she sighed. "I'm so hungry. We should have stayed in the city."

Her voice was soft and even younger-sounding in the dark. In her mind's eye, Celine conjured the picture of Yochanna on her hands and knees, heaving like a raccoon stricken by a paroxysm of rabies. The mess of inedible food strewn around her stained the memory in bright, noxious colors. She could not un-hear the grunt Paul let out when the giant smashed him against the table. It was the sound of fate putting another rip in Celine's safe reality—a rent in the canvas, letting artificial rain pour through the ruined cloth.

"Too late," Celine said.

The girl's fingers creased the fabric of Celine's shawl, folding it into pleats. Celine heard a faint snuffle. Silent tears were running down the girl's face and leaving wet spots on Celine's clothes. It didn't matter, she told herself. Whatever the monster had in mind for them was unavoidable. There was no way out of this. Let the girl ruin some silk. In the dark, there was nobody to see the stains anyway. She felt the girl finger the border of chrysanthemums that Celine's mother once added on a whim. The dots of their sepals were like a code, she said—a pattern for calming the mind. Celine herself had traced the same line many times when waiting on bad news. She was glad, in that moment, to know the magic worked on others.

"I'm such a fuck-up," Yochanna said. "I didn't want any of this. I did it all wrong."

"You look at your life and that's how you feel about it? You're young. All you have are opportunities to change your story."

"Not anymore."

Celine shifted closer and the girl moved into the space under her arm and folded her lanky frame like an umbrella. Her knobby knees clanked against Celine. Curled up, she made a parcel nearly as small as Robert Weiss. The hand that clutched the stippled shawl crept behind Celine's waist. Yochanna's sour breath came close enough to stir Celine's hair as she burrowed into the hollow between Celine's shoulder and her neck.

"I suppose your boyfriend didn't know about the pregnancy," Celine said. The girl's head was heavy on her breast. To lighten the pressure, Celine shifted and slid her arm around Yochanna's back. She could feel the shell-like ridge of the girl's ear against her chest. The unseen tears she'd guessed at began to seep into her clothes. When she felt the moisture against her skin, her hand seemed to move on its own, exploring Yochanna's face, wiping away the wet. This girl was so young; her cheeks were unwrinkled and nearly poreless. The deep creases of her features were well-formed, suggesting a face that—if not beautiful—was profoundly photogenic. Her lashes fluttered against Celine's palm. Celine remembered that once, people used to call these "butterfly kisses," though everyone knew butterflies were mythic creatures, like goblins or elves.

"I don't have a boyfriend," Yochanna muttered. "This wasn't something I wanted. I'm not even oriented that way."

"Does he know?"

She laughed, a light and bitter bark. "Nobody on the surface knows. I was supposed to be getting a termination, too."

Celine didn't point out the obvious—that she would still be getting one, like it or not. It was a black thought and it chilled her as it passed through her mind. Celine calculated their life expectancy; the guess came out as a disheartening collection of hours, at best. Her mother hated this cynical tendency of hers. It was instinct, sewn into Celine's lining, the same practicality that balanced the accounts of money, life, death, and favors with equal seriousness. The slanted wall behind them scratched at her, but she ignored the sensation and tried to breathe through the surge of fear that came when she contemplated their mortality. The cell was too small to avoid being scraped by the misaligned nasal bones and broken teeth of the skulls that covered the walls protruded at sharp angles, each jutting shard eager to take a bite out of the prisoners. Celine was glad for the lack of light. She could not have endured seeing the hundreds of empty eye sockets gloating over the last moments of their lives.

"You don't need the orientation to get a baby," she said to Yochanna, trying to ignore her own racing heart. "It's biological."

"Do you have children?"

"I'm not oriented that way, either," Celine said. She was a little ashamed of the prudishness in her own voice. She sounded like a judgmental old maid. She tried to amend her tone by adding that it was a lack of opportunity, that's all, but she could feel Yochanna pulling back. She squeezed the girl in an awkward hug.

"I wish I had, sometimes," she said to Yochanna. "My mother and grandmother raised me, and after me, there is no heir to Broussard's. I am the only umbrella-maker in the world, and it seems that I will be the last one, too. I have no apprentice. The technique will die with me."

Yochanna took the fabric of Celine's shawl in her teeth—Celine felt the tug of her mouth, a strange sensation, as though the girl was nursing. An eerie keen leaked from her throat. At the end of its spectral vibration, Celine heard another sound trickling through the air. It was high-pitched and seemed to be coming from under the brittle reeds strewn on the floor. Celine pressed her cheek to Yochanna's, signaling for silence.

> *Go and dream, on golden wings;*
> *Go find your rest on slopes and trees,*
> *Where lotuses touched by fisher kings*
> *Wave soft and fragrant in the breeze.*

The voice wavered in a melody Celine didn't recognize, but the words plucked at her ears. Where had she heard this before? She tried to listen past Paul's heavy breathing to catch the thread of the tune.

Remember the rivers of Maia lost to time,
My beautiful country, stolen by the dark.
Oh, our Maia, so pure and so sublime.
May you rise to life as the tide lifted the ark.

"Who's there?" Yochanna whispered.

Celine shushed her, but it was too late—the voice was silent. For a moment, the only sound was Paul's resounding snores echoing off the domed foreheads in the scullery's wall of bones. Celine turned her head from side to side. Maybe her ears, newly sensitized by the dark, would pick up a hint of the music again. She caught a subtle whine from Yochanna and gently spread a hand over her face to hush her.

Bring back the tide of our memories,
The sea crests relieving all pain.
From a breath to the width of a century,
We grieve the world, we remember her rain.

This time, Celine focused on the sound and followed it to the slick sandstone slab under their feet. The fiber covering parted under her eager fingers as she lowered her head to the floor and pressed her ear to the stone's chilly flank. A trace of sound drew her away from Paul's rumblings toward the door that sealed them in. She touched its surface with her hands and felt the ornamental engravings and gingerbreading that cluttered every surface down here. The marks were clearly deliberate but had no discernible meaning to her and offered no hint of what might be on the other side. She felt her way along the crack toward where she thought the hinge might be, hoping that her eyes might suddenly work in the impenetrable gloom.

The song came again, this time stronger. It was on this side of the wall, she realized. She traced it. Was she going crazy? Her fingers scrabbled over the sandstone and the bristly matting. She parted the reeds and felt an unusual shape that she didn't recognize at first. Her hands explored it, the fingers accustomed to straightening seams and unpicking knots. She sensed the sunken edges of the space and its texture and realized it was a grate formed like a series of inset stars. Warm air floated through the miniscule vents and brought the lilting harmony with it.

"Stranger," the voice whispered.

Celine recoiled with a yelp and skidded backward, bouncing off Paul. He was on his feet in an instant, blind and silent. Celine heard the change in his breathing; even blind and half-broken, he was awake and aware. She listened, probing the darkness for another signal.

"You want to go home?" the faint voice said.

She crept back toward the grate and put her ear against its screen.

"Yes," she said.

"The man who says he is God is lying to you about his powers," said the stranger. "We resist his wishes and his perverse laws. Maia loves her people who obey the truth of land. She will never forsake us."

Celine heard a tiny rasping sound as the screen underneath her cheek began to shift. This could be another trick, but nothing could be worse than dying here, among the bones. Paul was right beside her, and the girl—perhaps they would not have to die under the ground. She felt Yochanna's hand slip into hers.

"Please," Yochanna said.

Celine groped toward the screen and the opening was clear—a gap in the stone, darkness within darkness, with an unknown fate inside. But it was better than being flayed and eaten. She clasped her umbrella close, slid into the rough-cut hole, and felt gaunt arms embrace her. The scent of minerals, phosphorus. She was still blind and terrified, but the stranger's closeness somehow comforted her.

As she helped Yochanna ease herself into the vent-shaft, she realized where she had heard the song before—her grandmother, Helen, who used to sing while she was sewing.

"What is Maia?" Celine once asked her.

"It's the place rain comes from," Helen said, "and where all rain still is."

20

Up to this moment, Yochanna had never considered that she might not survive. Some people say that motherhood, like the will to endure, is genetic, but where this power truly comes from is impossible to say.

Yochanna's mind whirled in the dark. Her sense of direction slipped away and her eyes, deprived of pictures, colors, and light, seemed to spin inward in her skull to examine faded images of the past. As she padded through the tunnel after the invisible landfiller, she felt as though she was walking not through the mine, but through the passage of her life. The path she walked had led her here—a crooked line, with no sense of direction.

Yochanna could not claim to be born *this way* or *that way* but she did know that by the time she was five she craved motherhood with the senseless fervor ordinary girls reserve for fairy tale weddings. This urge may have been hard wired and may have been culturally stoked; it may have been an inexpressible urge to be better than her own mother, and enact the kind of mothering she did not receive. Either way, by 16, Yochanna knew that understanding this urge's origins would not make it go away, and by the time of her first pregnancy scare, she knew that it was a desire better left unfulfilled. Long before Mitch got his hands on her, she had come to believe that all desires were dangerous, and all to be avoided.

Motherhood was not rational, in Yochanna's opinion. It was at best a fact of life. She took birth control because her common sense did not suppress what she wanted. The medicine was a stop-gap; it did not take away the pain of being desired by the men who repelled her. If anything, each morning's sterilizing pill was a daily acknowledgement that she was delaying the thing she craved as well as the arrival of the person she wanted to be.

No matter what Yochanna did, mothering found a way into her life. One day, during her freshman year of college, she wandered off the Georgetown campus on a sunny afternoon. Early spring intoxicated her and she meandered like a nectar-drunk bee, in her too-small yellow polyester sweater. In those days, she got all her clothes from crates marked "free" at the edges of people's property lines. She was unusually tall, over six feet, but narrow as a rail. Her clothes were too short in the sleeve and she cuffed the pants to hide the fact that they weren't going to cover her ankles anyway. She was hungry all the time and ignored it. Sunshine fed her; she stole a daisy from someone's yard and put it behind her ear.

Yochanna found a swollen toy that held her interest for a block, juggling it from hand to hand as she walked. When she reached the next street, she left it balanced on top of someone's mailbox. She picked through a couple of bins, opened the lid of a trash can. When a well-dressed mother came out on her porch to watch, she waved. These people had money; they probably thought she was a landfiller. She walked on, following a trail of pastel balloons someone had tied to the intersection markers.

Two folding tables were nudged together in a driveway and covered in a thin plastic tablecloth, as though prepped for a church banquet. A boombox, connected to an extension cord in the garage, sprayed the ratty sounds of techno across the unmowed lawn. There was a dented red wagon, the usual box of dead media, and wads of secondhand shirts and pants spread on the grass. Yochanna looked for kitchen supplies—back then, pots and pans for the cooking she didn't do, in the kitchen she didn't have—but what drew her closer were the baby clothes. They were tiny, pristine, and bleached a blinding white. The newborn-sized socks were paired in knots the size of a buckeye in a lime colored plastic mixing bowl. She dipped a hand in, squeezed.

"Where's the baby?" she asked the host. His face was dark and lopsided.

"Napping," the man said. He frowned.

Yochanna wondered if he was lying. In her mind, an idea appeared: what if these were the clothes of a lost baby, or a baby who never was? What if these cotton suits were purchased for a baby that had failed to arrive? Her heart seized, and she found herself holding back tears.

"How much?" she asked. *She thought, I'll buy them all, so this surly man never has to be reminded of what he lost. He won't think to thank me, but I will have done a good deed.* She imagined holding a peach colored infant that slowly faded in her arms, the color draining from it like sludge from a clotted gutter.

"A dime each. No trades," he said, eyeing her. Yochanna pushed up her sleeves, disguising their shortness. Maybe she did look like a rag bag, but she had a little money. She put two credit chips on the table, and the man swept them into his lap as though they were a winning poker hand.

He told her to help herself, so she did. She picked out a tiny onesie decorated with yellow cartoon toadstools, with a hat to match. Another one sported pale spermatozoa with googly eyes.

She imagined her future baby. Boy or girl or something else? She chose only gender neutral images and colors: carrots, light-bulbs, lollipops, clouds. She wanted to hold each one up and check for stains and ripped seams, the way her mother would have, but the man was watching closely and she didn't want to offend him. She made her selections quickly.

"Do you have a bag for these?" she asked. She clutched fist-fuls of baby clothes. She was sure she hadn't taken too many for what she'd paid, but felt nervous that the man would count them and find that she was stealing. He fished a white plastic sack from under his chair.

"I wouldn't usually, since you only spent a little," he said.

In spite of his rudeness, Yochanna thanked him. It wasn't until she was back in her dorm that she realized he hadn't asked about *her* baby. He wasn't curious; maybe Yochanna didn't look like a mother to him.

She laid the newborn clothes across the bed and examined them. The fabric was softer than her own clothes, combed so fine that it wouldn't irritate an infant's nearly poreless skin. She rolled the hems between her fingers and marveled at the miniscule, decorative buttons. She practiced opening and closing the three silver snaps and let herself dip into the fantasy of having a baby to put inside these garments.

How hard could it be? Her own mother didn't have a crib; Yochanna had slept in a drawer, pulled partway out of her parents' dresser. She had played on the floor with whatever was at hand. Kids didn't need extra toys and gadgets, Yochanna thought. She remembered her own recent childhood and how a maple leaf could hold her attention for an hour, tracing the map of its veins as though it could lead her somewhere better.

She hid the baby clothes under her folded sweatshirts and forgot them unless it was laundry day or she was sad. When she finished at Georgetown and moved to New York, she brought the clothes along; *who knows,* she reasoned. There might be a baby someday. In that case, she'd be ready.

She once thought that babies simplified things by distilling life into its most essential ingredients: wake, sleep, laugh, cry, eat, grow.

It was a life she thought was possible for herself, once upon a time. Holding tight to Celine's cape as they edged along the vent, Yochanna was disgusted by her own past naivete. Pregnancy was a nightmare—how could she not have seen that? She had believed that she could somehow be an artist, on her own, with a tiny human to raise. The collection of baby clothes embarrassed her when she thought of them. The baby she dreamed of back then was easy and appeared as though by courier. It cost nothing, needed nothing. It was not foisted on her and did not incapacitate her with queasiness that made it difficult to even stand. It was not a terrifying question mark that hung over her whirling head.

The tunnel tracked to the left, then seemed to double back on itself. Yochanna's eyes crackled as she caught a few pale rays of frosted looking light. There were phosphorescent streaks on the walls and ceiling that glowed pale blue—not the warm looking lamps, but a type of paint or bioluminous pigment smeared over the earth's natural contours. She stroked a fingertip over it as they passed, picking up a few radiant grains. The light brightened as they went on. Soon, she could make out the bald, downy silhouette of their guide's head.

Tucked between the support beams, Yochanna could see long troughs of filtered water circulated through pump stations the size of microwaves. Thick roots floated in the blue solution. Some sprouted chewy-looking leaves and even a white lily or two. A whiff of dusty flowers touched her nose. One doorway revealed a storage larder filled with containers of seeds and labeled boxes of preserved food. There was enough down here to feed all of Brooklyn for a year or more. A brilliant bank of lamps shone on a mound of pinkish dirt. Slender white stalks slinked out toward the artificial sun—asparagus.

Some of the taller plants held cartoonishly red, round fruit like Christmas baubles. Others sparkled with tiny star-pointed flowers that emitted a pungent, fuzzy perfume that reminded Yochanna of warm summer mornings. Their red skin blushed near to bursting under the intense wattage of the sunlamps. They were not truly crimson, Yochanna noticed, but a rich orange shade created by a fruit so dense it pushed the blood-red juice to the surface.

Her brain searched for a referent and finally came up with an emoji. They were tomatoes. She realized this is what the pats of dyed gel on every slice of street pizza aspired to—what that red sauce was supposed to imitate, although they were dissimilar as a chip of broken mirror and the sun.

"What is this place?" she murmured.

The guide paused just long enough to glance over their shoulder. Their eyes were large and black, like the eyes of a wild crow, more pupil than iris.

"Just because the invaders eat human flesh doesn't mean landfillers do. Our hunger strike starves Dagda out. Those of us who belong here find ways to feed ourselves." Their pupils fixed on Paul. "This one has eaten flesh. The mark is on him."

Paul stopped dead. By some miracle, he was still carrying Robert Weiss.

"How would you know?" he rasped. "Like that savage on your throne?"

"The mark is plain," the stranger simply said. "You'll repay it soon enough."

"Why let us go?" Paul asked.

A hatchet mark formed in the center of the stranger's narrow brow. They barely came up to Paul's belt buckle, but they spoke to him with the serene authority of a saint.

"I can only deliver you to a means of getting free, flesh-eater," they said. "What deprives the enemy of meat is good for Maia. What taints the invader's table is a blessing to my people. Take your appetites back to the world that can feed you—we have nothing for you here."

"We need a ship," Paul said.

The stranger bowed and continued through the tunnel. More than once, Paul rubbed against the side of the walls. Once, a sulfurous burp escaped from the noxious parcel he still carried. Yochanna held her nose as she cast glances from one side to the other, trying to take in as much as she could before they were barred from the underground forever.

As they passed each room, Yochanna sniffed, savoring the scent of fresh vegetation. This must be how the ice-drinkers ate, she thought. The rich had real lettuce snipped from plants that grew from unpolluted soil. What they ate was organic, not threaded in agar and cultivated in petri-shaped patties. Her stomach moaned. She could not remember the last time she had eaten a fresh fruit or vegetable. The gummy bars she kept in her desk at work were nutritionally complete, but left her feeling somehow emptier than before.

The tunnel twisted down sharply. Yochanna slipped, then caught herself with a hand on the wall. Her palm came away blue, carrying a light touch of the luminous dust. The glow seemed to vanish before her eyes as the guide waved them into a chamber that stank of unrefined oil. It was brighter in here. The details of the room sharpened in the new light, but by the time Yochanna could focus her eyes, the stranger was gone.

She blinked again. Behind them, a tall panel sealed itself behind them, vanishing into the details of the wall around it. It was as the stranger had said. They were never here—they would leave nothing behind.

21

YOCHANNA TOOK IN the smell of industry—smoke, rust, and methane. The landfiller had brought them to a kind of hangar, crammed with parts. It looked like a graveyard for broken bird-lifts and defunct commuter planes. The carcasses of several ships lay strewn in pieces across the space. Some shed bolts into pools of leaking lubricant. One curricle leaned mournfully against the wall, as though grieving for its snapped aerofoil.

Paul put down the bundle that contained Robert Weiss. He set his hands under the dangling wing and lifted it, testing for loose plates. It seemed to have torn through the rudder, but was otherwise whole.

Yochanna watched Celine walk around the machine, which was an older model built for short sky-rides. These fog-hoppers were still common in the city, designed to transport people from roof to roof without descending below the penthouse level and getting into the dust and shadows between the buildings. How the craft had gotten this far into the subway tunnels was anyone's guess, but Yochanna spotted another metal door at the end of the chute. It likely led out to the filthy sky and whatever drones were circling, taking notes on the terrain below.

Paul's hands explored the broken wing and tested its limitations and the tensile strength of its surviving lugnuts. He pulled a tool from his jacket and began repairs, moving with robotic efficiency. Yochanna watched him work. Broken ribs and all, he was unstoppable; they'd be gone in no time.

But now that her nausea had faded and immediate danger was nowhere in sight, Yochanna found that she wasn't so eager to leave. Dagda seemed like a spectral giant from a dream—not a real threat at all. Her companions, on the other hand, were dangerous. Sticking with them had only gotten her in trouble, and worse.

She eyed the door they'd come through. On the other side was the art she'd craved her entire life, fresh flowers and plants, and enough food to last a lifetime. Why was it so peaceful here? She had seen vague figures rotating the plants under their lamps and counting the bags of seeds in one of the storehouses they passed, but this did not look like *work*. There were no desks down here. For all she knew, there was no such thing as money either.

She took a step back from the ship. All at once, she realized why she was willing to risk her life to stay here. She had found a world where her debt did not exist; here, she was not enslaved, nor was she a criminal. Deep underground, with her device unlinked to the networks of the surface, she was not a data point or an income generator. Even her load of stolen stickers was meaningless. Everyone had what they needed here. What she had witnessed in the hidden part of the mine—the strangest thing—was people taking care of one another.

"Just a few minutes, if the engine starts," Celine said in a whisper as she gave Yochanna's elbow a delicate nudge. When she saw Yochanna's expression, her eyes widened.

"I'm fine," Yochanna croaked. Her acidic tears felt like kaffir marmalade on her cheeks. She swiped at them and they smeared over her skin. The surface had loaded her system with non-toxic chemicals that slowed her lacrimal ducts and even changed the texture of her sweat. A shaky breath brought a lungful of landfill air into her system and it still tasted cleaner than the filtered vapor of Manhattan. Even the water in her body was poisoned, she thought. A gelatinous tear bubbled down her nose and landed on Celine's sleeve, where it wobbled—a perfectly round, pale yellow globule that was too viscous to absorb into the fabric it sat on. A toxic pearl.

"We'll get out of here," Celine said. She brushed the tear off her arm. Yochanna watched it bounce and then roll across the floor, gathering particles of dirt until it finally came to a stop in the shadow of the ship Paul was fixing.

"What if I don't want to?" Yochanna said.

Celine searched Yochanna's face. They were close enough that Yochanna could smell the faint odor of stress on the other woman's breath and see the softening flesh around her eyes. She couldn't have been more than sixty-five and her expression was made more sensitive by the lines in her forehead and between her brows, which intensified her look of concern as she peered at Yochanna. Her eyes were a silken hazel, with a deep brown ring around each iris that brightened their color and made Celine look as though she was peeking through a pair of bird-sized binoculars. A single whisker ornamented her chin. She did not look like a killer or someone who was accustomed to the limelight. Her hair was worn natural and was dry at the tips. Her earlobes were dimpled by piercings bare of jewelry. Yet, the hand that clasped Yochanna's was strong and steady, sure of itself. She was the only umbrella-maker in the world, a master craftsperson. Her palm was warm on Yochanna's wrist.

"It's so beautiful here," Yochanna said. "They have what I've been looking for."

She stumbled over the words. The wall-sized illumination still hovered in her mind, and underneath it, her memory contained a weaker layer of her failed ink and paper experiments, and the years she had spent scraping up the shades of New York City and trying to distill it into colors on the dented burner of her stove. She thought of the inks that caught fire and scorched the pan, inks that stained her palms with the pall of jaundice, inks that slobbered down her forearms as she painted swatches on the wall, inks irremovable, inks infuriating her landlord, inks that shimmered like a distant oasis, promising a creative future she could never reach alone.

But now she was *here*. As if by magic, she had been drawn into a place that was entirely constructed by hand, where the stressors of reality could not reach her. For an instant, she was grateful she'd come to the flower shop and been dragged along by these two felons.

Her decisions all brought her to this.

An engine sputtered, and she turned to see the big man yanking hard on a metal strut. Celine was right—they'd be gone in another minute.

"If you're found, that monster will eat you," Celine asked. Her gaze sought Yochanna's. Her irises shivered across the white space of her eyes. "Stay and you stop existing. You want to take that risk?"

"You saw what they had—that place away from everything else. The vegetables, real ones. Maybe it's worth it."

These people replicate the things they remember from above. This place is a tomb. If we hadn't gotten out of that cell, we would all be moving through Dagda's guts right now."

But the tyrant and his silver-tipped teeth felt murky and distant now. Yochanna was not afraid of him, just as in her childhood she only feared the claws under her bed at night. The daylight whisked those fears away. As she fretted, Celine touched her damp cheek and dabbed another jellied droplet away. If Yochanna didn't stop crying, they'd gel on her eyelashes and set into salty glue, blinding her. Somehow, this made everything worse—Celine's kindness, the nausea that still held her close, and Robert's crumpled corpse all piled up on her and made her throat feel like a clogged hose yearning to burst with stored-up tears.

To steady herself, Yochanna tried to make herself think about the tomatoes and the fruit that had enticed her. A plant could be fooled into flowering many times in one season. She imagined herself painting in an earthen chamber with illuminated walls, sitting under a sunlamp. She wondered how long she would last before she missed the real thing. The sun was something she took for granted; it was as consistent as the subway and gave more warmth than her apartment's radiator. This underworld did not seem like the kind of place that permitted coming and going. And although she had seen a vast representation of crafts in the tunnels, she had seen no artists; only people caring for the hydroponic slough and counting inventory bags. Where were the makers in Maia? Or was she fooling herself in hoping she'd stumbled into a new utopia, where she could devote herself to her dreams?

As if reading her thoughts, Celine said, "You think they have everything. But what are they missing? How long can they survive under that kind of oppression? You saw their faces. They're on a hunger strike until Dagda leaves, or they do. Even with all that food, they're wasting away."

Yochanna frowned, thinking. This place was a rich repository of created things, the materials she'd searched for since reading about them in college. It was the fulfillment of a promise. But Celine was right. There were no creatures that she knew. No sky, no filthy puddles. She tried to imagine herself happy in a place ruled by a monster and absent of birds. She knew from experience that she could tolerate enslavement, but birds? She would miss them—the Baird's Sandpiper that refused to be coaxed back into nesting near the Hudson and the dotty expressions of the pigeons who pecked around her feet, begging for crumbs.

To her, art was its own pair of wings.

"Don't end your life here," Celine said.

Yochanna felt as though it had never started. But she felt Celine's hand and her warmth, and in the delicate wrinkles of this woman's face she could read a message just as evocative as the one carved into the granite wall.

The engine cranked again and this time its motor purred smoothly into action. The ship's nose, reoriented toward the hangar shield, was dulled with neglect and its pod coated with dust but it looked safe enough. The shield itself was creaking ajar. Long slats admitted a breath of landfill vapors and Yochanna snuck her cloth mask back over her face. In an instant, the upper world had erased all her sensory memories of the mine and what she smelled and touched there.

When Celine headed toward the chamber's flapping port door, Yochanna hesitated. Inside, she could see the dark parcel of Robert Weiss' body leaking on the seat. The windows were grimed beyond opacity. The airfoil was graffitied with a single horrified eye scraped into its coating. The dual propeller shaft squeaked rhythmically as it rotated. Yet, if she stayed down here she'd never leave.

Celine reached out her hand and what could Yochanna do but run to her, and the mistakes they'd made—separately and together—and board the rusty curricle before it leapt into the air and vibrated toward the sky? The gondola was waiting. The hangar showed a slice of greenish light. They leapt into the craft and Paul aced the takeoff and in a moment they were speeding out of Gaspar up into the copper clouds.

Yochanna burrowed under Celine's sheltering arm as Paul grappled with the control bars to aim them higher and higher, toward the world above. The little ship nosed its way into the mists that spilled down into the hangar and lost their color in the dark.

The long door closed beneath them and within the period of two gummy blinks, Yochanna could no longer identify the camouflaged panels that concealed the magical world beneath.

The details evaporated with the celerity of a dream even as she groped to remember them. She buried her nose in Celine's shawl and squeezed her leaking eyes shut. Her fingers weaved through one another, drawing the shapes of things she'd seen. The lamp, with blown-glass bubbles. The arching nave. Freshwater feeding multicolored vines.

"Tomato," she whispered fiercely, unwilling to let the memory leave her. It was red, it was round. She traced its plumpness onto her palm. "Tomato, tomato, tomato."

Otzara

22

On takeoff, Celine's stomach lurched. She gripped her bent umbrella's handle and pressed herself into the bench seat. The rough repairs in the planelet's body creaked. Bolts around the windows rattled in time with the struggling motor, threatening to work their way out of their slots and creating a deafening vibration. As the planelet clanked down the makeshift runway, Celine watched the patched wing bend nearly in half, then correct itself and stiffen as the craft approached an irresistible velocity.

They blasted out of the hidden tunnel and ascended through the fingers of pallid mist, gaining altitude. The city fell away from the window. Celine saw how the setting sun shone on the shimmering panels and vents of the skyscrapers, making them glitter. Bare masses of steel and stone shouldered one another aside, like plants competing for sunlight, with hardly enough space between them for the planelet to squeak through. As they gained altitude, the shadowy streets darkened into puncture wounds, then valleys, then impenetrable crevasses that greedily sucked in the light; nobody could survive in such depths, Celine thought, under the pressure of those massive buildings. The topmost spires sharpened as they passed and the whole extent of the city scrolled out beneath them, so massive that it denied comprehension; it looked like a gloss portrait of a city, or the 2-D backdrop of a low budget Skin Series, not a real place at all but a metropolis that existed in the imagination of someone who had only guessed at the bright stars that crowned the steeples high above.

Celine could see that the sun was suspended inches over the horizon and lowered itself languorously toward the gently curving cheek of the horizon. At this altitude, the sunset lasted orange-honey hours longer than it did for the people on earth. The clouds were a peach colored gauze and as they crossed the northeastern sector of the city, Celine stared down into the cluttered grid that demarcated New York City and tried to make sense of the streets she'd been raised on, the ones she knew by heart. The canals were filled with slum-shops and cellular net-trees, their false foliage painted an artificial green that was nothing like the way New York had once been, a green and gentle place lined with avenues of elms that swayed in the breeze. Celine's grandmother had told her about that long-lost city and young Celine, already absorbed in her device's version of life, had not believed those stories until this moment, when she was able to see with her own eyes the layers of time that spackled the city. Its mottled patterns suggested the shape of the New York underneath the glass and photovoltaic prisms, an ancient place that was made by human hands of bricks and steel beams and welding flame. A fragment of stained roof tiles flickered far below and perhaps it was a color she recognized, an old school, though how would she know that, since she had never seen the city from the air? All the same, she whispered, "Look!" as though to a distractable child.

In a few more minutes, the dead river's sinuous banks were visible, and then the bloody stain of the coastline where the Atlantic pressed its burning lips into the Hudson's delta. The outflow was so dark with cinders and waste that it appeared purple in the fading sun; inky underwater clouds rolled like toxic silks into deeper water, which was a startling green that settled in gradually darker rings to the blackish blue of Robert Weiss' suit. And past that, like the brilliant gates of Hell, she saw the long plumes of fire from the reef of burning trash that the tides held offshore.

Out here, the city's brilliance faded and there was no moon; everything beneath them lay in stark technicolor, the setting sun warming past the point of comfort and turning the peaches to a scarlet, abraded wound that ran redder than blood. Had this world always been here? It frightened Celine to think that it had been suspended over her entire life; that, had she only been able to see it from above, she might have known that the zeppelin of time was levitating directly overhead, its incessant spin casting a shadow on what would be the future, what would always be the past.

Then, the sky dropped around them. The engine fluttered and the weak wing shrieked as its fulcrum bent under the pressure of flight. The land magnified through the pitted, broken windows. Celine's hands were rigid white crabs in her lap. Her stomach shifted, hiding inside her ribs. The girl gave a great, breathless sob that was somehow worse than a scream—it swallowed up all the air in the gondola.

"Grab something," Paul shouted just before they hit the ground. The already-broken wing busted off and skittered into a bank of ferns. They swirled sickeningly for several long seconds, bashed against the walls by the mixing forces of thrust and gravity. The whorling sound of its engine was replaced by the hollow tones of the wind. Were they dead? The panels were peeled up like Robert Weiss' fingernails.

Celine staggered out of the plane and collapsed on a sand-pit. Her legs were trembling. The girl crawled toward her on her hands and knees, mewling with terror.

They were alone.

The Meadowlands was an empty place—a landing pad gone to seed many miles outside the city. There was nothing out here, and Celine, who had never been under open sky before, felt her guts loosen with the weight of it, the potential. It was as if the world was staring down at her with a titanic, seeking eye whose gaze was heavier than the Chrysler Building, vaster than Midtown. She sank to the ground and when a pale green cloud glissaded through the air above their heads, she leaned back and pressed her spine into the hard-packed earth. The two others joined her and they lay there, breathing and silent, as the sky lost its final streaks of sunlight and receded into dusk.

"What are those lights?" Yochanna asked. Celine turned her head to see.

"Civilization."

The homes that bordered the park were illuminating in tandem, casting a dull glitter that did not pierce the place in the Meadowlands where the fugitives were hidden. People lived nearby, Celine thought. But they never came this far out, into the dark. Overhead, there were no drones. That meant they were safe for the moment. They could not be seen.

"What are *those* lights?" Yochanna asked again, pointing up into the night.

The first star—or was it Venus?—winked overhead behind a smudge of cirrus clouds. It beamed so intently at the earth that Celine thought for a moment that it must be a surveillance satellite, pausing in its endless lazy circle like a woman in summer sighing as she dips her sunburned feet into the shallow silt of a public reflecting pool.

"Are you sure we're going the right way?"

"Yes," Paul said. "We got closer than I hoped before it conked out. We'll be at their compound in another few hours. Maybe less."

Yochanna shrugged. "Their father isn't getting any deader, is all I know."

The heady scent of burned grass washed over Celine. She closed her eyes as the chemical smell transported her from the wasted field of the Meadowlands to the polluted shore of her childhood. She recognized the scent in the air—it was the smell of toys, the ones that came out of their packages carrying a distinct, tacky perfume that smelled like artificial strawberries and sweetened machine lube. Even in her half-dream, the inside of Celine's nose puckered. The name for the toxic smell was "nostalgia." Celine groped along those sensory rays in need of a word for loving something that you knew at the time was disposable, cheaply made, and meant to be thrown away.

She was young again. Playing on the studio floor. All the things she loved back then were trash. She had half a dozen action figures, a couple of naked dolls, and a translucent purple pegasus with a winged detachable saddle. She turned over the toys she retained, their faces worn away by endless thumbing. Everything she owned, including the umbrella-fabric blanket that her grandmother stitched with daisies, fit into a miniature suitcase. In the dream, she packed her case, its coral-red handle suddenly huge in her hand. It slapped her in the shins as her mother dragged her toward the gate where her ever-absent father was waiting for yet another promotion that was never going to come.

The shifting tide moved a lost ephemera across the surface of the human world in an immense gyre of discarded belongings that could cover Texas and was comprised of the trash that surrounded Celine her whole life, as though every disposable thing she'd ever touched lolled in the gentle waves. Celine was blinded by its expanse and crouched to plunge her hands into a foam of decorative buttons, trying to sift through her own detritus, searching for its secret hidden codes and the reassurance that humans were made of something better than the objects we loved. The waves whispered, *there is more to this than plastic, more of us, more of you, more.*

23

When Celine opened her eyes, she was stiff and chilled from lying on the ground. To her right, Paul was a sodden lump, rolled on his side, snoring. His shoulders rose and fell with his breath, which left his mouth in grating snarls. The corpse's shroud lay over him like a shawl. Celine blinked and the blades of crabgrass prickled into focus. Their dense, herbal scent clotted in her nostrils and made her eyes start with tears. She swiped at her face and sat up slowly. When she turned her head to coax her neck back into alignment, she could see the outline of where she'd slept in the sunken earth.

A few feet away, a shallow, sandy scarp jutted from the grass. Its exposed flank was pale yellow, the color of the curved bamboo canes Celine used for some of her umbrellas. A thick bank of ferns hung over the edge. Their blackened fronds tangled together, making a partial curtain over what was left of Robert Weiss. Paul had flung the body aside last night, hardly bothering to cover it, and now, the deflated bundle lay on its face, as though tasting the sulphuric gasses that seeped from the breast of the meadow.

Celine shuddered. She had not seen death up close since she was young, and the funerals she attended as an adult were sterile and solemn. The families who hired Celine for their rain parties also came to her for their other ceremonies: graduations, weddings, bar and bat mitzvahs, birthdays, christenings, promotions, mergers, retirements, and finally, funerals. She observed the life cycles of the rich from a tasteful distance. In her experience, the ice-drinkers enjoyed an experience of death that was opulent. Hygienic. Over the years, she had crafted dozens of black umbrellas made of sheer net to shield their users from the paparazzi's face-identifying lenses. Black silk, sprayed with a citric compound that would make the fabric dissolve in a body-temperature cloudburst. Black canvas with the deceased's name and face embroidered into one panel, to be cherished long after the event.

This was not a tycoon's end. Robert Weiss, who should have been lying with his arms crossed in a biometric pod, surrounded by the tender faces of freshly plucked orchid blossoms and real oranges, was folded into a parcel and rotting in the Meadowlands, miles away from the city where he commandeered his empire. His suit was torn and crumpled. Clods of mica-flecked soil clung to his clothes, the unobtrusive glitter embedding itself in the weave of the fabric. The hands were stiff paws. The fingers, Celine saw, were swollen with purple-brown blood that forced the curling nails out of their beds. Celine could see the pale skin of his scalp through his silvered hair, as though the skull underneath was bulging with rot and would pop under the pressure of the fetid gasses inside it.

One day, she would be dead like this too. She was grateful that she could not see his face.

She turned away and scanned their hiding place. Aside from the ferns, there was no cover. The crabgrass rioted in chewy tufts. In the distance, Celine could see the neon flares that marked a cluster of houses, but they were so far off that she had to squint to see them, and their light wavered in her watering eye, making them into a mirage. The pearly sky matched the luster of a rich man's cufflinks and seemed to hover only a few meters overhead. As the sun rose in increments, the air thickened with mist that tethered the meadow to the ambient gray and turned the world to one impervious piece of celluloid. At least they were out of drone range. And there was nothing to attract anyone's attention to them, lying on their backs in this marsh.

All the same, they could not stay here. Celine climbed to her feet and stretched her hands toward the blind clouds. Her spine creaked in protest and her hips ached, while her stomach revved its hopeful engine, making her think wistfully of the slice of chocolate cake she'd eaten only the day before. Even soylent sounded appealing, but she had nothing with her—just Paul, the girl, and the body of Robert Weiss.

Yochanna lay sprawled out at the foot of a crabgrass tussock. Her legs were splayed open and her hand was in her mouth, the middle two fingers collecting saliva as she sucked passively at them. A bead of drool lingered on her lip. Her dull hair was matted against one side of her head and strands of grass stuck out of it. She clutched her battered canvas tote against her belly with her free arm. Looking at her, Celine realized that her fashionable-looking shoes were only disposable spats, the kind you bought from sidewalk vendors. The green vinyl uppers were dull and their seams were coming unglued and peeling into ratty curls like dehydrated rhododendron leaves. The shoe underneath, Celine saw, was worn to near transparency. Its leprous sole was riddled with bald patches; a hole over the ball of the foot was mended with a slip of pasteboard, which itself was tattered and soaked with Meadowlands runoff. The canvas bag, too, had been mended so many times that it was more selvage than anything else. Its handle was discolored and the screenprint on its side was roughened to illegibility; as battered as the moon's face, its symbols and crests dull craters of faded ink. It did not look like it held a wad of stolen stickers, but Celine knew its grubby appearance belied the wealth inside it. The girl was the owner of a golden ticket—the value of those stickers was a digital reset button. Drip was useless out here, but in the city, what the girl carried was priceless. She could be anyone she wanted, with that stack.

No wonder her grip on the bag was so tight.

She began to stir as Celine gazed at her.

"What time is it?" she muttered, eyes still closed to the greasy dawn. There was dew in the crabgrass but its pale green tint told Celine the turf they slept on was laid in slabs over a copper dump. These landfills were hundreds of years old and held the layers of the past as they seeped their neon poisons into the strata of the earth. The back of Yochanna's skirt was damp with gangrenous dew.

"I don't know. We're off the grid."

A bearish yawn signaled that Paul was awake, too, and reaching up to the low-hanging mist to stretch the kinks out of his back. He rubbed his neck. His face was impassive, with the grooves of sleep still carved deeply under his eyes and around the irregular gash of his mouth. As Celine watched, he seemed to expand as his consciousness moved back into his body. The blood moved through his limbs and the pin prick scars that pocked his skin vanished like stars swallowed by the coming dawn.

He twisted his head from side to side, taking in the sodden turf and bank of ferns and the shriveled sack of meat and suiting that represented Robert Weiss. If he was sore from carrying the quadrillionaire's body out of Midtown or breathing through a set of cracked ribs, Celine could not tell. Privately, she sometimes wondered if Paul was automated, but when he stood up to raise his palms in the direction of the sun and sing the lines of the morning karakia, she knew he was all man. No robot understood gratitude; it was an emotion that was impossible to program, because it was not an emotion at all, but an action. Machines could not differentiate between work and reflection and never sat back, as Celine did at her drafting table, to contemplate the irregular, captivating pattern of the sliced silk or the bits of thread whose weft coaxed them into vague loops, as if spelling out a secret, illegible message.

Paul plucked a leaf of crabgrass, bent its blade under his nose, and inhaled.

"We should go. There's a lot of runoff here," he said.

"Go where?" Yochanna asked.

"Higher ground."

"There isn't any," the girl huffed. Aside from a few places where the garbage thrust into the turf and created an irregular steppe, covered in weeds and patches of glittering dust, the Meadowlands was as flat as the hardtop in Times Square. The houses were far off, but the trio might be detected, even at this distance, by searching drones or watchers who knew what to look for.

Without her device, Celine had no sense of time; all she knew was that the sun was worming into the sod, which sizzled as the copper beads heated up and fried in the toxifying swamp. They would never have been able to sleep here in the day, she thought. Each footstep pressed an acid exhalation from the earth. She copied Paul and tore off another square of her tunic so she could stuff the fabric into her filtration mask as a makeshift pad. Masks were designed, like everything else, to be disposable; this one would melt in a matter of hours as her breath turned it into corn fiber glue and broke down the vac mechanism inside. At least with the padding of her clothing against her nose, she could only smell her own body.

Yochanna kicked the ground in frustration, exposing a white root ball. Celine watched as she bent down and began to claw at it, trying to roll back the thick, resistant sod. The carpet of grass resisted her as she dug her hands into its fibrous pile. Suddenly, she yelped and fell backward, scraping her hands on her skirt. The tips of her fingers were faint green and her palms were leaking a spring-colored mist. They were over a copper dump. Under their feet, billions of the discarded pellets collected from the street sweepers' caddies were oxidizing into a burning pulp that would eventually devour the turf they were standing on. Yochanna blew on her hands, as if to cool them. The grass was hissing as the sunlight pierced the fog and heated the copper rounds packed solid under their feet.

"Makes people sick," Paul said. "Let's go, we've got a delivery to make."

"I don't," Yochanna said, slipping down from the fern and pushing her blockers back onto her head. "I'm not supposed to be here. It was a mistake."

"You think anyone will believe that story?" Paul said. "Besides, where would you go?"

"It's not safe to let her find her own way out here. She'll asphyxiate," Celine said.

Yochanna sucked her lower lip into her mouth. Celine watched her unblockered eyes dart from Paul's face to the city on the horizon. She knew Yochanna was thinking of the golden stickers she was carrying; imagining, perhaps, that she could swap them for an identity chip, activate her new life, and walk away from this whole disaster. A contraband chip would wipe Yochanna's slate clean.

Celine saw in her hesitation that the girl was daunted by the long walk to Manhattan. The swamp dew corroded the stitching in her bedraggled shoes and their tacky spats; its acids gnawed her nerve endings and shortened her breath, as they had Celine's. Her shoes could not survive more than a few hundred yards in the burning grass—and there was plenty of ground to cover. At this distance, with the mist so thick, it was impossible to guess how far away the cluster of houses was, or how dangerous the landscape might be between the village and their hiding place. Now, with the day's heat intensifying, Celine knew that Yochanna was just as disoriented as she was. Paul was the only one who seemed unaffected by the noxious swamp.

"Where are we taking the body?" Yochanna asked.

"Back to his people," Paul said. The sable stain of his breath seeped through his face-mask, and his eyes were screwed into a squint against the brightening day. "They wanted him. They'll get him, one way or another."

"It's the only way out," Celine said, though she more hoped than believed it would release her from the agreement she'd made with Henry. Perhaps, with the body delivered, the media blitz would end and with it, the manhunt. But even so, it was a gamble. There was no limit to what her umbrella clients could do when they wanted something. After all, they had the ability to create rain on demand for their own amusement; they peeled the skins off infant monkeys to harvest the freshest possible stem cells; they traveled the globe on a whim, spending their mornings in Beirut and eating dinner at Depoe Bay. The world turned on their wishes and nothing was beyond their grasp for long. The future was a place where the rules no longer applied, Celine thought.

Her shins still seemed to bear the bruises of her childhood and she felt the old impatience pounding in her feet, telling her it was past time to go, they would be late.

Paul had said that the only thing limiting the rich was a lack of imagination, and that the rest of us were lucky because they were so very stupid—but Celine knew from experience that ignorance was temporary, and all it needed was a spark of energy, whether it be rage, desire, grief, or greed, to power its engines and send it down the runway, picking up speed as it went, and leaving Celine and her mother trailing behind it with their bags flapping against their shins, hands raised to the departing craft as if to beg for another chance—a better chance—to do it right this time, even perfect, now that we knew what was really expected of us.

She remembered that the Weisses' property lay far west of the city. They were close, Paul said. The planelet had taken them as far as they could get.

Celine pointed toward the fog beyond the ferns, which was huddled in a venomous knot that resisted the sun's startling headlamp. The Meadowlands were caliginous, but even light found a way into them. *And out of them, too,* Celine thought. She nodded to Paul and Yochanna and, holding her umbrella, took her first steps into the west.

24

They set out across the wasteland, weaving their way between the oozing mounds of turf and jet-black ferns that jutted like lacquered eyelashes from the sodden ground. Celine felt fatigue settle into her joints as the sun crept higher and the adrenaline of the previous day seeped out of her body. The landscape overwhelmed her and made her feel blind; she could not seem to differentiate the surface from the sky. The Meadowlands was a shallow plain shrouded in a layer of mist that was thicker than the copper and dust clouds that gathered between the Bronx's skyscrapers.

She was used to reflective surfaces and hard pavement; the ambient softness that permeated even the blade-sharp fern fronds acted on her senses as well, muting them. The small wad of torn cloth inside her mask crowded her nose and upper lip, making her feel as though she was muffled in her sleep-quilt at home. She recognized this place from her dreams—a swirling, endless void of colors and patterns that confused and nauseated her. She shut her eyes, seeking refuge in the darkness behind her eyelids. Each time she opened them, she was dismayed to realize that she had not returned to her waking life. This was not her bedroom. Looking down, the soil sprang back with each step, filling her footprints and erasing every trace that she had existed.

If they died here, no one would find their bodies. They would melt into this landfill and cease to exist. Celine clutched her umbrella tighter and felt its joints creak in her anxious grip. If she lay down here and surrendered to the endless sleep that sucked people into nothingness, the umbrella would be beside her. Its ribs and hers would disintegrate in tandem. At the same moment, Celine and the craft she'd practiced her whole life—generations of Broussards, with their nimble fingers and clever hands—would sink into the mire of time. As rain had ceased existing, so would umbrellas.

She refused this—an anonymous fate. She plugged on, trying to remind herself that they were close to the border of the Weiss' stronghold.

Any moment now, and they would cross over into Otzara.

She was not as strong as Paul or as quick as Yochanna, and soon she had fallen behind them. The ground sucked at her shoes and made her feel like she was walking in slow motion, like the old people you saw muddling their way up the subway stairs, overloaded shopping trolleys in tow. Celine herself was in her mid-sixties and never felt the twinge of age, but the Meadowlands made her feel time's weight acutely.

When she looked over her shoulder, the distant reef of houses at the edge of the turf had vanished into the mist. They were alone out here. As long as they kept moving, there was a good chance they might come to the far side of the marsh before the fog turned from acidic to fatal.

She wanted to call out to the others to slow down and wait, but shouting would mean taking deeper breaths than she could tolerate. The air here singed her nostrils, and as she walked she felt as though she was being strangled by her own sheets. Paul's broad back seemed to be melting into the thickening mist and Yochanna was a butter-colored shadow at his side. The ground was invisible now, cloaked in a bitter tule fog that tangled around Celine's ankles and licked the hemline of her pants. She lost her balance in an invisible divot in a slick bank and fell sideways. As she tried to keep her footing, the tip of her umbrella jammed into the ground and sank; the metal ferrule vanished, then the fit-up, then the open cap. Celine looked down the stem of her creation and watched the turf gape like a mouth around the umbrella's notch and swallow its outside rosette. The scruffy grass divulged a fertile, rancid burp; pulling back, Celine could see the darkness directly under her feet, which could eat her up in a New York minute. The black hole made a sound like escaping steam and she remembered that this place was not solid, but a vast hydra of tunnels and tubes that hissed and breathed poison from its innumerable contorted necks. What looked like a barren field was actually a porous net, eager to swallow Celine up.

Though she knew the others were close by, her misstep slowed her even further. Looking around, she could not see any trace of them at all, not even a glimmer of movement in the mist. She scrabbled out of the depression and forced herself to keep walking. Her legs were stiff with fear and her knees locked; the adrenaline that had pooled in her glands the night before was half-digested and pinged through her nervous system, feeding her imagination fearful flashes of yesterday and the horrors she was certain waited for her on this blackened slough. She stumbled on mechanically, forcing herself to hurry in the direction of her friends. Had she walked fifty meters or five thousand? The padding inside her mask, which had at first felt so comforting, was saturated with steam and carbon dioxide. She felt whiskers of sweat trickling down the gutters on either side of her mouth, but she dared not adjust her filter. It would let the vapor in. She could smell her own breath and the traces of salt in it and distant bites of cake. Life decayed through aspiration, she thought. It was not a choice to hold your breath.

She side-stepped a crustaceous hulk that protruded from the ground and headed toward the wavering nimbus in the near-bleached expanse. Her eyes were watering; the knee she'd landed on when she fell was tingling. When she spotted the rolling pattern of Paul's stride through the pea soup, she felt her eyes prickle with leucine tears. His comforting bulk drew her along over the virescent sward and though she was nearing blindness from fatigue and fumes, she headed toward him with the certainty of a heat-seeking satellite. Her vision was bleached to an almost colorless lime as she pressed on, ignoring the burning in her knee and the exhaustion that dulled her senses until all she felt was the inexorable pound and suck of her feet extracting themselves with every step from the copper swamp.

No sooner had she put her hand on Paul's shoulder than the first of the MID-drones found them. They omitted a hum that was lower than the city curfew drones Celine was used to, a grating vibration which caught her ear an instant before the swarm blipped into view among the roiling copper mists. She instinctively ducked her chin deeper into her cowl and opened the shielding canopy of her umbrella. She felt frozen to the spot; her feet tingled as the icy runoff soaked past her stockings.

They must be closer to the garden than she thought, and she realized with horror that they had not headed straight through the marsh but taken a semi-circular path that meandered around the sinkholes and fern thickets; they had looped back into range of the scanners that surrounded every habitable place, protecting people from the dangers that spawned in the unmonitored wilderness.

The MID-drones flew in formation with their light-sensitive carapaces only a few meters from one another. Their dangling scanner lures seemed to entangle and then uncouple from one another as they harvested data from the surface of the meadow below. Even in the thickening fog, Celine could make out the ring of lights on the drones' underpanels, each one marking a sensor that collected temperature variations, color spectrum patterns, and even CO_2 density. The drones could not see human bodies, exactly: they were built for speed, not granularity. While their data might match a pool of identities, they weren't advanced enough to capture specific facial features. They recorded the unique fizz of chemicals bodies emitted; the breath, sweat, and UV radiance that signified existence. Their electronic eyes perceived how the dark red ring at the core of each person faded to a dissolute halo of pinks and oranges; lime colored flippers indicated arms and phalanges that flailed in the air.

Paul heard them coming, too. He grabbed the girl's arm and shoved her back, under the safe cover of Celine's umbrella. Her squawk was swallowed up by the mist, but all the same Celine saw his massive paw clamp across Yochanna's bandanna to seal her protests in. The umbrella could not screen all of them, but it was enough to keep their heads out of sight. The news only named Celine—the other two, anonymous, still had a chance to evade identification.

Drones had a limited battery range before they either lost power or their data web thinned to uselessness. With no sense of how far they were from a charge hub, Celine could not guess the degree to which she was perceived. Her hands started to shake with a mix of fatigue and anxiety that flooded her already-depleted adrenals. A drone zipped past them, mis-adjusted its rotation, and slammed into the ground. Its hull snapped shut and it caught on fire. A breath later, another burning discus landed close by.

"Run," Paul croaked. Still gripping the remains of the dead quadrillionaire and towing Yochanna by the wrist, he pivoted on his heel and took off at a full sprint across the waste. The girl's body bobbed behind him like a rag doll. Celine followed them into the murk, going as fast as she could in spite of her shaking legs. The umbrella clamped to her shoulder swung wildly as it caught the wind. Its tube whacked the side of her head but she hardly noticed; she pursued Paul, frantic. If she was left behind, she would never find her way out.

The drones' hum was thick in her ears and her breath coagulated in her chest. She pushed on, though she could not see more than a few feet in front of her. As long as Paul was ahead of her, she told herself, she must be going the right way.

She saw her friend's back waver amid the clouds. He was gone one instant, then rematerializing the next as he plunged back into the pollution like a needle through burlap. Every time he disappeared into the denser fog, Celine thrust herself after him without hesitation, fearing that she would lose his trail. He flickered ahead of her; she caught a glimpse of Yochanna's shoe, the tattered spats dangling from a slime-stained ankle, and the girl's eye, rolling back to meet Celine's own riveted gaze.

Overhead, motors whirred and Celine heard the deadly ping of surveillance as the devices parsed one unique characteristic after another. The clouds couldn't hide them forever. Their gender expressions, heights, and body types were noted, their elevated heart rates and the melanin composition of their uncovered skin. The umbrella obscured Celine, but at the same time, who else could she be? The object she'd chosen for protection took away her anonymity. No other person in the world would have one of these strange devices, outside a rain party. The drones didn't know that; but any sensible detective would. She was damned either way. They would die in this swamp. She felt the carbon dioxide settle into the stiff lobes of her lungs. If she gave herself up, the others could escape. And she could finally stop running. They were only—after all—looking for *her*.

There was another explosion overhead as two drones collided with one another. A handful of scorched silicone smashed into the ground near Celine's feet. She tried to run faster but her umbrella caught the drag of the air like a parachute, slowing her down.

She wrapped her hands around her umbrella's sweat-slick tube and reached up to unclip the top spring and bring the ribs down to their stem. Her chest felt as though it was squeezed by steel bands and she was dimly aware that her steps had slowed to a miserable shuffle. Her thumb found the button and released it and like a pair of wings the fabric collapsed down over Celine's head and her shoulders and folded around her, blinding her, saving her, dark. She tripped over a hummock and lost her balance again, this time stumbling several steps to one side and she slipped, then sprawled full-length into an inch of water that her clothes absorbed on contact. She felt the chemical burn before the chill hit her; she could not see, her hands itched as she flailed inside the umbrella's grasp.

A hand on her sleeve. Yochanna's voice.

She said, "We're here. Look! We made it inside the fence."

25

Henry's favorite part of each gardening cycle was the bi-lunar rain. It was a time to test the gutter-pipes and refresh the lily ponds by turning on the rain. He had attended—and hosted—countless rain parties in the city, but natural rain was a completely different experience. The industrial rain machines he designed for Otzara were thousands of times more powerful; instead of coaxing an hour-long cloudburst out of a corporate ballroom's ceiling, these juggernauts—each with turbines the size of the teahouse, which was the height of an adult dogwood tree and ringed with mature snowball bush viburnum—pumped out rain on a massive scale.

Here, Henry Weiss-Broms initiated the rain events himself, flipping a single switch that cranked the machines into high gear. The artificially generated clouds took hours to gather overhead; even the ultra-powerful generators needed time to transfer ambient water to condensation. However, once they'd reached their optimal revolution level, they could stay there for days at a time without overheating. Massive ports on both sides of the main tank drew hydrologic energy out of the air and deposited it into the holding chamber inside. Over time, the moisture in the air created a spider-silk effect as one hydrophilic molecule clung desperately to its neighbors as it was sucked into the tank. The copper dust that permeated the urban skies and the smoggy chemicals made the water behave magnetically; after a day of letting the machine run, Henry could collect thousands of gallons of water from the sky. The stolen compounds were charged by the machines and became gently ionic. They bonded in the sky, creating an atmospheric river that ran over Otzara.

It was real rain—the only rain left that streamed out of the sky, the only rain that would ever fall on this dry and dusty globe.

No one else had the authority to make this kind of rain. Henry created clouds that could cover more than half of the garden acreage and conjured thunderheads that were hefty enough to herd to the agricultural preserve to the west. Hours of rain, sometimes a whole day and night, fell on the gardens and filled the reservoirs to swollen.

After he initiated the mechanism, Henry sat back to wait, eager to test the gutter-pipes and refresh his lily ponds. He watched as mist filled the garden. From his vantage point on the Eastern Overlook, he could see the baby clouds thickening around the ankles of the trees below. Some of them were already beginning to levitate like rogue lambs. From dawn to late morning, these infant puffs worked their way toward the sky and intermingled, coalescing into fluffy, damp clumps. As they became denser, they darkened and thickened, becoming corporeal in a way that never failed to thrill Henry.

By afternoon, falling sheets of water darkened the roof tiles on the teahouse and stone gates. The lotuses transformed into upside-down umbrellas that caught each droplet and collected it in the palms of their leaves, so that each one swelled like a separate flower with a massive, glimmering diamond at its heart. Under the pressure of the falling rain, their broad green bowls dipped and swayed in a rhythmless, elegant dance. Henry loved to watch the pond they stood in rise slowly, dimpled by rain. The drops struck the water's surface with sufficient force to leave an instantaneous blip of themselves in the air, vanishing proof of their being. Blink, and you missed it—and all water was water, in air or as a collective. The transaction between the two was merely an optical illusion as water became one with itself.

From a great distance, the bluish cumulus giants might look like industrial test waste, blending with the dust storms that moved in patterns over the planet's mutilated face. However, from below, Henry felt he was looking at the underbelly of a whale that floated over him and the patchwork of greens and flowers he tended. The clouds reminded him of how small he was, and feeble. As far as most people knew, the Weisses had not procured a whale, or managed to replicate one—but that was only a rumor. Henry pondered his clouds, gloating.

Nothing was impossible for him.

He was looking up at the gathering sprigs of nimbus when a sizzling hunk of metal zinged through the delicate veil, clipped the branches in the high canopy, and blasted through the cedar-shingled roof and white fir rafters of his teahouse. The ridge buckled on impact like a freshly punched mouth and the gash the broken drone left behind it was hot and filled the air with acrid, stinging smoke as the edges of the tiles crisped against the corrugated visor and blades of the broken rotor shaft. Four more followed it, mechanical kamikazes that rocketed themselves into the teahouse and spread flames over its shingles.

Henry fell flat on his face. His cheek bounced off the smooth flagstones and the ground cover abraded his ear. He cowered on the ground. The trees swallowed the sound of the accident, but Henry detected a subtle crackling above him. The roof was catching fire and the paper window panes were blackening, turning to ash.

Henry rolled over and climbed to his feet. There was no chance of the boundary security cameras catching this—on the rain days, the smoke would be indistinguishable from the clouds, and no lens had capability to anticipate sōzu test conditions. Henry darted toward the near side of the teahouse and wrenched the fire extinguisher from its casing, but by the time he'd broken the brittle wire around its neck and aimed the nozzle at the burning shingles, the small flames had fizzled out and a massive, rugged figure was edging along the torn struts of the wrecked wall.

Even with the clouds behind it, the golem was a bleak silhouette that seemed to absorb light, more of an elemental emanation than a human being. Henry could see its thick neck and clutching hands as it found its balance and then reached back into the shrubs to extract the limp bodies of two significantly smaller creatures. It tossed a parcel into the viburnum and then lifted the two women onto its shoulders and began to shimmy around the porch. Despite its size, it moved with a spider-like assurance that filled Henry with terror. His legs suddenly felt as weak as the safety wire on the fire extinguisher and his hands were clumsy, as though wearing ox-hide gardening gloves.

The golem came closer and the dangling feet of the two bodies he carried dangled like the tails on a raccoon coat, making it look as if he was not carrying them but wearing their hides. One pair of feet wore a crispy-looking pair of patent green spats; a bloody patch of sole peeked through a hole in one of them. Henry could not see their faces. The top branches of the flowering bush rattled as the golem landed in its snowball bloom-laden grasp and as it landed, Henry's finger snapped the safety latch on the fire extinguisher and deployed a full-blast plume of freezing monoammonium phosphate.

The force of the geyser knocked him back a step on the paving stones but he held the lever steady. In an instant, the side of the teahouse and the luckless viburnum were both coated in several inches of pale-blue chemical foam. The emptying extinguisher canister chilled as the chemical reaction inside forced the dregs of dry ice and liquid ammonia out of the narrow spout. The smell made Henry's eyes cinch closed but he guided the stream over the spot where the intruders had landed.

Rancid foam drizzled down the frigid metal and over Henry's pants; he could feel its nip through the fabric as it soaked in and came in contact with his skin. He was shivering with a combination of fear and bicarbonate fumes and all he could think of was the foam and its pH—the way it would affect the soil and how it coated the shriveled leaves on the shrubs and the stained and broken skeleton of the poor teahouse.

And now it was all ruined by this monster from the sky, which not only pierced the clouds but left a burning crater in its wake, heedless of the centuries it took to nurture blossoms; destroying without thought a refuge that took thousands of hours to conserve and plant and grow. Resentment and ammonia brought acid tears to Henry's eyes and blurred his vision. The apocalypse he worked so hard to keep in check had broken through at last and brought with it an inferno of killing, pain, and the destruction of all natural balance.

For several long moments, Henry was certain that he'd frozen the intruders in place or somehow subdued them with his makeshift weapon, so when the foam-covered golem leapt out of the viburnum with its muscled arms outstretched and flew at Henry, he seemed to see it as though underwater, like a behemoth rising to the surface to tackle and swallow and subsume him into the foam and white swirling blossoms.

Henry rocked back on his heels in anticipation of the jolt and his hand fell to the handle of the hori-hori knife on his belt and slipped it free and then he was under the golem, whose shadow was colder than bicarbonate, as cold as a cloud carrying nothing in its belly but ice. A pair of massive hands swept Henry up and off his feet. He was pressed into its icy arms, lifted into the air, and they were tumbling through nothingness together but Henry was not unarmed, he was not powerless even though he was overwhelmed, and as the monster smashed him against the paving stones, he slipped the keen edge of the hori-hori into its neck, just under its mandible, in the soft spot that the strongest jaw cannot protect, and stabbed inward as though prizing a rotting bulb out of a lotus bed.

The knife was hot with blood, a sudden flow that turned Henry's hands to fire and the rest of him was ice and the world was a garden of colors as his spine smacked the flat stones and exploded with a sound of a long branch breaking under the inexorable weight of a long night of snow.

For a moment, he could not open his eyes. Inspecting the backs of his eyelids, he noticed how the collagen injections that kept his skin supple and plump caused his capillaries to glow as though filled with black-lit mercury. In here, there was no umbrella-maker to worry about, or half-brother trying to steal Otzara. In this state, Henry evacuated reality and drifted free of reality's demands.

He gazed at the crackled constellations inside himself. It was a pleasant disassociation—a night sky within him, untouched by the misery of sharing the garden he loved. He felt his spirit dissemble and sprinkle itself along the fragile veins inside his skull. There was only one truth in this unending twilight—that Otzara would persist, with or without Henry's permission. He rolled his eyes back further. Left, right. The dark went on forever in every direction, eating Henry, eating space, eating time. It sought the light and drowned it, turning all living beings into a throwaway handful of stars.

26

LATER, CELINE WOULD remember crawling toward Paul on her belly with the white petals of the hedges clinging to her hair and her clothes like sticky coins—*I found a wooden nickel*, she wanted to tell him. Her skin was blackened from the landfillers' dirt-pack engine and the crash that threw her halfway to unconsciousness. Elegant fingers that once cut through bolts of fine-milled satin and washi canvas transformed to blunt, gnomish paws. She patted Paul's face and pressed her nose against his, stricken with a sudden animal desire to lick him, kiss him, and nuzzle him awake.

From the beginning, Celine believed that nothing could kill Paul. He was too big, too strong to be vulnerable to anything less than a falling star. In the years since she had befriended him, he had grown in her mind to be larger than life—larger than himself, even, a figure that arrived outside Broussard's like something out of a myth. Explain how he appeared in front of Celine's studio one morning, a boulder of a man dressed in drab canvas rags, begging for a part time job. Explain how he knew how to fix anything just by turning it over in his hands. Explain how he held an innate sense of direction and could augur miracles in the flights of common pigeons. Explain how he was powerful enough to lift the front end of his own van straight off the pavement and scoot it off its axle. Explain how he found his way in and out of places with the ease of a rat snake, following his nose with an instinct that relied not on sight or even scent, but the steadfast intuition of a survivor. In the past forty-eight hours, she had seen Paul commit acts of unspeakable violence without flinching, and his own staunchness in executing these acts was so pronounced that it dulled Celine's own distress and drew her forward, under the umbrella of Paul's strength, his fearlessness, his protection.

It did not make sense that such a person could be dead.

Celine and Yochanna managed to roll Paul over. His hand was wrapped around the knife buried in his neck, as though he was on the verge of wrenching it out. With another instant to spare, Celine was sure he could have done it.

But now it was too late. In the end, he wasn't quick enough. For once, he wasn't ready.

Celine knelt beside Paul's body with her palm against his cheek. He was still warm, as though he had been sleeping in the sun. His right eye was closed but the left remained slightly open and she was afraid to nudge it closed, as though that would squeeze the remnants of his soul out of his body. His skull was massive and fragile, a papier-mache moon that she coaxed onto her lap. Under his chin, the handle of a hori-hori knife protruded stiffly. Stuck through his jugular, it was as rigid as a bone. When she squeezed the grip, she felt woozy and sick.

The man who killed Paul lay nearby, empty handed and shrunken. A whistling rattle burbled from his crushed lips, the song of his last breaths leaving his lungs. Celine told herself both this man and Paul died instantly, though she knew it wasn't true. The wheezes escaping from the other man's throat were proof of that.

"What about the other one?" she heard Yochanna say, and her voice was all thorny, as though pushed through the staticky wires of a subway speaker.

Celine could only shake her head. The stranger was dead, too. Nobody survived their run-in with Paul; that seemed to be his gift. Celine looked up at Yochanna—poor, morning-sick Yochanna with her two black eyes and the gutter between her nose and lip discolored with dried, brown blood—and found that she could not speak. Her voice died in her throat and anyway, what was there to say? Their rock, their protector, their Paul, was gone. No words were sufficient to express what she felt inside. An empty space ripped in the fabric of her heart. She heard herself crying but could not identify the source of the sound.

He was gone—it was over. This was how the world ended.

Yochanna squatted down beside her and put her hand on Paul's chest.

"We have to go," she said. "You saw the trees. The house. We're detectable here."

"I can't," Celine moaned.

"We will die if we stay here," Yochanna said fiercely. Her voice was like a slap.

Paul was a planet with its own gravity, a hundred times the strength of earth's.

"Get up," Yochanna said.

If they did not move, they would be found.

Paul died and nothing else was left to save them. He'd brought them to this Eden and now they were alone. Celine's sooty paws stroked her friend's somber face, his broad, bald head, and the perfect shells of his ears. Her thumbs left ashy streaks across his skin and painted him gray. The hollow rounds under his eyes were filling with fluid; with his heart stopped, his body no longer regulated its own tides and estuaries. His nostrils looked waxen, separate from the rest of his head. His leering eye rolled to its own outside corner as a ruby teardrop crept out from under its lid.

"We have to bury him," Celine rasped.

Yochanna looked at her with profound exasperation. "With what? There is no time."

"There is always time to do what's right," Celine said. "Take one of his arms. He is even bigger than he looks."

Behind the teahouse, rich, sandy soil in shades of henna and carmine opened in a deep trench that exposed the steel guts of a massive irrigation vent. Loose wires protruded from one end, as torn nerve endings hang from a partially severed limb. The pit was wide enough that when Yochanna and Celine rolled Paul over the edge, he fell hard into the dirt, arms outstretched like an angel's wings. He landed face down. Celine was grateful that she could not see his expression. She wanted to remember him not from this moment, but the way he'd looked before the rain party—her tall and stolid friend with the infrequent smile, whose face was placid and whose hands were sure. He could carry a hundred parasols in his arms, as though they were as light as daisies.

Celine stood at the lip of the pit as the mists of her memories threaded through the air around her. A moment later, a package flew past her and landed near Paul's foot with an audible crunch. It was the battered parcel that contained the remains of Robert Weiss. He had been broken, folded, bent, and wrapped so tightly that the cords that bound him bulged across the buttons of his once-swanky suit. A cufflink glistened from among the folds of his body. The staid tailored jacket and trousers were discolored with mud, gore, and spinal fluid that leaked from the snapped bones and severed vertebra; wadded up, the quadrillionaire made a malevolent bundle only as wide as his own pelvis and as half as long as his femur. He rolled once or twice and then settled in the dirt.

"Help me with the other one," Yochanna said.

Celine tore her eyes free from her friend's body and turned back to where the other man—a gardener, by the look of his clothes—lay on his back. His jaw was misaligned and the back of his head stuck to the paving stones when they tried to pick him up. Filler leaked from his cheeks. The impact of Paul's body seemed to have popped whatever cosmetic reservoirs were floating under the stranger's skin. Magnetic stripes scrunched just below his scalp, marking where a hairpiece usually sat. His face was smashed, unrecognizable. Paul had landed on him with such force that even his nose was bent out of place. His face appeared melted and his features were both flattened and smoothed, flowing toward the distended side of his head. One ear was a torn flap that fluttered when Celine took hold of his shoulders.

Yochanna retched, spat, and reached for his pants cuffs.

"It happened so fast," Celine murmured.

Yochanna grasped the body's ankles. As they lifted him, a boot fell off; his exposed foot was pale and curled up with the toes clenched together in a tight ball. Celine bit her tongue and forced her nausea to the edges of her conscious mind.

They staggered over the raked gravel and past a fragile Japanese maple and a series of small stone pots, each filled with miniscule evergreens. This body was lighter than Paul's—they overestimated the force of their throw. The gardener clanged against the steel flank of the metal tube and slid down into the pit on his side, as though asleep.

Yochanna pointed down into the pit. A sniper drone still smoldered on the roof of the little house; it steamed with acetone and fuel, threatening to explode at the touch of a wayward spark. The only way out, it seemed, was to go below the surface again.

From the sky, the land had looked so lush and welcoming, with its springtime colors of pale green and bursts of exuberant flowers. They'd seen a herd of zebras surging through a field of tall grass topped with golden seeds that glimmered as the animals pushed through them, black and white and moving like a ribbon against the earth. For a moment, Celine had felt suspended in time, before the engine fritzed and they were in a gut-twisting freefall that ended here, in another accident, with another loss, and another ignominious escape. She was getting tired of pushing on. Without Paul, she did not want to.

She felt Yochanna's hand slip into her own. Its grubby fingers interlaced with hers and gently squeezed their palms together.

"We can't stop now," she said to Celine. "We're so close."

"To what?"

"Look around and tell me what's not here," Yochanna said.

All Celine could see was Paul at the bottom of the ditch, lying in a grave they hadn't even dug for him themselves. She felt her knees loosen, and before she gave her body permission she was squatting and then sliding down the side of the pit, sand filling her shoes as she landed on her backside in the ditch. From here, she could see that the irrigation tube was as big as a subway car and ridged on both sides. It was not a single segment, but the opening of an unlit, industrial tunnel that curved down into the ground. An instant later, she heard a shower of gravel and the thud of Yochanna sprawling awkwardly beside her.

"There's no cameras," she said to Celine. "Or if there are, they can't see us. Usually there would be drones all over a place like this. But nobody has come."

"They should be here by now," Celine agreed.

"They would be."

They tilted their faces up toward the trees. The pale green underbellies of the leaves quavered against one another and crowded together on the branches, nearly blocking the view of the sky. Celine heard strange music—high notes that dripped into one another in a repeating nonsensical melody—and realized it was not synthetic, but a real bird standing somewhere with its matchstick legs akimbo and its head thrown back. The warbling wove through the trees and seemed to create a picture of another time and place, a now-lost age full of spring and eggs and babies and nests sheltered in the pits and knots of trees protected from the cold and birds who broke the news of dawn first by stretching their wings and singing joyfully to welcome the sunbeams that pierced the murky darkness and danced on the ground below. It was a song of hope that awakened Celine's heart and called to her through the mists of her grief, tugging her back into the moment. There were such things as birds who sang for love, she thought. Yochanna's hand was nestled in her own.

"We should lay them out before we go," she said at last.

The sky seemed to draw together over their heads as they arranged the bodies in the pit. They pulled on Paul's shoulders, rolling him over onto to his back. Celine tucked the tattered fabric of Robert Weiss' shroud into its bindings and straightened the pleats of the bundle. She crossed the gardener's hands on his belly and cleared the dirt from around his nostrils so that he looked more like he was sleeping. She traced the seams of his garment's sleeves with her razorblade and pulled a few scraps loose, then laid them in straight lines across the man's sagging brows and mouth, creating a death mask that shielded his face.

When she got to Paul, she kissed his battered hands and forehead before she covered him with a cloth. He did not seem truly dead until the moment she laid the fabric on his face. She had the strange sensation that she was tucking him under a warm quilt in his own bed. She placed her hand over the cloth and smoothed it, feeling the prominent bones of his cheeks and chin and the yielding cartilage of his lips and nose. When she first met him, he seemed like a man in trouble who was eager to avoid more problems. Within the last two days, however, she had learned that her reticent, helpful friend had never been a coward; he was merely biding his time. However he'd acquired the knowledge that ensured Celine's survival, she was grateful for it. There was more to Paul that she'd discerned; if there were angels, then he was one.

As Celine scooped up a handful of dirt, she glanced at the darkening sky. The mist was thickening into an impermeable, violet cloud that descended through the trees and filled the garden and the pit they stood in. Celine shivered. She groped through her memory for the prayers her grandmother had taught her, but could only remember one broken phrase. It was not enough—not good enough for Paul, who deserved the world—but she said it anyway.

"God, grant me serenity," she whispered. She sprinkled the earth over her friend, the parcel, and the stranger. Small clods rattled against the bodies' bloodstained clothes and settled in the folds of their burial coverings. It was a poor excuse for a funeral— hardly even half a prayer, or interment underground. But it was what Celine had. The sand clung to her fingers. She rubbed her face, heedless of the grains that scraped her skin and lodged in her eyelashes.

Suddenly, she felt an icy pinprick zing into her hair. She slapped the place where it stung her, hoping it wasn't a drone-dart or some new kind of bullet. Her hand came away wet, but she felt no pain. The droplet on her fingers was translucent. An instant later, another one fell on her shoulder and then a dozen more blasted into the dry dirt around poor Paul. Celine's ears rang as the soft patter of a million priceless raindrops fell through the mist and came in contact with the ground.

The rain stippled Paul's body with dark dots of water that soaked into his clothes and stained them the dusky shade of their cleaner selves. Celine opened her hands and looked up as the sky opened above her and released a torrent that washed down into the pit and over her. She felt the ground breathe a sigh of relief under her feet, as though the storm was a reprieve and a balm.

The scent she recognized from rain parties came strongly to her, a smell with a name like a Greek goddess—*petrichor*, the perfume of a dry place sighing in pleasure as its minerals and stones were gently opened by the tiny, seeking fingers of the rain.

"It's real," Celine whispered in wonder. She extended her hand, caught a few drops. They ran down her wrist like diamonds. In the city, these ephemeral little things were worth more than jewels. Yet, billions of them splashed on the earth here, as though it was still natural for rain to fall and plants to unfurl their thirsty leaves to receive it.

Celine pressed her fingers to her lips. Even mixed with the salt of her tears, the rain was fresher than any kind of water she had ever known. It held the flavor of the sky, the breath of trees, and the birdsong, all in one. It dazzled her as it dripped across her palate—the taste of a world that was continually refreshed, even in its ancientness.

How could something be so pure, and free to every person that it fell on? As Celine marveled, Yochanna grabbed her arm and coaxed her past the bodies to take refuge in the tube.

It was dry inside. Pinging rain bounced off its metal casing and made a ringing music of identical tones that overlapped in an infinite loop of tintinnabulation. The sound was a shield against Celine's ears and in spite of her sadness she found herself absorbing into its supple flow and the refreshing humidity that seemed to burst up from the newly forming puddles of the ground. The mouth of the pipe caught the echoes of the rain and swallowed it, sending ripples into the winding esophagus that led into the darkness behind them. She was grateful for Yochanna's proximity, her warm body that exuded the aroma of youth in spite of the grunge that coated her shirt and skin.

"Whatever is at the end of this is where we want to be," Yochanna said. She clung to the ratty shred of her tote bag; its printed crest design was eroded nearly to transparency. "We're almost there."

It sounded like a promise—though Celine knew it couldn't be. She turned away from the sodden lump that once held the spirit of Paul Anahera and walked into the velvet throat of the snake, headed to the center of Otzara.

27

THE IRRIGATION PIPE that swallowed Yochanna was blacker than a wolf's guts and darker than the sludge she scraped on Wall Street. It drew her stumbling steps down its metal slough for what seemed like many miles. Celine clung to her with such intensity that after a while, their bodies began to move in tandem. Their feet fell in rhythm and they edged along like a single four-legged organism through the belly of the garden.

To Yochanna's relief, the tunnel was incomplete; open vents and long industrial flues let in light and low-lying puffs. Cloudlets. A surprise burst of water drenched the women as they crossed between two segments, making Celine shriek. The sound echoed off the walls and traveled far ahead of them without boomeranging back.

Puddles of rainwater formed as the storm nosed its way into the tube. A flash of sunlight revealed the gradients of mineral color that washed up the sides of the metal. The highest demarcation was far above Yochanna's head, near the very top of the wall. It was pale gray, the same color as a pigeon chick's fluffy down. Beneath it, the tones deepened to the shades of concrete, morning smog, Mitch's coffee, and black sesame halva. With nowhere to escape, the water condensed around their feet and grew deeper by the minute. It was already past Yochanna's spats and was making its way up her socks. These pipes were set to be full of water again—flooded. And soon.

Although she'd dragged Celine in here with confidence, Yochanna felt lost underground. She was grateful for the cover of the pipes, which would protect them from surveillance. But there was no way to know whether they were going in the right direction, or even what was above them. In places, the trenches were open to the sky, and they caught glimpses of tall stalks of wheat or pampas grass; in others, formal gardens with fiercely trimmed boxwoods rebuked their ragged clothes. A breeze flowed toward and over them in a perpetual sigh that carried traces of pollen, construction, and rot in an alternating palette of scent that only offered a whiff of what might be happening on the surface.

Yochanna's pregnancy seemed to have fine-tuned her nose, making a map that only she could sense. With no sense of direction or distance, Yochanna counted her steps as she once had in New York, guessing the number of city blocks she covered as a way to feel less lost. Every 1,200 steps, the smell of the air changed slightly. They traveled from the dusty perfume of maple spores to a sharp, fresh-cut alfalfa. Mud enriched with herbs, a flower Yochanna didn't know the name of. When she caught the scent of roses, she paused in the tube with her nose lifted. Artificial rose—or even the airbrushed, single-bloom hothouse variety that florists packed in preservative—was easy to identify because it stank. Bathroom potpourri was more pleasant than that cloying cologne. Cheap, saccharine, and sour, it was sprayed everywhere, on bodies and buildings alike. This new scent was fragile and powdery and touched Yochanna's senses like a feather or a prayer. It bloomed slowly, with a tender richness that was both sweet and seductive. As Yochanna paused to sniff the air, the perfume's potency drifted down into the tunnel, as though a thousand roses were unfolding to embrace her.

"This is it," she said.

"How do you know?" Celine asked.

"I know the smell of money."

They waded through the rising water to the end-greave of the segment of pipe. It was askew from its mate, with the irrigation laces still loose. Rain flowed down its side into the basin of its belly. Half-finished solder linked metal struts to the two sections. There was enough space for them to slip through the gap and climb out. Celine was already gripping two stanchions and hauling herself out of the water. Her feet dripped onto the top of Yochanna's head as she balanced on the struts. Then, she vanished through the hole in the ceiling.

"Clear," she called back to Yochanna.

Yochanna slipped the handles of her tote around her neck and adjusted it so it hung against her front. She grasped the ladder. A wet chill entered her body like an electric shock. She gasped, but did not let go. If she stopped now, she would never begin again.

She forced herself to put one ruined shoe onto the first rung. Her foot was half-naked inside the once-shiny spats; half the sole was torn back and missing, and the pad of her foot felt as though it had been tenderized. The sharp edge of the rung cut into her toes, but she hoisted herself up and reached for the next piece of steel.

She tried not to look at her own fumbling fingers as they scrabbled up the welding. Her once-soft papermaking hands were now inept meathooks, so filthy and uncoordinated that they didn't seem to belong to her at all. The nails were caked with dirt clods that darkened the ridges around her knuckles and stained the webs between each digit. She tilted her face up and forced herself to keep moving.

Celine hauled her over the edge and suddenly, she lay on a plush, verdant lawn. A carpet of manicured tufts of grass cushioned her aching body and held her as she rolled onto her back. The rain was lighter here and fell in a sumptuous curtain. Moisture coated Yochanna's face and slid into the corners of her mouth. She could taste her own dried blood as the rain reconstituted it, like the powders she had once turned into ink on her tiny two-burner artist's stove. Thinking of her mini-kitchen, hundreds of miles away, she felt her heart wrench in her chest. She hated that apartment, hated the knowledge she'd be trapped there until she died, paying rent to a landlord who didn't need it or care who occupied the trashy shitbox on the eleventh floor. She had thought she would be eager to escape that life, the smallness of it, the misery. But all the same—in this moment, she wished she was there—standing over the boiling pannikin of black elm sap, canola, and bottled water, trying to cajole the hideous, stinking mixture into usable dye for the paper that wouldn't congeal from the wimpy pulps she mixed in the sink. She would have given anything to be there now with her slippers sticking to the tacky lino, sweating into the pot because the fan only worked in spurts.

She pressed her cheek into the bosom of the grass and felt it prickle against her ears. She had never felt such luxury—and all she wanted was the dingy sights of home.

Celine's voice seemed to reach her from a great distance. It pulled Yochanna from her reverie and tugged at her sleeve, dragging her against her will to the present moment and the Weiss family's lavish estate.

The lawn was so even that it looked computer-generated, with each chubby blade of grass evenly trimmed into a blunt point exactly the same height as its neighbors.

"Look at that," Celine said.

Yochanna squinted at the Italianate wedding cake that emerged at the other end of the garden. Turquoise cherubs, plaster-mold laurel wreaths, and carved garlands gingerbreaded each of its ornate tiers, while outsized Corinthian columns guarded the front door. It was crowned with a glass dome dotted with garish bubblegum-colored mosaics of nude nymphs who chased one another around the roof, carrying goblets to catch the shining pebbles of rain that fell over their pink lemonade flesh and embedded like tiaras in their elaborate coiffure.

Each story of the mansion boasted slender windows with floor-to-ceiling panes; the roof was real terra cotta, a rich Monticello clay that matched the slurry they'd waded through to get this far. The house leaned back on its foundation, as if looking down its nose at them across the vast field of blooming rose bushes that perfumed the air. Despite the weather, the ravishing scent seemed to suffuse even the rain drops, turning them sweet. The light itself was rosy, relaxing Celine's haggard face into the soft and pink expression of a much younger person—someone without problems. The weight of the previous forty-eight hours dripped off them both like rain. They were at the center of the priceless garden, the protected inner sanctum of the dynasty that owned the world.

Yochanna stood on her aching feet and surveyed the rows of roses. They were planted in triangles and trapezoids that interlocked to create a labyrinth. The whole garden was a mirage of waving and bending flowers that moved in an asynchronous dance as each of the million roses tilted from side to side. From outside, the pattern looked simple enough, but the high, thorny walls would make it nigh-impossible to navigate once they entered. Fog filled the avenues of roses and frosted the spiked trellises. Clinging brambles released fist-sized flowers into the rain; fragile cups, they collected the shining pearls until they became too heavy to remain upright. Then, their ponderous heads drooped to one side on their stems, slowly tipping until the rain ran out through the hidden crevices and onto the grassy paths below.

"Give me your bag," Celine said. She had stripped off her sweater and the shawl over it and was holding the tattered fabric in one hand. The other gripped her razor.

Yochanna instinctively shielded her tote, covering it with her ruined hands. The loose-weave canvas was saturated with rain and so dirty that it looked like the rags people wore in homeless camps. If she'd seen her tote on the street, she would have stepped right over it. But it was *hers*, all she had to prove she'd ever been worth anything—that she'd dreamed of art, of ideas bigger than the nightmare she found herself caught in now. Georgetown itself seemed like as much of a figment of her imagination as the fantastic garden she stood in, its memory as tantalizing and fatal as the perfume of the roses.

"What do you want it for?"

Celine mimed a series of small cuts with her razorblade and showed how the fraying edge of her cape could be teased free from its weft. She said, "Thread. So we can find our way out. I don't have anything else I can take off, and it isn't enough. We need the bag, too."

Yochanna envisioned them halfway through the maze, out of ideas and holding the end of a frazzled, natty strand. She stroked the shabby canvas tote and unlooped its handles from her head. She'd carried this for four years, then four more, so eager to show the world that she was worth more than she appeared. Yet, without it—they could be lost, trapped. She remembered how medieval monks were said to walk in labyrinths as a way of contemplating the unknowable principles of the divine. They imagined they were traveling through the mind of the deity who formed the universe and created logic from chaos, who strung gametes together like a child's beads, who knitted formless cells into bones and flesh, who separated the day from night; the holy one had made a world that was bewildering even in its orderliness. Explanations for the thorny partitions eluded Yochanna; after all, the same consciousness that inspired centuries of creativity could also smooth a person's brain to idiocy, withhold the power of speech, and thicken his tongue as it grew in his mouth. Maybe the labyrinth was not a mystery, but a punishment from God. The monks, though they'd rarely come out and actually say it, believed in retribution. They spent their lives making peace with the Lord for sins committed against Him from the moment of the very first breath.

As a student, Yochanna pored over holy books and searched the illuminations for hints of the world beyond what she could see and touch; these inky, coiled letters didn't point out where their troubles originated. They couldn't explain the current state of the world—a place without rain, where nylon-eating bacteria chewed at the landfill rafts that floated offshore and avocado cartels smuggled a fortune's worth of fresh fruit in five-pound sacks from one trade region to the next. It wasn't just sinning. Sinning could be stealing donor stickers from the locked case in the supply closet, or forcing the girl who made your coffee to become the receptacle for your transitory lusts. Real sinning attracted divine attention, and yet Yochanna knew from experience that retribution for ordinary acts, acts that went unremarked upon on earth, occurred. She had come to believe that small missteps could have special meaning to God—God the nitpicker, the giver of unfair detentions, the deducter of points. The heart of the maze was the answer to the riddle: what brings us here? Why seek at all, when the pain of looking is so profoundly hard to bear?

She slipped the contraband stickers out of the bag and hid them in her waistband, against her skin. Then, she watched as her own hand offered the bag to Celine. Her fingers felt as though they were controlled by another power. Celine's razor blade snicked into the canvas and in a few moments, the rain artist had transformed it into a loose coil of dingy-looking thread that she stuffed into her pockets.

The cape and garment disintegrated too, vanishing before Yochanna's eyes into long, multicolored strands of fringe that tangled around one another. They tied the end of the thread to an especially aggressive thorn bush and carefully unraveled it in handfuls as they processed a step at a time into the Weiss-Broms rose garden.

The grass here was as soft as the Meadowlands' turf had been, but instead of stinging Yochanna's soles, it yielded to her footsteps. Rose bushes bristled on both sides of the narrow path, some so flush with flowers that their thorns were nearly invisible. Glossy, blood-dark leaves flanked the blooms, which were as different from one another as strangers' faces on the subway. Bold sunrise yellow roses the size of a feral cat's head whose edges were tinted a violent pink snuggled against flowers that seemed transparent in comparison, a single flimsy layer of petals that held a couple of crude lumps of pollen in their center, as clumsy as a child's drawing. Every shade of red and pink and orange and yellow were represented, and as they walked, carefully unspooling the thread from their pockets, Yochanna noticed that the overlapping aromas were barely discernible. A particularly pungent rose might call to her, but otherwise they walked through a blanket of scent that blinded their senses as much as the labyrinth narrowed their steps.

Within a few turns, Yochanna could not say which direction they were facing. The domed house shimmered over the garden like an evil god, sitting in a cloud just out of reach. They doubled back, following the thread as they inched their way closer. The dome glistened with falling rain, which soaked the roses and gently turned the grass into pulp. The rain was cool and the air mild, as though adjusted for pH to maximum pleasantness; all the same, Yochanna found that she was stiff and shivering. In such a beautiful place, her body was remembering its fear and discomfort, and small waves of adrenaline ran down her back, chasing through her depleted nerves with no outlet or escape.

They turned left, then left again. Each time they encountered a dead end, Yochanna felt a part of her mind surrender to the idea that this whole garden was a high-budget illusion, designed to prevent them from ever reaching the mansion. Perhaps they would wander among the paths until the roses faded and dropped their petals and shriveled to wine-stain nubs under a winter coat of frost. Maybe they would have to drink the rain from the flowers and eat their fleshy petals to survive. It would not be the first time she'd made a meal of nothing but beauty.

Another dark hedge blocked their path, glowering. Celine sighed and tucked some of the thread back into her pocket.

"We must be close," she said.

The house seemed no nearer, but Yochanna was afraid to say it—to acknowledge the madness of their wandering would mean giving into it. Destabilized, the mind meditated easily and released its petty attachments to things like paper and ink.

Yochanna glanced at Celine, who stared at the sky with her hands folded, as though hoping to be rescued and plucked free from this terrible place. Her legs were mud-stained and Yochanna could see her knees trembling with fatigue. Her mouth was drawn in a flat line. The vague lines under her eyes deepened to pits tinted indigo and her cheeks seemed to recede into her skull. Her pockets were so stuffed with thread that she seemed to be wearing panniers, and they gave her silhouette an obscene curvature; she was a walking corpse, padded to look like a human woman.

"Only a little further," Yochanna said. She knew that if they sat down to rest, they would never get up; they would lie in the grass and sleep until the end of the world. She wished suddenly for Paul's presence and his velocity, his ability to drive on to the next safe place and carry them with him. Yet, perhaps this maze with its floral palisades would have flummoxed even Paul. Confused and exhausted, even he might have wandered in circles here, eventually succumbing to the irresistibly tender grass.

"It will have to be," Celine said. "I'm down to the last of the spool."

She pinched the loose, tote bag-colored thread and drew it slowly from her pocket, then tied it in an economical knot onto a nearby rose. The delicate lavender blossom bobbed as her hands looped and tied their lifeline to the flower's neck. Yochanna glanced back the way they'd come—a dark strand laced among the thorns marked their path, which vanished as it turned the corner at the end of the row. Starting over meant retracing their steps to the beginning and trying a completely new approach; the mere thought made Yochanna melt with exhaustion. This would have to be the right road—they did not have the resources to keep trying and trying, relying on repetition to solve the mystery of the maze.

She closed her eyes. In her imagination, the image of the labyrinth sprang into focus. She perceived it as a patchwork of triangles, loops, and stripes laid out in a pattern that oriented itself toward the house. The negative spaces between the roses flickered in her mind, as though illuminated with a black light. They might be halfway up the right side, possibly further. She tried to envision the exit that would release them from the impenetrable hedges and the now-sickening scent of the flowers that was more cloying than tantalizing. Left, right at the narrow fork, and left again—they'd be at the feet of the inner sanctum, ready to climb the steps of the porch that encircled the first story and sheltered its windows from the rain under a sloped ochre roof.

She grasped Celine's wrist and drew her along the route described in her mind. Sometimes, loose barbs snagged their clothes and scratched at them, but they pushed on, so fixated on their path that they were oblivious to the beauty around them. The rain pattered on the rose petals and the fleshy stalks that proffered them to the clouds, but its music faded to white noise in Yochanna's ears. She saw herself as a glowing blue dot, blipping along the linear track that would set them free. She was no longer blind. Her turns were angular; she trusted the cognition of her mind as it guided her first left, then right and between the vertices, which arose fully formed in front of her in a neat diagram, just as she had pictured them. Amid the syrupy fragrance of the flowers, she detected a smell she knew very well—burning plastic. Its polluted plume weaseled through the rose-scent and touched her nose, bringing tears of recognition to her eyes and then nausea, the sickness she felt every day in the city without noticing it. It signaled the proximity of poison.

"Close," she whispered. She pulled Celine closer, then slipped her arm around the older woman's waist. They leaned against each other like old confidantes, both too tired to console one another in any other way.

Staggering, they turned the final corner and tottered toward a hedge of brilliant yellow roses whose bloody core leaked sanguine beads into the marrow of their petals. There was a gap in the wall; beyond it, a four-foot bronze astrolabe on a stump of marble pedestal rotated its interlacing halos, collecting rain. A figure cast in bronze wrapped its arms around the supporting pillar clutched a burning torch; its head was broad and hairy, horned like a cow's, and its human hands offered the flame heavenward, as though it could set the twirling spheres alight. The fire stank of fuel and copper waste and carried the vaguely aqueous shimmer of the campfires Yochanna recognized from the neighborhood in Brooklyn. The minotaur's eyes were bulbous marbles and its guts leaked long agate necklaces from a rift in its torso. A garnet tongue lolled from its tortured mouth, and something about its expression so reminded Yochanna of Paul that she had to turn away from its torment. Her own belly writhed in sympathy; the stars rotated insensibly overhead, obeying their own mechanism. A golden arrow pierced the astrolabe as though spearing the cosmos and pinning it to a single point, the center of the turning earth.

She took the final piece of thread from Celine and tied it to the arrow's tip, anchoring them at last. There was no denying that they had finally arrived.

This was the seat of the gods, the givers of life and death, makers of decisions; the family that rotated the world at their whim, who transformed ice to fire and back again, who created rain and let it wash over the lands they stewarded for their own, exclusive uses. They remade the unicorn and kept the treasures of the snow; birds that would never survive the city's filth sang in their pristine trees.

Yet, as Yochanna placed her mangled shoe on the Weisses' porch, she heard nothing—only the rain, and its persistent silence, which was a thicker wall than glass, more impregnable than roses. Her mind was a blank page of vellum, wiped clean by the sky's tears and primed for the first stroke of a devoted, anonymous brush.

28

Heavy purple clouds clustered around the Weisses' house and reclined on its canted terracotta roof as they released sheets of storm-laden water that pelted Yochanna and Celine as they made their way onto the porch and found shelter under its eaves. Soaked to the bone and bedraggled, they were too exhausted to wring the water out of their hair and remaining clothes.

Celine's lips were gray with fatigue; her bare arms were coated in bloodless goose flesh that reminded Yochanna of the flabby tofu patties you could buy in the market, floating in agar preservative. When she put her hand on Celine's shoulder, the other woman was cold to the touch, as though her living self had receded below the surface of her skin and was hibernating beyond reach somewhere in the region of her bones. She had sacrificed her cape and her tunic to bring them both safely through the labyrinth; without the threads of her clothes, they would still be puzzling their way through the maze's innards. But now, half-naked, Celine shuddered like a leaf catching the spray of a rain spout. Her pupils shrank to single-pica points and the skin on her cheeks and brow were loose with exhaustion, as though she wore a poorly-made mask of her own face.

The rain, which had seemed so friendly at first, had beaten the warmth out of them with the millions of chilly drops shed on them. Ensconced in the artificial cloud, Yochanna felt herself distilled into separate parts. Wasn't the human body mostly water? If they didn't get warm, she knew she would liquefy into beads herself and run down the interlocking boards of the porch into the thirsty soil, vanishing forever into the body of a rose.

The door of the quadrillionaires' mansion was high and narrow and made of burnished oak. Golden and inches thick, it was polished to a sheen that suggested a life beyond its transformation by the carpenter. Yochanna touched its smooth grain in wonder—it had been cut in a single piece, taken whole from a living tree. Decorative spirals were cut into the panels, and as she fumbled for the handle she saw figures in the wood, miniscule people riding on gargantuan rabbits and snails, roses with teeth, and in the center of them all, a knot of clouds that issued a diadem of lightning bolts.

The doorknob was buttery metal and turned without protest in her palm. In a moment, the gleaming door slid open and admitted them to the house. The rain faded to a distant sibiliation, dampened by the barrier of wood and glass and warmth inside. Luxurious carpets underfoot were as plush as the avenues of rain-fed grass they'd tread to get here; the creamy sunlight filtered through stained glass windows that depicted amethyst irises, bold sunflowers, and more roses that clambered up the panes on unruly, leaded vines.

Here, the walls were covered in paintings protected by real wood frames and glass. Small statuettes cluttered every available flat surface. As they passed through the foyer, Yochanna saw a wrought-iron clothes tree whose branches were loaded with warm-weather clothes. She tugged an aubergine coat loose and draped it around Celine, buttoning the fur collar around her neck as though dressing a child. She took a black overwrap off its hangar and put it on her shoulders. Its weight was reassuring and it smelled vaguely of a woman's skin and lily soap. The warmth began its return to her body, creeping along the silk lining to the ends of her hands and heating her skin so that the rain that soaked her turned to humidity and filled the wrap, making Yochanna feel like a cloud herself.

After a few minutes, Celine's face was less drawn and the color was returning to it; her eyes lost their icy sheen and she seemed to see the details of the rooms as they passed through. Goddesses cavorted with satyrs in some of the paintings, or dipped their hands into pools of water, dabbling with their own reflections. Staid, weak-chinned people dressed in clothes stitched with copper wires and platinum microchips gazed out of their frames; these must be the Weisses of the past, the generations that had guided the family to their current place of power. Their expressions made Yochanna aware of her sodden clothes. Her right shoe was degraded to the texture of a banana peel. She kicked it off, discreetly hiding its ruined rind under an easy chair upholstered in silks.

"Those are from Broussard's," Celine said, pointing out a metal stand shaped like a bear. The bear embraced an armful of umbrellas and wore a gaudy birthday hat, although its demeanor was serious. It offered them the party favors solemnly. Celine caressed the handles she had crafted, saved from rain parties over the years. White, yellow, pale green, and the deepest turquoise, each one was distinct from its companions, designed to be an unforgettable reminder of the event that marked a transition in the life of a beloved family member. From their bris to their birthdays and finally, their burial, a single person would accumulate as many as a dozen umbrellas over the course of their existence. It was not simply the shared ritual or its accompanying opulence, Yochanna realized, but the continuity that the umbrellas provided.

They seemed to say at each of life's junctures, *The rain is here for you, always. Learn to dance in its abundance.*

By the time they reached the great room at the center of the house, the sensation had returned to Yochanna's hands. Her clothes were losing their moisture and the stickers in her waistband were beginning to itch against her skin. Her blistered hands clutched at Celine, the door jambs, and even caressed the picture frames, as though looking for something to steal. She caught a glimpse of her reflection in a pane of glass as they passed and was horrified. She looked worse than the hat-wearing bear. In the stolen overwrap, her body appeared to have grown a hump like a buffalo's. Her lapels flapped loose, dragging on the sumptuous rugs like a pair of jagged, broken wings. Her bare foot was swollen to such a degree that it appeared leprous; her hair sprouted in clumps from her head like a crown of tumors. Her eyes were liquid pits that searched wildly, glancing from the grandfather clock in one corner to the collapsible telescope in another. She did not look like a nice girl who had gone to college; she hardly looked like a girl at all. She turned away from this image of herself, but she could not escape her sense of her own beastliness.

The great room was in the center of the house, under the crown of the glass dome Yochanna had spied from the maze. Light filtered through the multicolored panes and dappled the richly colored divans, cushioned benches, and ornate coffee-tables that filled the space. There were no screens here; an aquamarine cast tinted the lamps' light. Overhead, a tubular aquarium ringed the rotunda; jeweled fish flickered inside it, and Yochanna gasped as she saw a trio of dolphins circling through the tank, swimming in an infinite loop over her head. Before, she had only seen them in drawings where dolphins appeared as spouting whales or sea-bound creatures with many rows of teeth. Once, dolphins were said to rescue drowning men from shipwrecks and carry them to shore. But they had supposedly died off when the ocean co-agulated, the ultra-saline environment making it impossible for most marine mammals to survive. In school, Yochanna learned about the mass die-off when hundreds of thousands of whales and dolphins beached themselves in protest of industrial mistreatment of the planet; now, salt flats stretched for bald miles where these animals once raised their babies and chased flickering shoals of anchovies.

"They're supposed to be extinct," she said.

"Not here," said a voice.

His deep blue suit blended into the paisley velvet of the sofa where he lounged in the shimmering reflection of the water over-head. Small, lemonade-colored lenses covered his eyes and he wore a pair of silver neuro-spec gloves that were dimpled all over with sensors, like the body of an urchin. He extended his lanky arms in a catlike stretch and then curled his hands into claws as he unkinked a single bony finger at a time. His feet were naked and repellently pale, like the painted feet of Christ's corpse in a sacral Pieta. Smooth and white as polished quartz, his skin seemed to have no veins or even tendons. However, his toes gave away his real age—despite his artificially youthened complexion, his nails were yellowing and the knuckles on his feet cramped into spherical bearings from years of being shoved into tight slippers and dancing at rain parties.

"Dolphins were the largest cetaceans we could replicate," the man told them as he slithered off the sofa. "But soon, we'll have a whale."

He came closer, weaving between the shin-tall tables loaded with bric-a-brac and candy dishes. He skirted the discolored boulder at the center of the room and the shallow pool beneath it, which caught droplets of water that cascaded from its mossy flanks. The giant rock was unmilled and neither reflected light nor seemed to fulfill any function; it was an ugly, raw thing. But the pool beneath it was crystalline-clean and so pure that it was nearly invisible to the eye. Yochanna could only detect its presence when a drop of water ran down the rock and entered the pool with a ripple. She thought for a moment that there must be a leak in the dome overhead, or a faulty panel in the dolphins' tank—but no, the water came from the stone itself.

Laszlo Weiss-Broms slid a bony, gloved digit over the boulder's rough surface and stuck it into his mouth, sucking the moisture from his fingertip. The taste of real ice seemed to vitalize him.

Celine took an involuntary step back as Robert's half-brother closed in, looming over them like a cobra staring down at its next meal. His poreless skin was drawn taut across his jaw, which worked compulsively as he forced it into a predatory grin.

"The umbrella maker," he hissed.

"I did what Henry asked," Celine stammered.

"What have you done with our father's body?"

In her mind's eye, Yochanna saw the crumpled wad that Paul had carried under his arm, night and day, since the killing on Thursday. Robert's remains were lying in an irrigation ditch now; his bones had been pleated many times inside his clothes and pressed into a portable shape that was hardly identifiable as human: head nested inside ribcage and femurs broken in half, the most economical form a body could take.

How Laszlo would receive this information—his father's ignominious transport through city, swamp, and crawl-space—was anyone's guess. His eyes glittered as he spoke and his demeanor was gleeful, not the bereaved gravity of a son who recently lost his father.

"You can have him back when you hold up your half of our agreement," Celine said. "You promised me ice."

"Did I? I believe Henry mentioned chocolate," Laszlo said.

"Both. But the police are looking for us," Celine countered. "This was not our bargain. I should not have agreed to remove the box."

Laszlo shrugged. One silver glove crept across the back of a nearby chaise. Its sensory nodes flickered on contact with the tufted velvet. Yochanna noticed a brightly colored magazine open on the cushions, spine broken, pages torn. It was made of real paper; the glossy cover featured a graphic of two people water-skiing. She had seen one like this in college, years ago, kept behind glass in the library's archives. To leave such a valuable object out, to be sat on and torn up and bent in half, was a more meaningful gesture of power than the rest of the house put together. Each line of type had been set by hand, inked a letter at a time and pressed into the pages' fiber as though it would last for all time. Celine wanted payment in chocolate, which seemed insufficient to Yochanna; but if this family offered her a library of print, she would have committed a thousand crimes much worse than removing Robert.

"You're the one who killed him," Yochanna interjected. "Aren't we finished with this?"

Laszlo's head rotated smoothly on his neck as he fixed Yochanna in his uncanny gaze. She was unidentified in the news broadcast, officially nobody. He took in her tattered clothes, missing shoe, and tangled hair with a bemused expression on his face.

"A ragamuffin," he said. A thin smile momentarily creased his face.

"You broke your promise. The least you could do is let Celine go home. If you're powerful enough to make rain, you can hit the reset button on all this, too."

The smile vanished into the injected flesh around Laszlo's mouth. He was not used to being talked to this way, by such an ignoble person. Yochanna sensed his disgust at her presence, her appearance. It was as though a fleck of dandruff had shouted at him from a perch on the couture shoulder-shelf of his jacket. His lips flattened into a smirk.

"And who are you?"

"Not important," Yochanna said, but they both knew her bluster was meaningless. One security scan would reveal her entire history: the good grades, appalling debt, years of purpose-less employment, credit score, buying habits, residential address, and even her search history, all captured in a virtual cache of links and data that was as un-impactful as the rest of her life's activities. Laszlo could hold Yochanna up to the light, and see that she was trivial—a string of ones and zeroes that added up to nothing.

"I can see that. Would you like a fresh start, too? Your own iceberg, like mine?"

He flung a spidery hand into the air, taking in the sumptuous-ness of the room, from the dolphins to the rain that still rattled on the rotunda's decorative roof and the chunk of ice that bled its life out into an ornamental drinking-pool.

There was nothing beyond the Weisses' reach. With time, their searchers would discover Robert's corpse, tucked beside the bodies of Paul and the gardener he'd killed. And Laszlo had time, all the time in the world—the power to paralyze the passing minutes and rework them to his purpose. In this place, the climate was that of many centuries before the crisis. He commanded the clouds. That splayed silver glove held the world in its synthetic palm.

But he could not know everything. Yochanna shifted on her aching feet and felt the corner of a sticker snag inside her waist-band. It was right against her skin and its sharp edges pricked her, a reminder of the trapdoor she'd tried to construct for herself to escape her miserable, meaningless life.

"No," she told the quadrillionaire. "I want you to let her go."

"Why would I do that?"

There was no reason. After all, Celine was part of the conspir-acy to dethrone Robert. She had witnessed the stabbing and trans-ported its victim over municipal lines, evading capture; she had collaborated with off-grid separatists, trespassed into a restricted haz-waste area, and acted as an accomplice to a former convict. The instant she affixed the barbed ferrules onto the two umbrellas that became the murder weapons, she had been drawn into this plot and was central to its execution. Perhaps she had engineered it herself—it could certainly look that way, if Laszlo wanted it to. With enough money and power, facts became circumstances. The shape of the story could change at his every whim.

The gardener's face flickered into Yochanna's mind. Its smashed features rearranged themselves, resolved, and clarified into focus. The mashed brow had a glimmer of Laszlo's expression. The two men could be twins—or half-brothers. Yochanna swallowed hard. Even in death, the "gardener" Henry looked selfish and cruel, wearing the same smirk his brother sported now. She realized that she and Celine had buried Henry with his father and a felon in a ditch out by the lilies. It was an accident—of course, it was an accident—but that twist of fate had given Laszlo everything he ever wanted.

"Henry is as dead as Robert is," she said. "We delivered both bodies, and now you're the only one who's left. The whole world belongs to you."

"Even the rain is mine," Laszlo mused. A strand of translucent hair slipped from his carefully arranged quiff and fell across his forehead. He tucked it back into place with his glittering glove and fixed Yochanna in the crosshairs of his eyes.

He said, "Henry harnessed the clouds, but he had no respect for the free markets. He wanted to flood it all, drive commodities out of existence. He couldn't understand that the economy relies on us—on me. It's a closed system. One button makes trade begin and end. It keeps the estate, *my* estate, as green as Eden."

"If you can do that, you can end the manhunt," Yochanna argued. "That's worth what we gave you, isn't it? You can turn Celine back into nobody."

"Of course I can," he snapped.

A dolphin reversed course overhead, swimming in a lazy pas de deux with its partner. A tremor of thunder shook the dome and startled Yochanna, making her reach for the support of a nearby chair. Her foot was beginning to ache and she had the sick sensation that she was bleeding into the priceless hand-tied rug, creating a stain that would be nearly impossible to remove. Yet, she didn't mind leaving a trace of herself behind, she thought. If it was the only mark she made in this world, she might say she'd spent her life fairly.

"We'd never say a word," Yochanna promised. "She did what you asked, and more. She doesn't even want the ice anymore, do you, Celine?"

She could hear the whine in her voice, the sly keening just under the words as irritating as the song of a cat in heat. Laszlo Weiss-Broms heard it; it pricked his face into a sadistic moue that hovered halfway between a scowl and a pout. With so much cosmetic surgery, it was difficult to read his expression, but there was no denying the menace in his body as he drew even closer to Celine and wrapped his bony hands around the arms she raised to protect herself as she dropped the shredded body of her last umbrella to the floor.

The mini sensors on Laszlo's gloves began to flicker in a murderous pattern and his yellow eye-lenses flashed as he tightened his grip on Celine. Whatever was programmed into those neuro-specs—paralyzing toxins, Fen-Ten—had the power to blast the life out of her body, one electric pulse at a time.

The gloves tightened on Celine's arms. Their silver surface blistered with electric golden pustules that exploded into an autonomic network, flowing up the metacarpals toward Laszlo's fingertips, where the light intensified to a high-spectrum white that burned Yochanna's eyes. She fell back, shielding her face as she took shelter behind a sofa. Her hand groped over the objects on the table beside her. Blindly, she picked up the heaviest one and began to squirm toward Laszlo, who was lifting Celine off her feet and saturating her with terminating pulses that shook her body like a doll.

His feet may have seemed as smooth as marble, but when Yochanna slammed the figurine into his toes with all her strength, she was relieved to see how the skin split open and released a geyser of blackish-green blood. Laszlo screamed, so she hit him again as hard as she could, driving the granite statuette down with all her weight behind it. There was a sickening crunch as the piano-key bones on the top of Laszlo's foot fractured; one pierced his pale skin like a broken needle. Laszlo's marrow was not red but the color of concrete.

He reeled back, clutching his ankle with the awful gloves and hopping amidst the clutter toward the faraway door—but he was too slow for Celine, who lunged at him, caught him around the waist, and tackled him to the rug. He raised his glowing hands to protect himself, but she shoved them aside. Her artist's razor was in her hand and then Laszlo's face was bleeding too, long hair-thin cuts that bisected his vitamin-plump lips and cheeks, turning the manicured brows and injected nostrils into a spiderweb of blood. His hair seemed to fall out in clumps as she sliced ruthlessly, cutting him to ribbons. He bucked wildly, trying to throw her off, but she was irascible and stuck the blade deeper and deeper, hooking into his shirt and collar, nuzzling for the soft parts of his neck. Tattered gloves hung from his shredded wrists.

Laszlo's strength gave out as he reached the shallow steps that encircled the hunk of ice and the central pool. He curled on his side like an embryo—his screams were feeble now, the cries of an infant who knows nobody is coming to help. A lucky shot punctured his lung and Yochanna could hear his wheezing breaths leaking from his torso.

"Please," he rasped. "Anything you want, it's yours."

Celine's razor did not hesitate. She jammed its point into Laszlo's belly and leaned into him, skewering him to the marble steps. His howl echoed in the rotunda; even the dolphins paused in their languorous dance as though to hear the dying wail of the man who, for a few brief hours, was the sole owner of the world.

Yochanna knelt beside him holding the statuette. Laszlo's eyes sought hers, pleading.

Did this monster deserve her mercy?

She grabbed the remnants of his shirt and dragged him up the steps and into the glacial runoff. When it came right down to it, killing someone was simpler than making paper.

Yochanna's hands gripped his skull and Celine sat on his chest as they held the quadrillionaire to the floor of the tiled pool. His gloves sparked with daffodil static and flapped uselessly. His many wounds spat viscous clots of blood. Supplements and life-extending chemicals leaked out of Laszlo and tinted the once-pure water a violent chartreuse. His amber glasses floated loose. Small opals of air gathered around the roots of his hair. Yochanna felt the water take him, turning his body buoyant as the last bubbles left his mouth and his muscles softened, turning clumsy to their touch.

When the women climbed out of the pool, they were even wetter than they had been before and their sore muscles felt like sodden boulders. The fawn-colored fur collar on Celine's stolen coat was bedraggled. There were no cameras in here; if there was a security system, it was inoperable. Nobody would find them, idling next to the body of the third quadrillionaire they'd disposed of in mere days. They had the rotunda to themselves—everything, in this moment, belonged to them. Doomed cetaceans swam in circles in their translucent tanks. A priceless stone wept pure glacial tears into a pool of human blood.

This was privilege—this was wealth.

The storm outside seemed appropriate for an occasion like this, a special party for the passing of Laszlo, Robert, and Henry— the world's three richest men, the owners of a dynasty that touched every aspect of every single human life. No other type of acknowledgement would do. Every type of rain should be spilled in honor of this: three deaths worth a hundred thousand diamond mines.

A cobalt thunderhead nosed its way over the mansion's terracotta roof, chortling.

"What happens if the rain doesn't stop?" Yochanna asked.

Celine wiped a dab of blood off the back of her hand. "You mean if nobody turns it off? It just keeps going, I guess."

"Do you think it will come to New York?"

Celine smiled. "Everything goes to New York, darling. It's the only place to be."

⚊

Days after the death of Laszlo Weiss, the wind would finally carry this rain across the wastes—it was coming to fill the Hudson, to restore the beaches where sandpipers made their nests. Yochanna imagined the distant sounds of shouts and panicked horns as the leviathan entered the city, turning once-dusty windows the color of a dolphin's eyes. But for now, she heard nothing but the rain. She was grateful for the silence and for the sense of peace that washed over her, refreshing her.

Celine led her to the golden door and chose two umbrellas from the stand in the foyer.

"You can be whoever you want to, now," she said.

"Well, then. I'll be with you."

Yochanna slipped her fingers around the carved ivory handle. The effervescence inside her fizzed as the tiny sprout danced, rolled, and wriggled. A new identity and a fresh start were all she could offer this growing person—but that felt like enough, and more, at least for now.

Outside, the sky was the color of glossy agate, threaded with rivulets of light. As the first rain began to fall, Yochanna popped open her umbrella's hand-stitched canopy and raised its panels to the sky. She pushed her belly even further out and let the rain dabble her skin with joyous, gentle fingers.

The Rain Artist

This was her future—the rain, Celine, and hope.

Drops fell all around them as the sky became a celebration.

Claire Rudy Foster is the author of short story collections *Shine of the Ever* and *I've Never Done This Before*. They've co-authored three nonfiction books with Ryan Hampton, including *American Fix: Inside the Opioid Addiction Crisis and How to End It*; *Unsettled: How the Purdue Pharma Bankruptcy Failed the Victims of the American Overdose Crisis*, which was named the "best bankruptcy book in the world" and one of Ralph Nader's top picks of the year; and *Fentanyl Nation: Toxic Politics and America's Failed War on Drugs*.

Shine of the Ever was a finalist for the Foreword INDIE Awards and chosen for the ALA 2021 Over the Rainbow Fiction and Poetry Longlist. *O: The Oprah Magazine* listed the collection as one of the best LGBTQ books of the year. Foster's essays and fiction appear in many places, including *The New York Times*, *The Guardian*, and *The Washington Post*.

Acknowledgments

No book comes into being without help. *The Rain Artist* evolved from a dream to a reality with the support of many people and co-conspirators. Kayli Scholz, Wanda Boda, Dan Berne—thank you for offering the encouragement that kept me going, for your unremitting support, and for your faith in my creative process.

Thank you to the authors, scholars, experts, and researchers whose writing helped me craft my own dystopian New York, especially: the graduate students at Institute of Medieval and Early Modern Studies, Durham University; *Make Ink: A Forager's Guide* by Jason Logan; and forensic genetic genealogist Deb Stone.

Most of all, this book is for my son Lev—who deserves a future rich with rain.